AMBUSHED IN THE ALPS

AMBUSHED IN THE ALPS

TRAVEL P.I.
BOOK TWO

ZARA KEANE

BEAVERSTONE PRESS

Published by Beaverstone Press GmbH (LLC)

eBook ISBN: 978-3-03938-012-1
Paperback ISBN: 978-3-03938-013-8
Hardcover ISBN: 978-3-03938-014-5
Large Print Paperback ISBN: 978-3-03938-015-2
Large Print Hardcover ISBN: 978-3-03938-016-9

To Luigi Lucheni, whose misadventures with Woolite inspired a scene in this book. And to his person, Kate Tilton, who had to clean up the mess.

1

In the four months since I'd moved to the French Riviera, I'd helped unmask a catnapper, apprehend a killer, and stop a blackmailing scheme dead in its tracks. Sound exciting? It was—for the three whole days it lasted.

After my action-packed first weekend in Nice, my life stalled to soul-crushing tedium. I started work as a yarn shop sales assistant and moved into an awkward houseshare. My new roommates included Luc, a hunky French private investigator; Sidney, an English drama school graduate; and Mélisandre, Luc's prissy Persian cat. Of the three, the easiest to live with was the cat.

On this rainy Wednesday evening in early November, I was at the café-bistro Luc ran as an extra revenue stream. My presence at the café was no novelty. I stopped by most days to grab a takeout coffee or a bite to eat. But my reason for being here tonight was different. I was doing something I never thought I'd be doing—knitting.

Can you picture me, Angel Doyle—a semi-reformed thief and accidental P.I.—as a knitter? No? Neither can Maurice, the manager of the yarn shop and my new boss. For spacing reasons, Maurice hosted the Yarniacs meetings at the café. For keep-the-grumpy-boss-happy reasons, I'd agreed to attend. I regretted that decision.

"*Non, non, non,*" Maurice exclaimed in French, regarding my ragged stitches as one might a boa constrictor on the loose. His bald head, elaborate mustache, and fussy clothes reminded me of Agatha Christie's eccentric sleuth, Hercule Poirot. "This is terrible. You must improve your tension. Some of your stitches are loose enough to drive a steamroller through. Others are so tight I'd need a microscope to see them. You must relax your hands, find your rhythm, and have fun."

"In my world, the words 'fun' and 'knitting' don't belong in the same universe." I blew out my cheeks and glowered at my work in progress. "This looks more like a headband than a hat."

"It'll look like a hat once you've completed the crown." Sidney sat beside me, the rhythmic clicking of his needles producing row after row of perfect stitches. Like me, he'd been roped into joining the Yarniacs,

Maurice's monthly knitting club. Unlike me, Sidney could actually knit.

"Easy for you to say. Your scarf looks like something a person might willingly wear." I stared mournfully at the tangled mess on my lap. "Remind me why I'm here, Maurice? As a living, breathing blooper reel of *How Not to Knit?*"

Maurice made a tut-tutting sound. "While you're working at La Belle Laine, it's important for you to learn more about yarn. Otherwise, how can you advise the customers?"

"I do advise them. I advise them to ask you."

Maurice's entire head turned Pink Pizazz, this season's must-have yarn shade. "I don't know why Desirée insisted you work at the yarn shop. You know nothing about yarn."

Heat stole over my cheeks. He knew exactly why my mother had foisted me on him. When I'd arrived in Nice, I'd discovered my ex-porn-star parent helped run a super-secret international P. I. agency called the Omega Group. Was I itching to join her team? Definitely. Did she want me? Sure—out of sight and out of trouble. Getting me a job at the yarn shop was her reaction to me wanting to train as a P.I.

"You have to admit I'm good at accounting," I said to Maurice. "Your books were a mess before I showed up."

The man gave a Gallic half-shrug. "My role is to

order stock and serve the customers. I leave the bookkeeping to Jerry."

"Jerry's not exactly in a position to deal with the shop's accounts." This was an understatement. Two months ago, Jerry Gallo—my former stepfather and the brains behind the Omega Group—had been the victim of a vicious assault. He was still off work, recovering from his injuries.

Maurice sniffed. "That's no reason to let you loose in the shop. Desirée should've known better than to hire someone with no retail experience."

I doubted my retail experience, or lack thereof, had played a role in my mother's decision to put me to work in La Belle Laine. "I might not dazzle the customers with extensive knowledge of yarn and knitting accessories, but I can keep us afloat until Jerry's back in action. Wouldn't it be easier for both of us if we at least tried to get along?"

The man's pout conveyed his skepticism, disdain, and sense of superiority with one nonverbal gesture. His rejection of my olive branch stung. I'd done nothing to warrant his rudeness. Okay, I hadn't a clue about yarns and knitting accessories, but Maurice hadn't exactly helped me learn on the job. And as I'd pointed out to him, I was a whiz at keeping the accounts.

Maurice compounded my sense of ill-usage by turning his back on me and picking up Sidney's knitting. "Exquisite work. Perfect stitch definition."

Giving a moan of ecstasy, he ran his fingers over the intricate cables and color changes, practically caressing the blasted scarf.

I fanned myself with a menu. "Easy there, boss. The atmosphere in here is becoming X-rated."

Ignoring my quip, Maurice continued rhapsodizing about Sidney's scarf. "You have a natural aptitude for knitting. It's a pity Desirée didn't assign *you* to La Belle Laine."

I didn't bother to defend myself. Sidney would've rocked the yarn shop job, just as he was proving to be a hit at the costume shop, one of the other businesses that acted as a front for the Omega Group. I didn't fit in at either establishment, and it was grinding me down.

Sidney cast me a look of sympathy. "I'm sure Angel does her best."

Maurice didn't dignify this statement with a response. He returned the scarf to Sidney. "Keep up the good work. I look forward to seeing the finished product."

"Thank you." A note of bashful pride crept into Sidney's voice. "I honed my knitting skills during my years backstage, waiting for my cue to go on."

"Dude," I whispered in English, "just think of the number of scarves you could've knit by now if you'd stuck with acting instead of sewing costumes."

"Tut-tut. If you're not careful, I'll knit you a scarf for Christmas. I'm thinking hot pink glitter with sewn-on sequins to match your sparkling personality."

This made me laugh. "Knit me one with a skull and crossbones, and I'll gladly wear it."

Sidney turned to Maurice and switched back to French with impressive ease for someone who hadn't grown up bilingual as I had. "Love the new bow tie. Lavender is your color."

My manager preened at the compliment. "Thank you. I try to look my best."

He looked like a dog's dinner to me, but what did I know about high fashion? Maybe Maurice's lavender three-piece suit with navy pinstripes represented the pinnacle of this season's trends.

Sidney aspired to similar sartorial elegance, but his colors were louder than Maurice's. This evening, Sidney had opted for a bright orange waistcoat and pants, paired with black high-topped Converse and a skintight white T-shirt. He'd brushed his fair hair forward and had blasted it with enough hairspray to make my lungs burn.

Maurice moved to another table to critique his next victim, an elderly lady knitting a lime-green toilet paper cover, complete with a crocheted gnome on top.

I leaned into Sidney. "Watch out, mate. If you keep sucking up to him, he'll force you to join his jigsaw club."

He looked suitably aghast. "Maurice is into jigsaws?"

"Not only is he into them, but he's also the president of the local dissectologist society. That's a hardcore fandom."

"Dissectologist is a new word for me. Jigsaw puzzle lover?"

"In Maurice's case, it's more like a jigsaw puzzle obsessive. He has so many jigsaws that he's started storing them in the yarn shop's stock room. I had the misfortune to knock over a pile and got the pieces jumbled. When Maurice found out, he lost what's left of his hair."

Koffi, my fellow yarn shop assistant, detached himself from the chatty woman he was helping and reclaimed the seat to my left. He gave my arm a reassuring squeeze. "I'm sorry Maurice is giving you a hard time."

"You overheard?"

Koffi's warm smile brought out the deep crinkles around his dark eyes. "Your facial expressions when he critiqued your knitting told me all I needed to know. For what it's worth, it isn't personal. Maurice is rude to you because you're an easier target than your mother."

Even though he'd lived in France for almost thirty years, Koffi's deep rumble still held traces of a childhood spent on the Ivory Coast. I'd warmed to the older man the instant we'd met on my first day at the yarn shop. I still knew very little about his life before he'd started at La Belle Laine five years ago. From what I'd gathered, Koffi was a former stockbroker who'd opted for a radical career change after a bad burnout. If it hadn't been for Koffi's calming presence at the yarn shop, I'd have lost my cool with Maurice weeks ago.

"What's Maurice's deal with Desirée?" Sidney asked, dropping his voice to a murmur. "Do they not get along?"

Koffi counted the stitches of his knitting project before answering. "It's complicated. Maurice used to work for Jerry and Desirée in a...different capacity."

"*Maurice* used to be a—?" I stopped myself in the nick of time and mouthed the words, *private investigator.*

Koffi inclined his bald head. Apart from being roughly the same age—mid-fifties, give or take—baldness was the only thing the men had in common. Maurice was a small ball of anger. Koffi was his tall, rangy, eternally calm counterpart.

Sidney leaned closer. "What happened? How did Maurice wind up managing the yarn shop?"

"An assignment went awry. Someone got hurt." He spread his palms wide. "I don't know the specifics, but that's the gist. After that, Jerry decided Maurice needed a break and put him to work at the yarn shop. The break became permanent."

I felt a reluctant pang of sympathy for the angry little man. "If he'd rather take a more active role, I imagine he's frustrated. Still doesn't excuse his behavior toward me."

"No, it doesn't. Hang in there. Unlike Maurice,

your situation is temporary." Koffi patted my hand and rose from his seat. "Carine is having issues with her hat. I'll go and help." He ambled over to a dark-haired woman with a tight, 80s-style perm.

I turned to Sidney. "I hope Koffi's right about the yarn shop being temporary. It's not like my mother made any promises about our P.I. training."

Like me, Sidney dreamed of training as a private investigator for the Omega Group. I'd first met him on the Eurostar from London to Paris. He'd been on his way to start a sensible career at the British Embassy. I'd been on the run from a London gangster. A series of crazy circumstances had forced us to work together to catch the criminals and avoid the morgue. After that first wild weekend, Sidney and I had been well and truly bitten by the crime-solving bug. We'd accepted my mother's offer of jobs and accommodation as a stopgap solution, but I'd run out of patience by the time summer had turned to autumn.

Fortunately for him, Sidney was of a more easygoing disposition. "Have faith, Angel. Your mother said she'd discuss our training when she gets back from her latest assignment."

"Her latest assignment has dragged on for months," I replied gloomily. "Don't get me wrong. I'm grateful for the home and the job and the chance of a fresh start."

"You just feel like that fresh start is in permanent waiting mode," Sidney finished for me with a wry smile. "I get it. I feel the same. My family hasn't spoken to me since I ditched my embassy job. I need to prove to them I made the right decision."

"At least your family cares in their own strange way. My father hasn't spoken to me in over two years, not since I helped get his boss's son sent to prison. As for my brothers..." I trailed off, brooding over my fractured family. I was my mother's only child, but I had four half brothers on my father's side—three older, one younger. All had gone into the "family business," Dad's tongue-in-cheek reference to his career as a London gangster's longtime lackey.

"Have you decided what to do about Del's birthday?" Sidney's tone was soft and understanding. "It'll do no harm to send him a message."

I pulled a face. My twin from another mother, my brother Del, had been born three months before me. We'd been tight as kids, and that connection had stayed strong throughout our teenage years. Once we'd hit our twenties—and especially after my falling out with Dad—we'd had less contact.

Yet Del had been the only member of my immediate family who'd kept in touch after I'd helped the police convict Dad's boss's son. Del's failure to respond to my messages after my brush with death in July hurt, and I was still smarting over the rejection. I was now torn about sending him a message for his birthday, thus sharing my new phone number with him and, potentially, the rest of the clan.

"I'm trying not to think about Del. His birthday isn't until Friday. I'll decide what to do then."

Picking up on my reluctance to pursue this topic, Sidney switched back to our job situation. "Our current gigs aren't ideal. But, hey, at least Nice is a lovely place to hang out while we wait for your mother to decide about our future."

He was right. I was in a gorgeous city with sun and sea galore, money in my pocket, and a roof over my head. Even in November, the temperature rarely dipped below ten degrees Celsius, plenty warm to get away with a light jacket rather than the heavy winter coat I'd worn last year in London.

I regarded my knitting and sighed. "Right. Time to woman up and deal with this tangle."

For the next half hour, I attempted to fix my hot mess handiwork, ripping back rounds of knitting and starting over. Lather, rinse, repeat. I kept at it until Luc materialized in front of us with a tray. Luc left the café's day-to-day management in his assistant's capable hands while he was away on investigations. Last night, he'd returned from an assignment in Italy.

Yeah, I was jealous. And not just because of his assignment. Luc confined his role at this meeting to serving food and drink. While he looked mad, bad, and tattooed behind a tray, I struggled to knit my first hat.

Luc served our neighboring table their drinks. Then he handed Sidney a brandy Alexander and slid a strawberry margarita in front of me.

I blinked at the red drink. "I didn't order anything."

He stood close enough for me to smell his trademark spicy aftershave. A smile played over his annoyingly kiss-me-now lips. "Considering that tangle of yarn in your hands, you look like you could down ten."

I hated guys who assumed they knew what I wanted. And ordering for me? A cardinal sin. But the worst part? Luc nailed what I liked. Every. Single. Time. I glared at him but reached for the drink. I took a sip. It tasted good. Seriously good. And it took me every piece of my willpower not to show it.

And it wasn't as if Luc had shown the slightest interest in me. Maybe that was part of the problem. But why did I care? The last thing I needed in my life was a know-it-all boyfriend. Actually, any boyfriend. After my previous relationship had crash-landed, I'd promised myself I'd stay single until I found a man who was the polar opposite of my usual type. I had an unfortunate tendency to fall for bad boys, and Luc's broad shoulders and wicked smile ticked all my happy boxes.

Luc picked up my wannabe hat, and his lips twitched. "What's this supposed to be? A tea cozy?"

"It's a hat," I said with dignity and snatched it back. "Did you come over to insult me, or do you have an ulterior motive?"

He fixed me with his electric blue stare. "Why do you always suspect me of being up to no good? You don't even know me. How often have we even been under the same roof since you moved in?"

Twenty-three nights. Not that I was counting. Luc was my mother's semipermanent house-sitter for her beachside villa. When she'd invited Sidney and me to stay in Nice and work for her, she'd made Luc accept us as his new roommates. I'd expected him to be grumpy about sharing the place with two strangers. However, it transpired that he spent most of his time away on investigations for the Omega Group. He considered us to be convenient cat-sitters.

I jabbed the air with a knitting needle. "I may not know you well, Luc, but I can always tell when someone messes with me. What's up?"

"Not messing, I swear. Do you two still want to become private investigators?"

Sidney and I exchanged wary looks, then nodded in unison.

An impish grin spread across Luc's overly handsome face. "In that case, I have a job for you."

2

That grin did a number on what remained of my self-possession. For an instant, the smells, sounds, and sights of the café receded, and I was aware only of Luc and me. A burning blush crept over my cheeks, pulling me back to reality. "I knew it. You are messing with me. What's the job? Investigating the case of the missing sugar shaker? Newsflash: the gnome lady did it. I saw her slip it into her knitting bag five minutes ago. But, hey, maybe you'll luck out, Luc. She might gift you a gnome-topped toilet paper doily as compensation."

Luc regarded the woman in question and groaned. "Not again. Madame Benoit has a touch of the klepto."

Sidney winked at me. "A trait she has in common with you, Angel. Are you sure you don't have a stray sugar shaker hidden up that enormous sweater?"

I tugged at the hem of my oversized long-sleeved T-

14

shirt, suddenly hyperaware of my dowdy outfit. Knowing Luc would be at the café tonight, I'd dressed down for the meeting. I hadn't wanted him to think I'd made an effort to impress him. Now I was irritated with myself for caring what Luc thought of my appearance. This irritation made my response to Sidney sharper than his teasing warranted. "I haven't nicked so much as a toothpick for nearly two months."

"You're a reformed character," Luc drawled. "Perfect for the job I have lined up for you."

Sidney placed his knitting on the table and leaned forward. "Come on, Luc. Don't leave us in suspense. What is this mysterious case? Do you need us to search for Mélisandre's missing chew toys again?"

"This has nothing to do with my cat. Have either of you met your knitting comrade Ghiselle Dubois?" Luc pointed at a wiry forty-something redhead who was currently quizzing Maurice. I couldn't hear what they were saying, but I could tell she was obsessed with getting her complicated colorwork sweater right.

I pulled a face. "Oh, yeah. We've met. She's pretty...intense."

"Ghiselle, the Seaside Psychic?" Sidney squinted through his black-rimmed glasses. "I've seen her around, but we haven't exchanged more than a *bonjour*."

I perked up at the mention of Ghiselle's profession. "She's a seaside psychic? As in, she tells fortunes on the beach?"

"As in, she makes a living scamming tourists." Luc's tone was wry. "Enough of a living to hire your amateur detective services. How do you two feel about taking on an unofficial case?"

I side-eyed him hard. "A case not sanctioned by Jerry or my mother?"

He struggled to control his facial muscles but failed to hide his smirk. "Okay, 'case' might be an overstatement. Let's call it a small side job. Don't you two want to try out your sleuthing skills?"

"Why does Ghiselle need us? Can't she pull a tarot card and have a vision or something?"

"Hang on, Angel. Let's not dismiss her just yet." Sidney sounded serious. "If we want to convince your mother and Jerry to train us as P.I.s, we need the practice. Besides, Ghiselle's supposed to be uncannily accurate. If the idea of getting my fortune told didn't scare me rigid, I'd stop by her tent."

I wrinkled my nose. "I can't believe any half-rational individual would take that claptrap seriously."

"And yet newspaper horoscopes are perennial favorites," Sidney pointed out. "Not everyone who reads them is a fool."

That was a matter of opinion, but I could see I wouldn't convince him. "Regardless of what we think of Ghiselle's chosen profession, she doesn't strike me as easy client material. When I met her at my first Yarniacs meeting, she scrutinized me so thoroughly that I felt like I'd been strip-searched."

Luc's dirty laugh sent a prickle of awareness zinging through my veins. I took a deep breath. Nope. I would not fall for this man. He spelled trouble in all-caps, blazing neon letters.

"Ghiselle can be full-on," he conceded, "but she pays well. And she's willing to pay you two."

Sidney regarded me with a hopeful expression. "Come on, Angel. It can't hurt to talk to the woman."

I wasn't as sanguine. We both wanted to score our first official Omega Group assignment. A successful conclusion to a sideline case might help us persuade my mother. Unfortunately, I had a sinking feeling that any job Luc offered us would be more Austin Powers and less James Bond.

"If Ghiselle needs a private investigator, why don't you take the job?" I asked Luc. "Or one of the other investigators at the O—" I dropped my voice, "—at the place that shall remain nameless?"

This time, nothing was appealing about Luc's grin. "The sort of investigating she needs doesn't require a professional. Just someone with good internet search skills."

I mimicked a cat scratching the table. "Meooow. Sharp claws, mister."

"I'm not saying that to offend you. You guys aren't licensed investigators. You just happened to get lucky during all the action in July."

His words unraveled the loose threads of my patience. "Seriously?" My voice rose with each syllable. "We used our brains to solve not one but *three* cases. Three *big* cases."

"Sure you did." Luc's easy drawl pushed my anger up into my rib cage. "You did well...for amateurs. I'm sure you'll do a great job for Ghiselle."

Walking away from a challenge was never easy for me. Walking away from a challenge issued by an alpha male? Never going to happen.

I was out of my seat before I had time to think. "You bet we'll do an awesome job for Ghiselle. Sidney, want to talk to her now?"

Luc's expression went from amused to smug. I wanted to quick-knit a lasso and then hog-tie him to the chair. Instead, I turned my back on him and marched across the café.

Sidney and his long legs wasted no time catching up with me. He grabbed my arm and drew me to a halt in the middle of the café. "Steady on, partner," he said, keeping his voice low. "Do we have a plan before we tackle Ghiselle?"

"We don't need a plan. We'll tell her we want to hear more about the job. If she doesn't want to spill her guts at tonight's meeting, we'll arrange a time to chat later. Then we decide if we want to take her case or not." I cast a black look back at the still-grinning Luc. "However much I want to annoy our beloved housemate, I'm walking if Ghiselle wants us to help her scam clients."

"If that's the case, I'll walk with you. But we don't

know what she wants from us yet. Try to keep an open mind, okay? And let me take the lead. You're pricklier than a cactus this evening. We want the woman to confide in us, not run screaming."

I opened my mouth to object to being called prickly but closed it again. Sidney had a point. I'd been on edge all day, and not just about Luc. "I'm sorry for being grumpy. I've had my brother's birthday on my mind, and Maurice has been particularly trying today."

"I'm sorry about Maurice. That's all the more reason for us to handle Ghiselle with care. If she hires us, we can dazzle Desirée with our investigative skills. Then she'll have to agree to let us train to be private investigators. That'll get you out of the yarn shop and away from Maurice forever."

A tantalizing prospect. I eyed our quarry and squared my shoulders. "Okay, partner. Let's do this thing."

In a few strides, we were at Ghiselle's side. She sat alone now that Maurice had made his escape, frowning at her knitting. The pattern was a gorgeous winter scene and something I could recreate only in my dreams.

"Hi, Ghiselle." Sidney turned on his money-making smile. "I'm Sidney. We've seen each other in passing, but we haven't been introduced. I believe you've met Angel already? Luc mentioned you wanted to talk to us." He stretched out a hand, expecting her to shake.

The woman recoiled like he'd sucker-punched her in the abs. "I don't shake hands. Too many germs."

Sidney let his arm drop. "Okaaaaaaay."

I fought back a laugh and schooled my features into calm and professional. Time for my prickly personality to prevail over his practiced charm. "Can we sit at your table? Or would that be another faux pas?"

"Sure. Sit." She pushed her chair as far back from us as the wall would permit.

I exchanged a loaded look with Sidney. I wanted excitement, sure, but I wasn't convinced Ghiselle Dubois was our ticket to Funland.

We took the seats opposite Ghiselle, trying to play it cool. With the weird tension in the air, I wasn't sure we succeeded. I placed my hands on the table and spread my fingers wide. "So...what's this job you want us to do for you?"

Ghiselle darted a nervous glance around the café, then dropped her voice to a funeral-home whisper. "I need you to find my late husband."

3

We stared at her, stupefied, for several long seconds. The sounds in the café receded, leaving me hyperaware of this weird woman and her outrageous request.

Finally, Sidney broke the silence with a series of rusty-hinge-style squeaks. "Late husband? As in, late to meet you? Or late of this world?"

"She means he's dead." I looked across the table at Ghiselle. "That's right, isn't it? You want us to look for a dead man?"

Ghiselle cocked her head to the side, reminding me of a robin redbreast perched on a branch. "My husband drowned in a boating accident five years ago. I need you to find him."

The woman sounded crazy, but she looked sane. But her request? Totally in the crazy-pants territory.

No wonder Luc hadn't wanted to take on this case. No wonder he'd been amused when he'd dumped it on us.

My gaze slid to the bar. Luc leaned against the counter, watching us and clearly enjoying the show. When I caught his eye, his gotcha-grin widened. My middle finger itched to flip him the bird.

Instead, I curled my fingers into the palm of my hand and focused on Ghiselle. From her deer-in-the-headlights eyes to her white-knuckled fingers, everything about the woman screamed neurotic desperation. I hated to add to her burdens, but I couldn't string her along. "I'm sorry for your loss, Ghiselle. We're the wrong people to turn to. We have no idea how to find a body that went missing so long ago, especially one that fell into the sea. That's a job for the police."

She dismissed my suggestion with one expressive jerk of her head. "The police? They're useless. They think I'm a fraud."

I was no friend to the police, but in this instance, I was Team Cop. I tried to keep an open mind about most things. However, I had a reason to be wary of anyone claiming to be a psychic. When I was a kid, a woman my grandmother believed to be a medium had conned her out of several thousand euros. The incident had made me distrust horoscopes, tarot cards, and anything smacking of hocus pocus.

Despite my misgivings, Ghiselle's mad request intrigued me. Even if we didn't take the case, I had to know more. "Have you been searching for his body all these years?"

"No, of course not. Like everyone else, I assumed Pierre was dead."

"And now you don't?" Sidney practically bounced in his chair, toddler-style.

The fine lines across Ghiselle's freckled forehead deepened. "Two weeks ago, Pierre started appearing to me in visions. He's not in the afterlife. I'm convinced he's in this world, and he needs my help." Her doe eyes filled with tears. Either she was a talented actress, or she was genuinely upset.

"Even pro psychics must have dreams that are just dreams," I said. "Why are you convinced what you saw was the real deal?"

Ghiselle let her guard down for the barest moment, and I caught a flash of contempt in her eyes before she slid back into her dizzy-neurotic routine. "These are visions. Pierre's hair is shorter and graying around the temples. He's grown older. Dead men don't age."

Ghiselle's wild story had hooked my interest. Her incongruous flicker of disdain had reeled me in. What game was she playing? What was the cause of her stress? Her late husband? Or a living man she regarded as a threat? "If you have psychic powers, why can't you contact Pierre and find out where he is?"

This time, there was no mistaking her annoyance. "Clearly, you understand nothing about psychic abilities. The closer I am to a person or situation, the less I can see."

I looked at Sidney and tried to mentally message him to bail us out of this situation. His mouth twitched once, then twice. Message received.

Now that he'd recovered from his initial shock, he'd shifted into one of his many public personas. It was a trick of his I found both admirable and alarming. I had a hard time blunting the edges of my personality when dealing with people. In contrast, Sidney dug into his treasure trove of acting skills and presented the persona best suited to the situation.

He leaned forward in his seat ever so slightly and adopted his wise-counselor act. "Do you have someone to talk to about all this, Ghiselle? Like a therapist?"

His sotto voce delivery had the desired effect. She unhunched her shoulders. Her lips trembled, and the floodgates opened. If this was an act, Ghiselle was in line for an academy award. Unfortunately for her, I was a picky critic.

I pulled a pack of tissues out of my bag and gave her one.

She took it and honked her nose. "No one understands me. No one wants to listen. I know what I saw, and I know it was real."

"I want to listen. I want to know what you saw. And I want to know what happened the day your husband died." Sidney drew his phone from his pocket and swiped the screen. "Is it okay if we record this conversation? It's easier to chat if Angel and I don't need to take notes."

Sidney's soothing voice softened the tension lines on the woman's face. "Sure. Record away." She waited until he hit the record button. Then she took a deep breath and began her tale. "One morning, Pierre went out in his speedboat and never returned. A passing fishing boat found the capsized speedboat and contacted Search and Rescue. They looked for my husband for two days but never found him. Everyone assumed he'd drowned." She curled and uncurled her fingers, seemingly unaware she was doing it. "For months, I waited for a phone call telling me his body had washed up somewhere. That phone call never came. Eventually, Pierre was declared legally dead."

"Did you believe he'd drowned?" Sidney asked. "Or did you suspect he was still alive?"

"It took me a while to process what had happened. I tried to connect with Pierre's spirit and never received a response. That's not unusual—it's easier for mediums to connect with strangers' spirits than those of loved ones. So yes, I accepted my husband's death." Her eyes grew large and held a manic glint. "These visions tell a different story. I now know he's alive."

Even if Pierre was alive, why did Ghiselle want to find him? Love? Closure? Revenge?

After exchanging a look and a nod with Sidney, I took up the conch. "Assuming Pierre *is* still alive, why hasn't he come forward in all the years since the boat accident?"

"Isn't that obvious?" Ghiselle's sigh was deeper than the Mariana Trench. "He was kidnapped and forced to work at a casino."

I slow-blinked and swallowed the *what the...?* that hovered on my tongue. "Let me get this straight. Pierre was trafficked to work at a casino? Why in the world would anyone want to do that?"

"My husband could've been a professional poker player. He was that good. And he spent a lot of time at the casinos in Nice and Monte Carlo."

I seized on this information, the first logical-sounding tidbit she'd provided so far. "Do you think Pierre's death, faked or real, was connected to gambling?"

Ghiselle shrank back in her seat and instinctively turned to sympathetic Sidney. "Pierre just liked to play poker. He didn't run up debts. He had no enemies."

"I'm sure he didn't," Sidney replied in a calming voice. "What was Pierre doing in your visions? Playing poker?"

She shook her head, loosening the lone gray curl in her vibrant red mane. "He was working as a croupier at a roulette table."

"That's great, Ghiselle." He gave her an encouraging smile. "Keep the details coming. Did you notice anything to indicate where the casino was located? Like the language people were speaking? Or the landscape visible through a window?"

Ghiselle fluttered her eyelashes at him. As in, actually batted them. And then she inched her chair a little closer, a clear indicator of her growing trust. Jeez Louise. How did Sidney do it? He was a natural at getting people to confide in him.

"Almost all the people around the roulette table spoke French," Ghiselle said, "but Pierre addressed one man in English. I didn't see any windows in the room. A series of photographs on the walls looked like mountain landscapes. I'm certain one was the Matterhorn, but I didn't recognize any others."

I turned this info over in my mind. "Assuming the photographs were of local mountains, the casino could be in Switzerland, most likely in the French-speaking area."

Ghiselle fiddled with one of her rings. Now that I looked closer, I identified it as a wedding band. "Switzerland would make sense," she said. "Pierre sometimes went to a casino in Geneva. Clearly, a gangster wanted to use Pierre's card skills to make money and kidnapped him. It all makes perfect sense."

Maybe to her, but not to me. "If Pierre was kidnapped for his poker-playing prowess, why wasn't he playing poker in your visions? You described him working as a croupier. That's a whole other level."

"How should I know why he was working at a roulette table instead of playing poker?" A note of testiness crept into her voice. "Perhaps he was helping out. All I know is he wore a uniform—a waistcoat with a candy cane pattern. Pierre would never wear a jacket like that voluntarily. He prided himself on looking suave."

"Candy cane pinstripes?" Sidney's face expressed undiluted horror.

"Forget about the waistcoat." I shot him a keep-on-track look, then turned my attention to the woman. "You said your visions began two weeks ago. Was there anything significant about the date? Was it Pierre's birthday? Or the anniversary of his accident?"

"No, nothing like that. The first vision came to me totally out of the blue." Ghiselle chewed her bottom lip, a look of intense concentration on her face. "I was lying in the bath. It hit me like a lightning bolt. Suddenly, I stood by a roulette table, stark naked and dripping wet. No one present could see me, but I could see and hear them. Pierre took bets from the people at the table and spun the wheel. He looked an older, grayer version of the man I married. But it was definitely him. And he was frightened. Of something, someone—I don't know. I could tell he needed my help."

"Did he interact with you at all during the vision?" Sidney asked.

She shook her head. "He didn't look in my direction. He didn't need to. I make my living through my ability to read people. I knew Pierre was stressed, frightened, desperate."

I leaned back in my seat and regarded her hard. Was I seriously considering taking this job? Common sense warred with the first bubble of excitement I'd experienced in weeks. Ghiselle was wacky, but her story intrigued me. "To sum up, you want to hire Sidney and me to determine if your husband is still alive."

The look she shot me was pure irritation. "I *know* he's alive. I want you to find him and bring him home."

"We can't make any promises, Ghiselle," Sidney said gently. "Even if we find Pierre, he might not want to come back to Nice. We can't force him."

Her jaw adopted a stubborn jut. "He'll come. He loves me. He'll want to come home."

I refrained from pointing out that a man who'd faked his own death, leaving his wife to assume the worst, was unlikely to embrace the idea of a romantic reunion. "If Sidney and I take this job, we'll need money to cover our travel expenses as well as our fee."

Ghiselle's mouth curled into a smile of pure irony. She drew a business card from her purse and scribbled something on it in a generous cursive. Then she shoved the card across the table. One glance at the sum was enough to seal the deal for me. I wasn't particularly mercenary, but I had bills to pay and no savings.

Judging by Sidney's intake of breath, he was of the same opinion.

I checked Sidney's phone to make sure it was still recording. "Can you tell us exactly when Pierre's accident happened? And give us a list of friends and coworkers to contact? Also, personal details about Pierre—full name, date of birth, occupation, etc."

"A photograph would also be useful," Sidney added. "Preferably one of him around the time of the accident."

Over the next fifteen minutes, Ghiselle reeled off names, dates, and addresses. Pierre Matthieu Dubois had been a forty-seven-year-old civil servant at the time of his disappearance. The photo she sent to Sidney's phone showed a forgettable face: dark hair, dark eyes, tanned complexion, average features. He looked like a million other guys in the south of France.

The life history Ghiselle recounted was equally mundane. Pierre had been an only child, and both his parents were now dead. He'd been born near Cannes and had lived most of his life in Nice. After school, he'd joined the civil service and had enjoyed an undistinguished career in the births, deaths, and marriages department. Any promotions he'd received had been based on seniority, not merit. The only exciting nugget of information Ghiselle shared about her husband was his poker talent.

By the time she'd finished, the Yarniacs meeting was over. The club members were dispersing. Sidney returned his phone to his pocket, and we rose from our seats. "Thanks for all the info," he said. "We'll be in touch by Tuesday. Sooner, if questions crop up."

Ghiselle's eyes filled with tears. "Thank you. Whatever mess Pierre is in, I'll help him out. All I want is for him to come home."

Despite my wariness toward the woman, I couldn't help feeling sorry for her. Nut job or not, her anguish felt real. I didn't know if Sidney and I could alleviate that distress. In the unlikely event Pierre was still alive, would he *want* to come home? And if he was dead, how could we convince Ghiselle to accept his death as a fact?

4

The day after we agreed to take Ghiselle Dubois's case was a rainy Thursday. Sidney was due to work at the costumier for a few hours in the morning, but I had the entire day free. I would search for info on the accident and meet Pierre's former coworkers while Sidney used his coffee break to call some people on Ghiselle's list.

Although Nice was busy all year round, the summer crowd was long gone. I zipped through the traffic in the little Peugeot I'd borrowed from Luc and found a parking space close to my first destination. Despite today's downpour, the temperature was a pleasant fifteen degrees Celsius —several degrees higher than I was accustomed to at this time of year. I was still adjusting to a warmer climate, and my T-shirt and skirt outed me as a non-native. I opened my umbrella and made my way from my parking space to the library.

Besides housing Nice's largest public library, the Bibliothèque Louis Nucéra was a popular tourist attraction. Its administrative offices were located inside La Tête Carrée, a massive sculpture of a cube covering a man's head. Yes, it had to be seen to be believed. This monstrosity had been designed by Sacha Sosno, whose massive sculptures could be seen all over the Côte d'Azur. I considered the square head an eyesore, but it never failed to send Sidney into raptures.

The library buildings open to the public were far more prosaic than the head. They were also massive, occupying a ten-thousand-square-meter extension of the Museum of Modern and Contemporary Art. Being a digital book kind of girl, this was my first time inside the library's ultra-modern interior. Frankly, I wouldn't be here if I'd had the money to pay for home access to newspaper digital archives.

I'd spent hours scouring the internet for information on Pierre Dubois last night. The result? A whole lot of nothing. I'd unearthed a few mentions of the accident on news sites, but nothing detailed. Pierre had had no social media presence, and no one on social media had commented on his death.

It was frustrating. And weird. I could buy the quiet Pierre avoiding a web presence, but surely his accident should've garnered more attention online, at least from his friends?

I headed to the front desk. An ultra-efficient receptionist furnished me with a spanking-new library card and directions to the public computers. It didn't take me long to discover articles on Pierre Dubois's boating accident—there weren't many to find. Like the mentions I'd found online, the reports were brief and devoid of sensation. Apparently, the death of a mediocre civil servant elicited little interest.

The details of the accident took me all of a few sentences to scribble into my digital notes app. Five years ago, on a morning in early June, Pierre Dubois had gone out in the secondhand speedboat he'd picked up at an auction a few weeks prior to the accident. He'd been alone and had told his wife to expect him home in time for their evening meal.

At three o'clock in the afternoon, a fishing boat spotted Pierre's speedboat capsized a few nautical miles from the Île Saint-Honorat, the second largest of the Lérins Islands. The captain immediately radioed for assistance and searched the water around the speedboat for any survivors. Search and Rescue arrived soon after, but found no trace of Pierre Dubois.

According to two witnesses, Pierre had enjoyed an early lunch on Île Sainte-Marguerite, the Lérins Island made famous by a fortress that had once held the Man in the Iron Mask. No one had seen Pierre leave the island, and no witnesses reported seeing him on another island or at sea. The man had no criminal record, no history of depression or addictions, and no known extramarital romance.

I left the library no better informed than I'd gone in. The only exciting tidbits about Pierre Dubois were his poker prowess and his speedboat, and those I'd learned from his wife. Even Ghiselle's job as a psychic didn't add flavor to the man's bland biography. She hadn't started her seaside psychic gig until after being widowed.

My second stop was a café near the library. I'd arranged to meet two of Pierre's former coworkers for coffee. Zaineb Gharbi and Claudine Berset were both women in their fifties. They'd worked with Pierre for twenty-two and twenty-seven years, respectively. Despite seeing him day in and day out for all that time, their only impression of Pierre was that he'd been punctual and quiet.

For the first teeth-grinding twenty minutes, I drank indifferent coffee and admired photos of the women's grandbabies and grandpuppies. I tried to steer the conversation back to Pierre every time they digressed. It was an exercise in frustration.

When Claudine, the older of the two, produced another photo of an infant resembling a peach-clad beach ball, I didn't even pretend to be interested. "What can you tell me about Pierre's wife?" My clipped delivery hovered on the border between direct and rude, but it had the desired effect.

Still clutching the photo, Claudine pulled her

yellow cardigan across her generous bosom and peered at me through her frizzy gray fringe. "Ghiselle is the Seaside Psychic."

"She wasn't the Seaside Psychic back then," I reminded her. "I believe she was working as a nurse."

"That's right." Zaineb, the younger and bubblier of the two, leaned across the table, narrowly avoiding spilling her cappuccino. "That's how they met. Ghiselle looked after Pierre's grandfather before he went into a care home. She was his private nurse."

I raised an eyebrow. "Private nurses don't come cheap. Was Pierre's grandfather wealthy?"

They regarded me with amusement.

"Absolutely loaded." Zaineb's soft Tunisian-accented French added a melodious lilt to her words. "Ever heard of Bonnier-Dubois?"

"The pharmaceutical company?" The stirrings of excitement lent my voice a musical tone. "Was Pierre's family part of it?"

Zaineb dumped a third sugar cube into her cappuccino and stirred vigorously. "Arthur Dubois, Pierre's grandfather, is one of the co-founders. He led their research and development department for decades."

"Pierre's parents also worked at the company," Claudine supplied. "They were pharmaceutical engineers."

I digested this new information, my mind in overdrive.

Regardless of Pierre's lack of a social media presence, the death of a local magnate's grandson should've been big news, both on social media and mainstream outlets. Why was information about his accident so hard to find?

I sipped my coffee and returned my attention to my companions. "You two claim to know very little about Pierre himself, yet you sure know a lot about his family."

"Well, yeah." Zaineb pointed at a rack of magazines the café supplied for their customers to peruse over coffee. "Pierre's grandfather is famous. And René and Caroline Dubois, his parents, were often photographed at high society events."

"We probably knew more about their private lives than Pierre's," Claudine mused. "Funny, that. But then, Pierre blended into the background."

"How did the grandson of a multimillionaire—"

"Billionaire," Zaineb corrected. "Arthur Dubois always makes France's Top Fifty Wealthiest People list."

"Mega-wealthy, in that case. Why didn't Pierre follow his parents into the family business? No interest? Or no aptitude?"

A flicker of a smirk played over Claudine's broad face, but she killed it fast when she caught Zaineb's warning look. "Pierre wasn't academic. He was an average student at best. Average doesn't cut it if you want to work at Bonnier-Dubois."

"Not even if you're the boss's grandson?" I pressed. "Couldn't Arthur have found Pierre a desk job?"

Claudine shrugged. "If he'd wanted to, sure. But Arthur Dubois had a reputation for excellence. He only wanted the best at his company. Pierre wasn't the best at anything."

Ouch. I felt a pang of sympathy for Pierre. I was all too familiar with failing to live up to familial expectations—or down to, depending on your perspective. I'd been estranged from my career criminal father since I'd given evidence against my ex-boyfriend—his gangster boss's son. Dad had taken his boss's side, a betrayal that still stung. My relationship with my mother had always been strained. She had an uncanny knack for making me feel less-than, and I had an unerring aptitude for making her lose her legendary cool.

I skimmed the notes I'd taken so far. "I assume Arthur didn't provide Pierre with a private income. Ghiselle's home is in a pretty average part of town."

"Oh, no." Claudine's tone turned blade-sharp. "Arthur is a self-made man and a miser to boot. I doubt he gave Pierre a cent."

"What about Pierre's parents? Ghiselle mentioned they were dead. Didn't Pierre inherit money from them?"

"That's the irony of the situation." Zaineb's smile was the barest twist. "Arthur has always been a miser.

His son was the opposite. He and his wife left all their money to charity."

Double ouch. "Wasn't that rough on Pierre? Didn't he resent being cut off from his inheritance?"

Claudine shrugged. "If he did, he didn't show it. But then, Pierre showed little emotion."

"From what the papers said at the time of their deaths," Zaineb added, "Pierre knew the terms of his parents' will in advance and was okay with it. Besides, he was aware he'd inherit his grandfather's fortune one day."

"You speak of Arthur in the present tense. I assume he's still alive?"

She shrugged. "He must be. If he'd died, it would've been all over the news. Right, Claudine?"

Her friend nodded in agreement. "Definitely. Arthur Dubois is well known in these parts."

And yet his grandson's fatal boating accident had barely warranted a few lines in the local newspapers. I tapped my stylus pen against my tablet screen. Something didn't add up here. Even if Pierre had been as boring as they claimed, his famous name should've attracted media attention, especially if he was the heir to a fortune—a fortune his widow had failed to mention. "Let's go back to Ghiselle. What do you two know about her relationship with Pierre?"

Claudine's lips twisted into a smirk. "Very little. Pierre met Ghiselle while she was nursing his grandfather. They fell in love and were married within a month."

"It was the most exciting thing Pierre ever did." Zaineb didn't try to hide the catty note in her voice. "However, I suspect Ghiselle was the driving force in that marriage. She knew Pierre was Arthur's only heir, and she wasted no time becoming Mrs. Dubois."

Ghiselle hadn't struck me as the mercenary type, but who knew? She earned her crust duping fools with fantasies of the future. A woman like that had to be skilled in the art of deception. I wasn't easily taken in, but maybe she'd played me last night. Had made me believe she was neurotic, vulnerable, gullible.

Her act hadn't been perfect. She'd shown a few cracks—the flashes of irritation when I'd expressed my doubts about her story and sharpness when I'd asked probing questions. Did Ghiselle's annoyance stem from years of being disbelieved? Or was there a deeper reason for her instant wariness? And scrolling back to the subject of finances, the fee she'd dangled in front of Sidney and me had been higher than I'd expected her to afford, but not outrageously so.

I pulled my thoughts back to the present. "Now that Pierre's dead, who inherits Arthur's money?"

"No idea," Zaineb said. "The state, I guess. Pierre was Arthur's only heir, and Pierre and Ghiselle never had kids."

Claudine regarded me with calculating eyes. "You

said Ghiselle hired you to take another look at Pierre's death. Does she think it wasn't an accident?"

I chose the following words with care. "There's a rumor Pierre might still be alive."

The women were agog at this news.

"Ghiselle thinks Pierre faked his own death?" Zaineb snorted. "No way. He didn't have the brains."

"Or the imagination," Claudine added. "Pierre was a simple guy. If anyone faked a situation, it would be Ghiselle. I can't deal with her pseudo-psychic nonsense. Defrauding innocent people out of their money and plying them with false hope? It's shameful."

"People consult Ghiselle of their own free will," I said, forcing myself to be reasonable even though I shared Claudine's opinion. "I don't believe in psychics, but clearly, many people do."

Neither woman looked convinced. Claudine snuck a peek at her watch and drained her coffee cup. "I need to collect my granddaughter."

I was on borrowed time. I had to bring this conversation to a constructive end. "Can either of you imagine a situation that might prompt Pierre Dubois to fake his own death?"

Zaineb shook her head. "No way. Pierre wasn't the type. He could've filed for divorce if he'd wanted to escape Ghiselle."

"Isn't it possible everyone underestimated him?" I

watched their reactions closely. "Maybe he wasn't the boring, unadventurous man you thought he was."

Their denials were prompt and decisive.

"Pierre's personality was a lot like the color beige," Zaineb said with a wan smile. "Unexciting. Inoffensive. Not the sort of man to lead a double life."

I wasn't so sure. Their description of Pierre reminded me of my former stepfather, Jerry Gallo. I'd written Jerry off as a sweet, well-meaning bore. And then I'd discovered he headed an international P.I. agency. What was that old saying my Irish grandmother had used? Still waters ran deep? I thought of Pierre Dubois, the depths of the Mediterranean Sea, and shivered.

I picked up the bill for our coffees and said goodbye to Claudine and Zaineb. I made my way back to the car, turning over the conversation in my mind. Sparks of excitement zipped through me, stronger even than the enthusiasm Ghiselle's fat fee had elicited. There was more to this case than a delusional widow. And I was determined to find out what.

I'd arranged to meet Sidney at Luc's café for lunch and a brainstorming session. When I stepped inside the café, Sidney had saved us a corner table. He pressed his phone to his ear, a wrinkle of concentration etched across his forehead. He nodded to me when I dropped into the seat across from him, and he gestured for me to remain silent.

"Thanks so much for your time, Elaine. I appreciate your candor. Yes, absolutely confidential. If I have follow-up questions, I'll be in touch. Enjoy your weekend."

I ran through the list of people Ghiselle had supplied us with last night. Elaine Ayari was married to Asad Ayari, Pierre Dubois's closest friend. From Sidney's cat-got-the-cream grin, I guessed his conversation had been fruitful. "Well?" I prompted when he lowered his phone. "What did Elaine say?"

His grin widened. "That Ghiselle was economical with the truth."

"That tallies with what I've learned this morning. Can you be more specific?"

"At the time of Pierre's accident, he was couch-surfing. His last known residence was Elaine and Asad's spare room."

This news surprised me into an arched eyebrow. "Pierre and Ghiselle had separated? His coworkers didn't mention this."

"Neither did Ghiselle." Sidney gestured to the phone. "According to Elaine, Pierre told Ghiselle he wanted a divorce a month before the accident. She flew into a rage and threw him out of the house."

"Not exactly surprising," I remarked. "Would you want to keep living with your soon-to-be ex?"

"Yeah, but Elaine describes Ghiselle as unhinged.

She claims the marriage was a living hell for Pierre, and he'd been anxious and depressed for months before his death."

I caught Sidney's drift in a millisecond. "Elaine believes Pierre took his own life?"

He spread his palms wide. "She didn't say so directly, but it was heavily implied. She's inclined to believe the suicide theory over Ghiselle's claim that Pierre is still alive."

"It's certainly the more plausible of the two hypotheses. If they were separated, why did Ghiselle tell the police Pierre was supposed to eat dinner with her on the day he disappeared?"

"Apparently, that part was true. Elaine said they were due to meet to discuss the divorce."

"If Elaine knows so much," I said archly, "perhaps she can tell us who inherits Pierre's grandfather's money if Pierre is out of the picture."

At Sidney's expression of confusion, I filled him in on my morning, with particular attention to what I'd learned during my coffee date with Claudine and Zaineb.

"So what we need to find out is who's the heir to the Dubois fortune?" Sidney asked when I'd finished.

"Exactly. And does it have any bearing on Ghiselle's sudden desire to find out if her husband is still alive?"

Sidney scrunched his forehead. "Why did Ghiselle hold so much back last night? She must've known we'd find out about Pierre's inheritance and their marriage problems once we spoke to the people on the list she gave us."

"The charitable interpretation is that she didn't want to say too much in the café in case we were overheard. But it makes me wonder what we'll discover when we question people Ghiselle *didn't* include on her list."

The jangle of the bell above the door announced the arrival of another customer. It was lunchtime. The café was busy. And yet my instincts screamed that this jangle was significant.

I was right.

I smelled her before seeing her—a musky perfume with a rose base note. Desirée Chablis. Former porn star, sometimes spy. And my mother.

Desirée looked magnificent, as always. Today's outfit was a curve-hugging scarlet dress and matching stiletto heels. She glided across the room, catching the eye of every person in the café, and making me painfully aware of how homely I was in comparison to her glamor.

I schooled my features into a semblance of a smile. "Hello, Desirée."

A flicker of irritation flashed in my mother's baby-blue eyes. She'd never liked me calling her by her first name. Which, of course, was why I persisted in doing so. "Darlings." She air-kissed us both, careful not to smudge her expertly applied makeup. "I'm so glad I caught you. I need you next door at once."

Sidney sighed. "Did Francine lock herself out of the cash register again?"

"Oh, no. Nothing to do with the costumier." My mother bent over the table, enveloping us in her scent and her cleavage. "I've called an emergency meeting. I need you two to be there."

Sidney and I looked at one another.

"Of the O—" I swallowed the name at my mother's look of warning. "You want *us* to be present at an agency meeting?"

A sly smile curved my mother's lips. "Not just present. I want to brief you on your first assignment."

5

My first official Omega Group assignment? The news should've blown me away. After all, this was the moment I'd been waiting for since I'd learned of Desirée's secret career. Instead of jubilation, my pre-programmed wariness kicked in. Like Ghiselle's case, there had to be a catch. There was no way my mother would allow Sidney and me to do anything remotely interesting. Not before we'd received formal P.I. training, and probably not even then.

Despite my skepticism, five minutes after Desirée's dramatic announcement, I sat on a cheap plastic chair, armed with caffeine and attitude. The meeting took place in Jerry Gallo's office. No super-secret underground room with fancy security. Just a casual coffee in a room that looked like it'd been cryogenically frozen in the 70s.

Sidney and Luc sat on either side of me, the former talking a mile a minute and the latter blandly bored. Maurice and Koffi inhabited the two armchairs. Maurice fidgeted in his seat, radiating discontent. Koffi sat with his eyes half-closed, serene as a meditating monk.

"I'm so nervous about this meeting that I worry I'll soon be reacquainted with my lunch." Sidney spoke super-soft and hid his words behind his coffee cup. "I can't believe we finally get to do something exciting."

"Don't hold your breath," I whispered. "If I know Desirée, she'll land us with the least desirable task."

Luc's rumbling chuckle reminded me he understood English perfectly. "Very likely. How do you feel about polishing my boots?"

I dropped my gaze to his military-style boots. He'd buffed them to a shine. "Seems to me you've got that under control."

My mother swanned across the room, wafting expensive perfume and Old Hollywood glamor. She placed her coffee on the desk and claimed Jerry's high-backed leather chair. The chair ought to have dwarfed my petite mother. Instead, she occupied it like an empress on her throne.

Maurice glowered across the desk at me and even shot a nasty look Sidney's way. "Why are you two here? Only agents should be present at official meetings."

"Guess that rules you out too. Or are you in the habit of taking down criminals with needles and yarn?" I kept my tone powdered sugar sweet.

The barb hit home. Maurice's egg-shaped head reddened from his bald pate to his weak chin. He opened and shut his mouth several times, enhancing his resemblance to a carp. "I might not be active in the field anymore, but I'm a qualified P.I. with years of experience. Even Koffi's a trained P.I."

This was news to me. Koffi met my questioning look with a hint of a smile before turning to Maurice. "I'm retired," he said. "Happily retired."

Maurice jerked a thumb at us. "All the same, *they* shouldn't be here."

My mother's expression underwent a metamorphosis. Goodbye, Queen of the Red Carpet. Hello, Queen of the Tundra. Her cool gaze swept over us with icy precision, effectively freezing our tongues. "I decide who needs to be present, Maurice. If this meeting was just for active agents, I wouldn't have invited the four of you. You all have a role to play in this assignment."

Her words should've been welcome, but they came as a sharp slap. I was pretty sure I wouldn't like whatever role she had in store for me. Judging by Sidney's stricken expression, a similar thought had dawned on him.

Luc gave an extravagant yawn, breaking the

tension. "Shouldn't we get started? I need to get back to the café by two thirty."

Desirée's perfectly made-up eyes narrowed a fraction and her gaze strayed to the door. "We're still waiting for Valentina. She's late."

Luc's rumbling laugh reminded me of how close his chair was to mine. "Valentina is always late. She'll lope in before long."

One of the Omega Group's star investigators, Valentina was a sulky-looking Spaniard with a penchant for tight clothes and loose men. Valentina had been away on an assignment when Sidney and I had arrived in Nice. When she'd returned and learned that we'd moved in with Luc, she'd taken an instant aversion to us. Not even Sidney's natural charm had won her over.

As far as I knew, we'd done nothing to incite her ire apart from existing. At first, I'd wondered if she was jealous of us living with Luc. Even though she flirted with him when he was in town, she had a seemingly endless supply of men to lure into her lair.

In the distance, church bells chimed the quarter-hour. Valentina chose this moment to make her grand entrance. *"Buenas tardes."*

She paused in the doorway, giving us time to admire her figure-hugging wool dress and thigh-high boots. A slim brunette with legs up to her armpits, Valentina was my physical opposite. Where I was short and curvy, she was tall and slender. Where my hair was a mad mass of unruly curls, hers was sleek and straight.

With her smooth, perfect golden skin, Valentina could've been anything from her mid-twenties to her mid-thirties. Given her seniority in the group, I guessed she was around Luc's age. Thirty-two, thirty-three.

Once Valentina was satisfied with her effect on the assembled company, she glided to the spare chair next to Luc's.

My mother's scarlet lips tightened, then relaxed into a smile. "Nice of you to join us." The unspoken *finally* hung in the air like a foul smell. This was my first time seeing the two women interact, but I didn't need Ghiselle's clairvoyance to pick up on their rivalry.

"I just got back from Rome." Valentina parted her full lips, revealing her sharp incisors. "By the way, Rocco says hello."

It took me a moment to remember Rocco Casetti. He ran a competing P.I. agency based in Italy. He'd also dated my mother.

If Valentina's mention of her former flame irritated her, Desirée didn't show it. She tapped a manicured nail on the sheaf of papers in front of her. "Now that we're all here, let's get straight to the point. Are you familiar with Crofton-Lowe?"

"The auction house?" My knowledge of auction

houses, prestigious or otherwise, was next to none, but even I recognized their name. "Are they a new client? What case do they need to have investigated? A suspected forgery?"

My mother's tinkling laugh set my nerves twanging. "Someone's keen. Let me finish talking, okay?"

Heat crept up my neck at this public rebuke. I caught Maurice's smug smirk and itched to flip him the bird.

"Our case concerns a theft at Crofton-Lowe's Zürich branch," my mother continued. "The branch CEO has hired the Omega Group. Our mission is to retrieve a cache of priceless Egyptian artifacts stolen from their vault."

My stomach performed a flip and roll worthy of an Olympic acrobat. Egyptian artifacts? Stolen treasure? Images of a Lara Croft-style adventure danced before me, luring me into a satisfying daydream.

Luc's low whistle dragged me back to the here and now. "Crofton-Lowe allowed thieves to waltz off their premises with an entire cache of valuables? Heads will roll if this gets out."

"Which is where we come in." My mother leaned back in Jerry's chair, looking every inch the boss. "Discretion is an integral part of all our operations. It's especially crucial for this one. The stolen artifacts are part of the Roulez estate. They're due to be auctioned next week. At the moment, the family is unaware of the theft. Our job is to make sure they never find out."

"Roulez?" Sidney's slo-mo jaw drop had perfect comedic timing. "As in Bernard Roulez, the arms billionaire whose family is at loggerheads over their inheritance?"

I'd never heard of Bernard Roulez. Judging by the faces around the desk, I was the only one.

"Yes," Desirée said to Sidney. "That Bernard Roulez. You can see why it's important we get those artifacts back before anyone realizes they're gone."

"It's also in the auction house's best interest," Luc added, his tone sandpaper dry. "They won't want their stellar reputation tarnished."

I looked at the papers under my mother's hands, straining to read the small print. "Does the auction house have any idea who stole the goods?"

"Yes." This time, no slap-down from Desirée. She must've approved of my question. "We have several suspects, but my money is on the Jones gang."

Reading my blank expression, Luc filled in the gaps. "Colin Jones runs an international crime outfit. They specialize in stealing and selling valuable artifacts on the black market. He's a smooth customer— think of a typical James Bond villain, only minus the violent streak."

"What a boring name for a master villain," Sidney remarked. "You'd think he'd have chosen one with more panache."

"Stop digressing," Desirée snapped, showing her impatience. "We need to focus."

"Sorry," Sidney said meekly and mimed zipping his lips. "I won't say another word."

"Jones," my mother continued, "has a history with Urs Hauri, Crofton-Lowe's Zürich branch CEO. Hauri spotted Jones at an auction a few years ago and notified security. This led to Jones's arrest. In retaliation, Jones 'dropped in' to Hauri's ex-wife's house and had coffee with her and their daughter. Jones made no direct threats, but the message was clear: 'Mess with me, and I'll hurt your family.'"

Cold discomfort crept over my shoulders. "That's creepy. If Jones is the smooth customer Luc says he is, he didn't steal the artifacts just to annoy Hauri, right?"

"Oh, no. Jones only goes after items that promise him significant financial gain. He wouldn't do a job just to annoy an old adversary. However, he's not above using an opportunity to taunt one." Desirée's gaze dropped again to the papers in front of her. "Hauri has received anonymous emails, hinting that the thieves plan to dispose of the goods at a black-market auction on Monday. We need to prevent that from happening."

"What's the location of this alleged auction?" Valentina demanded in her sulky, sultry Spanish accent.

"Switzerland."

I exchanged a loaded look with Sidney. Two days,

two cases, two mentions of Switzerland. Yet the cases weren't connected. Couldn't be connected. Right?

"Our information isn't more specific than naming the country," my mother continued, "but I've made a few calls. My hunch is the auction will happen in Geneva. Our job is to locate and retrieve the stolen goods and, if possible, apprehend the thieves."

"That sounds like a big ask," I remarked. "Do you think we can pull it off?"

Valentina treated me to a withering stare. "If you were a trained P.I., you'd know we could."

"Angel's right. It is a big ask." Luc sat forward and addressed my mother. "The Omega Group doesn't accept jobs on this scale."

Desirée didn't flinch under Luc's critical stare. "Jerry and I have talked about expanding the group for a while. Pulling off a job like this will help our reputation."

"And if we fail? What then?" Luc placed the palms of his large hands on the desk, spreading his long fingers. "We can't afford to damage our reputation, especially not while Jerry is out of commission. We're only just regaining traction after the Rocco Casetti debacle."

This incident had occurred just before Sidney and I arrived in Nice. Jerry had considered joining forces with Rocco's agency, but had backed out of the deal when he'd realized Rocco skated too far into the legal gray zone. Given the bad blood between the two agencies, Valentina openly hanging out with Rocco surprised me. It didn't seem to surprise my mother.

Desirée sat back on her temporary throne and regarded Luc with a steely smile. "We're well able to handle this job, Luc." Her tone was whiplash sharp. "Especially with a quarter-million bonus at stake."

6

For a held-breath second, we all stared at my mother in open-mouthed incredulity.

"A quarter of a million euros?" Valentina swore in Spanish. "Just as a bonus?"

"It's more of a finder's fee. Herr Hauri is prepared to pay for results." Desirée's jaw tightened. "He's hired us *and* Rocco's agency."

Valentina's lips recoiled in a snarl. "Rocco didn't mention this when I saw him yesterday."

"Rocco didn't know yesterday," my mother said. "The Crofton-Lowe vault wasn't robbed until last night."

Maurice clutched his pudgy hands. "This is a terrible idea. Having two rival P.I. agencies on the same job is a recipe for disaster."

"Or a recipe for results." I turned to my mother. "I assume both agencies get paid their base fee no matter what, but whichever group gets to the goods first makes bank?"

"Yes, that's exactly Hauri's thinking," my mother said. "Now to practicalities. We'll have teams of two. Luc with Valentina, and Armin with me."

Armin, one of the senior P.I.s, was so in demand that I'd never met him in the four months I'd been in Nice. I only knew him from the team photo, which showed a stocky man in his mid-thirties with a dark complexion, heavy beard, and ginormous muscles.

"What about Cho?" Luc asked. "Is she still in Denmark?"

Cho Chen, the sixth active-duty P.I., had been the most welcoming team member, and I'd have liked to get to know her better. Pity she was hardly ever in Nice.

"Cho won't be back until December," my mother said. "She's on a top-secret undercover assignment."

"Does that mean Angel and I are the third team?" Sidney's eagerness was palpable.

Valentina's cackle of laughter died in her throat when she caught sight of the milk-curdling look my mother shot her way. Next, Desirée fixed me with her steely stare. "I need you and Sidney to watch over Herr Hauri's daughter. We doubt she's in any danger, but given her father's history with Colin Jones, he doesn't want to take any risks."

"What are Angel and Sidney going to do to protect her?" Maurice glowered at me. "They can't defend themselves, never mind anyone else."

Prickling anger zipped through my chest. "We managed just fine in July," I reminded him, my tone clipped. "And don't you dare tell me it was beginner's luck."

My mother raised a palm. "Enough. We don't have time for arguments. The last time Jones tangled with Hauri, he showed up at Charlotte's home unannounced. As Jones has never had a history of violence, everyone assumed the implied threat was just posturing. All the same, you can understand that Urs Hauri doesn't want to leave anything to chance. Sidney and Angel, you'll drive to Höllenberg in the Swiss Alps. That's where he has a holiday home. Charlotte is due to spend the weekend there. She's been told you're coming to teach her English."

"How old is this kid?" I asked warily. "I'm not a kid person."

"You're not a people person, darling," Sidney whispered, softening his words with a wink.

My mother glanced at her notes. "Charlotte is sixteen. She's a weekly boarder at a school near Sierre. She usually splits her weekends between her parents, but her mother is working in New York for the next few months. Urs Hauri was supposed to collect his daughter from school tomorrow afternoon and drive to their chalet in Höllenberg. In light of the theft, he needs to stay in Zürich to do damage control."

"Wouldn't Charlotte be safer if she stayed at school over the weekend?" Sidney asked.

Desirée shrugged. "The chalet has a live-in housekeeper and two security guards. With so many adults watching her, she's unlikely to come to harm."

I spread my palms wide. "If Charlotte has two security guards in residence, why does she need us?"

"Adding you two to the household is merely an added layer of protection."

"And an added fee for Crofton-Lowe to pay you." My quip earned me a laugh from Luc and a glare from my mother. "There's no reason for Sidney and me to be there. This is the sort of assignment that keeps us out of the way. We want to help."

"Believe it or not, this is helping," my mother said with a touch of impatience. "Urs Hauri is anxious about his daughter's safety. She's his only child and they have a close bond. I agree with his security team that the threat is negligible, but having you two with Charlotte will ease Herr Hauri's mind. Frankly, he has enough to worry about at the moment."

"I assume Charlotte speaks German," I said. "My school German is rusty. Sidney's fluent, but I don't want to rely on him to translate all weekend."

"You won't have to," my mother replied. "Charlotte is bilingual. Her parents speak German, and she attends a school in a French-speaking area. According to her father, she also speaks English well." She rose to her feet, signaling the meeting was at an end.

"What about me?" Maurice stayed in his seat, his

egg-shaped head shiny with perspiration. "What's my role in the mission?"

"I need you and Koffi to hold the fort here. Make sure everything's running smoothly. You know what Francine's like. She hasn't been herself since..." My mother trailed off, deliberately not meeting my gaze.

"Since she shot a man and saved my life," I finished for her. Francine had also grazed Sidney's ear, but that had been an accident—kinda.

"Yes." Desirée delivered the word on a sigh. "The shooting coming so soon after Jerry's attack was too much. She's skating on the edge of burnout. If it weren't for Sidney helping her run the costumier, she'd already be there."

"I understand Francine is struggling—" Maurice's tomato-red head and quivering mustache said the opposite, "—but you promised I could return to field assignments, at least part-time."

"Now's not the moment for this discussion." Desirée's words were innocuous enough, but I knew that tone. She was crossing the border from controlled irritation to losing her temper.

Maurice beat her to it. He leaped to his feet, knocking over his chair in the process. "This isn't fair, Desirée. I haven't been on a proper assignment in almost two years. I've done everything you and Jerry have asked of me. Now it's time for you to fulfill your side of the bargain."

"What bargain?" My mother spun around on her

stilettos, practically leaving sparks. "You're lucky we didn't fire you after the Florence fiasco."

"You've reminded me of that fact every second since. Jerry promised me another chance in the field if I lay low for a while and helped run the yarn shop."

Desirée gestured to the now-empty leather chair. "As you can see, Jerry isn't here. I'm in charge until he gets back. You should be thankful you still have a job, not berate me for not allowing you to put more of our investigators in danger."

What danger had Maurice caused in the past? Sidney looked at me, one eyebrow raised. I answered with a beats-me shrug.

Valentina's cat eyes glinted with mischief. "I'm with you, Desirée. I don't feel safe having him as a partner in the field. And his lack of tech skills means he can't even help us with pre-assignment research. Face facts, Maurice. You're a has-been."

His complexion went from tomato red to mottled purple. He curled his pudgy hands into fists and took a step toward Valentina.

Luc intervened in an instant. "Settle down, Maurice. Go next door to my place and have a cup of tea. Or something stronger."

"No need to hurry back to the shop, my friend." Koffi's slow gestures matched his calm tone. "I've got you covered."

"My treatment is outrageous," Maurice spluttered, not placated by his coworkers. "I have every right to be annoyed. Especially when I'm verbally abused by a fellow investigator, and no one defends me."

Valentina merely laughed and sauntered to the door. "You'll email me with the details for the Crofton-Lowe case, right, Desirée?"

"Of course," my mother replied, her tone stiff. "I always do."

The Spaniard cast us all a sultry smirk and made her exit, leaving the rest of us to deal with Maurice's whining.

The little man bounced from foot to foot, reminding me of a toddler performing the I-need-to-pee dance. "Why do you let her speak to me like that, Desirée?"

A muscle in my mother's jaw tensed. She pointed a red-tipped finger at the chair Maurice had recently vacated. "Sit down. We need to talk."

Koffi sidled up to Sidney and me and propelled us gently toward the door. "Let's leave them to it."

"Yeah." Luc ambled after us. "Maurice will be even more of a grouch to Angel at the shop if she witnesses his next tantrum. Desirée can contact us with the specifics of our assignment later."

We trooped downstairs, reaching the bottom in time to see the front door swing shut behind Valentina. I instinctively slowed my steps. Interacting with the Spaniard was never high on my wish list, and I hoped to quiz Luc about Ghiselle.

Sidney jerked a thumb at the side door that led into

the costumier. "Francine has a dental appointment. I promised I'd cover for her for a couple of hours." He raised an eyebrow at me. "I'll text you, okay?"

I understood the unspoken implication. Sidney would continue to work through his half of Pierre Dubois's contacts. "Sure. I'll see you back at the villa."

Outside the building, rain bounced off the pavement. Koffi headed next door to the yarn shop and unlocked the door. "Stay safe, you two. I'll see you next week." He went inside, leaving me alone with Luc.

An awkwardness descended, as it often did on the rare occasions when Luc and I were alone.

He tugged up his hood. I opened my umbrella. Neither of us moved.

"So..." he began, "how's the Ghiselle case working out?"

His teasing tone broke the tension and made me laugh. "About as well as you'd expected. Seriously, though, what do you know about Pierre Dubois and his accident?"

Luc's grin vanished, replaced with a frown. "Not much. Which is weird, given his family's prominence. As I recall, it was a five-minute wonder in the papers. Not the front-page sensation I'd have expected."

"Right? I thought that too. Pierre's former coworkers had way more interest in his famous family than in the man himself. They even seemed to know more about Ghiselle than a person they'd worked alongside for over twenty years."

We took the few steps that divided Jerry's building from the café. Luc paused in the doorway, his hand on the handle. A sheepish look crossed over his face. "You've probably guessed I fobbed the case off onto you and Sidney for a laugh. I didn't expect you to take it."

I met his gaze with a challenge. "I know you didn't. After all, who'd be crazy enough to go chasing after a dead man?"

His grin returned, turning my knees to mush. "You two, apparently."

Warmth flooded my cheeks. I wouldn't rise to the bait. A teasing Luc was a sexy Luc, and I didn't need that emotional confusion. "Taking the psychic part out of the equation, do you think Ghiselle believes her husband is still alive? Or is this part of a scheme to get...what? His inheritance?"

"I assumed she was serious when she approached me," Luc replied. "I didn't get the impression she was lying."

"Why did she approach you, by the way? Isn't your P.I. work supposed to be hush-hush? Or did it come to her in a vision?"

Luc laughed. "You try keeping anything hush-hush in this town. Yes, the Omega Group is discreet, but people are aware I'm a private investigator. They just don't know who I work for."

"Even if Ghiselle didn't lie, she was economical with the truth. She conveniently forgot to mention that she and Pierre had separated before his accident. And she didn't list his grandfather as a person to contact."

"The man's got to be ancient. Isn't he in a nursing home? Maybe Ghiselle didn't list him because he's *non compos mentis.*"

A customer approached the café door. Luc greeted the man with a smile and held the door open for him.

When the man had gone inside, Luc turned back to me. "I'd better get back in there. We're short-staffed with Louis out sick. Hey, don't mention the Ghiselle thing to Desirée, okay? She'd disapprove of you and Sidney taking on an investigation on your own."

"Thanks for the warning, but I wasn't planning on telling her. At least, not before we've cracked it." I grinned at him. "You had no worries about Desirée finding out yesterday evening."

"Desirée wasn't in Nice yesterday evening," Luc pointed out. "Now she is. And she doesn't like us moonlighting, not even for a dotty ghost whisperer."

"Until or unless my mother trains Sidney and me to be private investigators, we're not moonlighting. We're just lowly shop assistants looking to make some spare change."

Luc snorted. "Desirée won't buy that excuse."

"She'll have to deal. Speaking of my case..." I dolefully regarded the rain dripping down from my umbrella. "It's not exactly a day for the beach, but that's where I'm headed. Liar or not, Ghiselle Dubois has some explaining to do."

7

*M*adame Ghiselle's tent was on a beachside promontory just off the Promenade des Anglais, or La Prom, as it was known to the locals. This walkway stretched for seven glorious kilometers along Nice's beachfront, offering spectacular views over the Mediterranean. Even off-season, it was packed with people, noise, and activity. For much of the twenty minutes it took to walk from the café to Ghiselle's tent, I dodged dogs, skateboarders, cyclists, and the odd truant toddler. Despite the wet weather, I relished the view and the salty tang of the sea breeze.

Ghiselle's circus-style tent was impossible to miss, especially on a gray day like today. With its bright orange-and-white stripes, the tent reminded me of an oversized traffic cone. Despite the rain, a line of people waited outside for an audience with the great Madame Ghiselle. Their expressions ran the gamut from excited to terrified. A large "on a break" sign hung over the entrance. Ignoring the protests from the front of the queue, I parted the flap and marched into the tent.

Ghiselle was in full pro psychic regalia. Floaty purple robes enveloped her thin frame. A dramatic ruby turban obscured her curly hair. A profusion of necklaces and bangles hung from her neck and wrists. Surrounded by a teapot, a crystal ball, and a pack of tarot cards, Ghiselle sat at a small table, nursing a cup of tea. Her delicate features settled into an expression of annoyance when she recognized me. "Angel, I'm working. Can't this wait?"

"According to the sign outside the tent, you're on a break." Without waiting for an invitation, I dropped into the chair opposite and fixed her with a hard stare. "I need to clarify a few points about your case. You left out pertinent details concerning your relationship with Pierre Dubois. Why didn't you mention you'd separated from your husband at the time of the accident?"

The woman broke eye contact, suddenly finding her herbal tea fascinating. "It wasn't relevant. All couples argue. Just before he went missing, Pierre and I decided to give our marriage a second chance."

"Is that so?" I leaned forward and rested my elbows on the table. "According to Elaine Ayari, Pierre wanted a divorce."

Ghiselle's mouth moved, but no words came out. She picked up the teapot and refilled her cup with an unsteady hand. Now that I was closer, I picked up on the distinctive gin aroma that the herbs couldn't hide. No wonder her hands shook.

"Is your response to Elaine's claim a 'No comment?'" I prompted. "If you want to get rid of me, you'd better start talking. I'm not moving until I get answers."

She took a long drink from her cup before answering. "Elaine's never liked me. She'll say anything to make me look bad. You should talk to Asad, her husband. He knows Pierre and I had a complicated relationship."

"Would Asad deny Pierre was staying at their house at the time of his death?"

Ghiselle's bony fingers clutched the porcelain cup so hard I thought it'd shatter. "How many times do I have to tell you? Pierre isn't dead."

"I'm more concerned with what you *haven't* told me. Why did you try to give Sidney and me the impression your marriage was solid?"

"Because it was." She chewed on her lower lip. "*Is*, now that I know Pierre is still alive."

I debated challenging her on the alive part but opted against it. I needed her to open up, not shut me out. "Claiming you're a happy couple when you haven't seen the dude in five years is pushing it, Ghiselle. You included Asad Ayari's name on your list of people we should contact. You must've known either he or his wife would mention the separation."

"So what?" She delivered the words in a snap. "They have their version of the truth. I have mine. No one knows what goes on in a marriage but the couple themselves."

"I get that, but if you want our help, you need to be honest with us. You can't leave out inconvenient facts. Frankly, it's a waste of our time and your money."

She exhaled a sigh. "Okay, I should've mentioned our living arrangements. I didn't think it mattered to your investigation."

"Don't you see that any relationship worries are crucial to getting a picture of Pierre's state of mind? You want us to find him and bring him back to you? Assuming you're right and he's still alive, he had a reason for doing a bunk. Happy-clappy people don't fake their own deaths."

"He was kidnapped." Her voice rose in pitch with each word, and a pink flush stained her pale skin.

"How can you know? The kidnapping didn't appear in your visions. You're just guessing."

"Given the circumstances, kidnapping is a logical supposition. I told you Pierre is a talented poker player."

"His poker prowess was one of the few things you shared about your husband. You failed to mention Pierre wasn't just a pen-pushing civil servant. He was the sole heir to a vast fortune. Why didn't you tell me he was Arthur Dubois's grandson?"

She blinked her large doe eyes. "Pierre and I lived a simple life. Yes, he had a privileged upbringing, but his family didn't do handouts. They expected Pierre to support himself once he finished school."

"Even so, wouldn't his family money be a much-bigger motive to kidnap him than his poker-playing prowess?"

"If that were the case, his grandfather would've received a ransom note. None came."

"Surely Pierre stood to inherit a lot of money when his grandfather died."

Ghiselle shook her head, making the beads on her turban bounce. "Pierre wasn't part of the family pharmaceutical business. He never expected to inherit a lot of money. When they died, his parents left their money to charity. As far as I'm aware, Arthur intends his money to be used to build a research facility in his name."

I wrinkled my brow. "In Pierre's name?"

Ghiselle's bitter laugh corrected that notion. "Oh, no. Arthur Dubois is a born narcissist. He wants his own name commemorated."

"You're saying Arthur Dubois cut his only grandchild out of his will?" I blew out a breath, feeling a renewed sense of pity for the unknown Pierre. "That's harsh. Were they estranged?"

"No, but they weren't close." Ghiselle paused a moment. "Arthur didn't cut Pierre out of his will. He mentioned leaving Pierre a small legacy, just not a vast fortune."

I pounced on this tidbit. "Small is relative. What amount are we talking about?"

She shifted in her seat, palpably uncomfortable by my probing. "What can that matter to your case?"

"Money is a motive for many crimes, Ghiselle. If you want Sidney and me to take another look into Pierre's case, we must consider all possibilities, not just focus on him maybe, possibly still being alive. Besides, you haven't exactly been consistent in your story. First, you said Arthur wasn't leaving Pierre money. Then you said he'd get a legacy. Which is it? And how much was it worth?"

Her shoulders relaxed a smidgen, but her wary expression remained in place. "I believe the legacy would've been a couple million."

"A couple *million*?" I whistled. "Not exactly chump change."

"Arthur is worth billions," she pointed out. "It's a small legacy seen in that context."

"Fair enough, but I could do a lot with a couple million euros. I bet you could too." A flicker of uneasiness passed over Ghiselle's face at my words. Had I hit upon a nerve? Time to press harder. "With Pierre officially dead, who stands to inherit that legacy when Arthur dies? You?"

Her flush deepened from pale pink to deep red. "Arthur will leave me a little something, yes. I don't know that it'll be the amount he'd intended to leave to Pierre."

"Can't you ask him?" I demanded. "You nursed Arthur, didn't you? Are you still in touch?"

Her hand went to her throat, her fingers fiddling with her many necklaces. "Arthur hasn't been himself for the last couple of years. He's an old man and somewhat...forgetful."

"In other words, he's dotty, but no one wants to say that out loud because he's a financial bigwig."

A bemused smile broke through her serious expression. "You're very direct."

"Direct saves time. If Arthur's not capable of talking finances, couldn't you ask his solicitor?"

"I don't know his legal representatives. I assume he has a team."

"What about Pierre? You didn't include a lawyer on the list of people to contact. Did he have one?"

She opened a drawer under the table and took out a pen and pad of paper. "Her name is Jeanne-Claire Maret. Here's her address, but I doubt she can tell you anything useful. Pierre and I had wills in each other's favor, but we had very little to leave beyond a heavily mortgaged apartment."

I took the piece of paper and glanced at the address. The lawyer's offices were a couple of streets away from the yarn shop. I'd call by this afternoon.

"Thanks," I said, pocketing the paper. "When I was looking at newspaper archives to see articles about the accident, something struck me as strange. Why did the presumed death of a local billionaire's heir get so little attention? Surely that should've been big news."

"Arthur dislikes any negative press about his business or family, and he has contacts at every media outlet." Her words were spiced with bitterness. "He was afraid Pierre had killed himself. Any sign of weakness, physical or mental, is unacceptable to Arthur. He preferred to risk the accident not being investigated properly rather than have it revealed that his grandson had committed suicide." She drained her teacup and pushed back her chair. "If you've finished interrogating me, I have to get back to work."

I took the hint and followed her to the door of the tent. "One more thing before I go."

The lines on her forehead deepened. "Make it quick."

"Sidney and I will be in Switzerland over the weekend, and we'll follow up your suspicion that Pierre is there, working at a casino. Switzerland has four official languages. It makes sense that Pierre would work in a location where he understood the language. Apart from French, what languages did he speak?"

"His Italian is fluent, and he has tourist Spanish. He struggles with English, though."

"Then I'll add casinos in the Ticino region to my list. What about German?"

She shook her head. "No. He said it was even more barbaric than English."

I stifled a smile. "Thanks, Ghiselle. I'll be in touch, but not until next week."

"Wait a moment, Angel." Ghiselle drew a small bottle of hand sanitizer from the depths of her robes and rubbed some on her hands. Then she grabbed mine, gripping them with surprising strength.

Remembering her reluctance to shake hands at our last meeting, the move surprised me. Her touch sent odd electric energy through my hands, and I instinctively tried to pull free.

Ghiselle's grasp tightened. "Stay still a moment." Her tone was urgent enough for me to obey, despite my longing to get away. She forced my hands palms-up. Her intense stare seemed to sear into my palm lines. "You'll face great danger in the near future. Beware of the bear."

A sick sensation crept over me, leaving me slick with sweat. I didn't believe in the sixth sense. And I definitely didn't believe in anyone who pimped out their so-called gift for financial gain. And yet, that lingering doubt... "What bear?"

Ghiselle's gaze met mine. Her pupils were enormous black orbs. Had there been more in that tea than herbs and gin? "Beware of the bear," she repeated, her grasp on my hands tight enough to hurt. "The bear means danger to you. And Sidney. And the man you love."

This time, she relaxed her grip when I pulled away. The strange tingling in my hands remained even after we broke contact. My heart beat an unsteady rhythm, and my breath came in ragged bursts. "I don't love anyone. And there are no bears in this case."

Her mocking smile chafed at my frayed nerves. "Are you sure about that, Angel? I've seen the way you look at him."

A searing heat thawed through the icy sensation I'd had since Ghiselle had grabbed me. She had to be talking about Luc. I noted she didn't mention Luc having feelings for me. The question lingered on the tip of my tongue. I bit it back and marched to the entrance of the tent. "Thanks for the advice, Ghiselle. I've got this."

"It's not advice. It's a warning. My visions aren't always clear, but they're never wrong."

I eyed her now-empty teacup. How many of her visions were of the gin-soaked variety?

Ghiselle followed my gaze and interpreted my thoughts correctly. "Don't be so quick to judge me, Angel. I know you don't believe I'm psychic. You're entitled to your opinion. Just know this: alcohol doesn't fuel my visions. It dulls them. I don't always see what people want me to see. If I add the odd drop of gin to my tea, it helps to make my job more bearable."

Don't overdo the violins, Ghiselle. "Message received," I said, straight-faced. "And thanks for the warning. I'm not planning on visiting a zoo this weekend. However, if I encounter a bear, I'll know to be wary."

8

Sidney and I left for Switzerland at the unconscionable hour of four on Friday morning. The extra-early start had been my idea. I regretted it the instant my alarm went off. Still, if we had to go to Switzerland this weekend, it made sense to use the opportunity to check out a few Swiss casinos and look for the allegedly undead Pierre Dubois.

We zipped out of Nice and followed the A8 to the Italian border, passing seamlessly from one country to the other. Despite traveling on a motorway, the views on this stretch were spectacular. I'd visited Genoa a couple of weekends ago, and the journey had been part of the fun. This early in the morning, it was too dark to see farther than the car headlights allowed, but I knew what was there. To our left, the Alps loomed in the distance—majestic, otherworldly, and appearing closer than they were in reality. To our right, we hugged the coast and the Mediterranean Sea. The water glinted in the darkness, inviting and menacing. And I loved it.

Ten hours and two casinos later, I felt less Zen and more stressed.

"That was a total bust," I said between mouthfuls of baguette. "And now we're running late."

We'd grabbed takeout sandwiches and energy drinks after visiting the casino in Montreux. Sidney had wanted us to sit on a bench overlooking the lake. I'd insisted we press on for Crans-Montana, the last casino on today's list.

Sidney steered the old Peugeot 107 we'd semipermanently borrowed from Luc through the snow-dusted streets of Montreux. "Of course, it was a bust. Did you expect anyone to recognize a guy who's been dead for five years?"

"No, but I hoped this side trip wouldn't take so long. Okay, maybe shooting for three casinos today was overly ambitious. I assumed our early start would give us enough time."

We'd made the journey from the villa to our first stop in Meyrin, Switzerland, in good time. Unfortunately, our visit to the casino had taken more than the thirty minutes I'd allotted it on today's itinerary. When we'd arrived, both the manager and the assistant manager had been in a meeting, and we'd had to cool our heels before speaking to them. Not that they'd had any information to give us. Neither they nor anyone on staff this morning had recognized Pierre's photo. Our stop at the casino in Montreux had lasted less time but had proven to be equally fruitless.

"At least we get a gorgeous view." Sidney pointed to the Belle Époque buildings on our right and the lakefront to our left. "Isn't Montreux lovely? I was here the summer after my exchange year at a Swiss boarding school. Friends from my school invited me to the summer jazz festival. We stayed a few days to go boating on the lake."

"We have no time for jazz or boating today, alas." I swallowed the last bite of my sandwich and washed it down with a sickly-sweet energy drink. "I hope we'll have better luck at our next stop."

Sidney side-eyed me from behind the wheel. "Do you? I thought we didn't believe Ghiselle's tall tale." He grinned. "Apart from her bear prophecy. I fully expect to see one prowling about the chalet."

I'd given Sidney an abridged version of Ghiselle's strange warning, leaving out the part about Luc and the peculiar electrical sensation I'd experienced when she'd held my hands. "One of the Swiss cantons has a bear on its flag," I said, "but we'll be nowhere near Bern this weekend."

"Bears aside, why are you determined our casino visits should turn up a clue? I thought we were just going through the motions of looking for Ghiselle's dead husband. Do you think she's on to something?"

"No, I don't believe Pierre Dubois is still alive. However, we might at least help Ghiselle find closure.

Once we've ruled out all the casinos, she'll have to accept Pierre is dead."

We reached the motorway and headed toward Crans-Montana, the location of the third and last casino on today's list. As we drove, snow coated our windshield, forcing Sidney to increase the wipers' speed. "Is the weather forecast still predicting heavy snowfall in Höllenberg this evening?"

I checked the weather app on my phone. A prickle of unease crept over my shoulders. "They've upgraded it to a snowstorm. What are the odds of this car making it up the Alps if the weather worsens? It's not a four-wheel drive."

Sidney grimaced. "At least Luc put the winter tires on before he went to bed last night."

"He also put snow chains in the boot. Do you know how to put them on the tires?"

"No. Do you?"

I shook my head. "Thank goodness for the internet."

He slid me a look. "You seem confident we'll have cell coverage. Are you sure we'll get a signal once we get higher in the Alps?"

"I researched Swiss cell coverage last night. It's excellent. Unless we're literally at the peak of a mountain, we should be fine. But you know me. I'm paranoid. I've already downloaded a video for us to watch."

The snowfall increased steadily during the hour it

took to drive from Montreux to the valley town of Sierre. When we reached Sierre, we began the ascent up the mountain to Crans-Montana and our third casino visit of the day. Crans-Montana was one of Switzerland's more famous ski resorts, with locals and tourists. The road was busy despite the lousy weather.

The road wound up the mountain, past charming snow-covered villages, ice-encrusted vineyards, and twisty hiking trails. As we climbed higher, the deeper the snow and the more distance between towns. The Peugeot objected to frequent gear changes, and the ever-deepening snow meant we had to keep our speed to a minimum. For once, I had no objection to Sidney's slowpoke driving. My position in the passenger seat gave me a skin-crawlingly clear view of the steep drop beyond the crash barriers.

"I bet Luc and Valentina aren't having this problem," Sidney said. "Luc's SUV looks like it could tackle the hairiest of situations. I bet they'll get cooler toys too. Like spy glasses and serious ammo. What do you think will be in our bag of tricks?"

Late last night, Desirée had sent me an encrypted email containing the chalet's address, a brief file on Charlotte Hauri, and instructions to collect a bag from a locker at the train station near the chalet.

I wrinkled my nose. "My guess is self-defense paraphernalia. Neither of us has a permit to carry a weapon in France, let alone across the border into Switzerland. She'll kit us out with pepper spray.

Maybe batons and knuckle-dusters. Tasers, if we're lucky."

"I learned a few judo moves as prep for a play. Do you think they'll come in useful?"

"I doubt we'll need to bust out *any* moves. If trouble comes calling at the chalet, the security guards can deal. We're just glorified babysitters, not Charlotte Hauri's personal SWAT team."

"True." He sounded almost wistful.

I checked my watch. "At this rate, we'll be late collecting her."

"We can call the school to let them know. I doubt we'll be the only ones late in this weather."

He was right, but his words didn't reassure me. I hated being late. And I had a bad feeling about our weekend assignment. While Sidney looked forward to fancy chocolate and cheese fondue, I dreaded dealing with a teenage attitude.

The final stretch to Crans-Montana wound through a winter wonderland of snow-laden trees, ending in a picturesque town filled with traditional Swiss chalets and a charming shopping street.

When we got out of the car outside Crans-Montana's casino, the difference in altitude was striking. As was the temperature. I put on my hat and gloves and sucked in a deep breath, trying to get as much ice-laden air as possible into my lungs to combat my light-headedness. It only took a few breaths to start feeling normal again.

Sidney tugged on his earlobes. "My ears popped on the drive here. I should've remembered my altitude sensitivity and brought chewing gum. It's crazy to think these Alpine regions were famous for their tuberculosis sanatoriums back in the day. I can barely breathe."

"You'll get used to it fast." I popped open the boot and unzipped my case. The coat I was wearing was suitable for a winter in the south of France, but it wouldn't cut it in this climate. I exchanged it for the orange eyesore I'd purchased yesterday in preparation for our Swiss trip. I switched my pocket essentials from one coat to the other and zipped the oversized ski jacket.

When Sidney eyeballed the jacket, he took a literal step back. "Wow. Where did you acquire that crime against good taste? The dump?"

"I unearthed it at a charity shop yesterday afternoon. I know it's fifty shades of fugly, but it only cost twenty euros—including a matching pair of ski pants."

"Twenty euros? You were robbed. Seriously, Angel. That style of puffy jacket hasn't been in fashion since the 90s, and they were bad even then."

Trust Sidney to focus on the fashion aspect. Anyone else would comment on the hideous color and the fact the coat was several sizes too large for me. In contrast to my fashion disaster, Sidney wore a perfectly fitting sapphire blue shell jacket with a faux fur-trimmed hood.

I pushed up a too-long sleeve and checked my watch. "It's already ten to three. We need to be back on the road by three thirty, or we'll never get to Charlotte's school on time."

Sidney stretched his back and inhaled deeply. "Okay," he said on the exhale. "Let's go in there and flash our spanking-new business cards at reception."

The business cards had been Sidney's brainwave. The printing place he'd visited after work yesterday had had a discount on glittery purple cards, inspiring Sidney to call us Sparkle and Shine Investigations. Our new name thrilled him. I was less enthusiastic.

"Same cover story as last time?" I asked, pocketing the card.

"The people in Meyrin and Montreux seemed to buy it, so, yeah. Let's go for a lather-rinse-repeat."

When we walked into the casino, the manager, a sleekly groomed blonde, was at the reception. She recoiled when she saw my coat, then belatedly tried to mask her reaction with an overly friendly greeting.

We introduced ourselves, gave our alleged reason for looking for Pierre—an adopted son had hired us to look for his biological father—and pulled out the photograph.

The manager took a long look at the photo, sniffed, and shook her head. "I don't recognize him, but I've only worked here for three years. Perhaps he was here before my time." She turned to the middle-aged woman behind the reception desk. "Madeleine, you've been here longer than me. Do you know this man?"

Madeleine wore a pair of glasses attached to a chain. She put them on before looking at the phone screen. "No, I don't think so…" She squinted at the screen. "Can I zoom in, please?"

"Sure." Sidney handed her his phone.

The receptionist frowned at the photograph. "I can't be certain. The hair's wrong. And this man doesn't have a mustache. But his profile reminds me of René."

A stirring of excitement tiptoed over my body. "Who's René?"

"He worked here a couple of years ago. Now, what was his surname?" The woman tapped the reception desk, frowning. "Hey, Paul, come here a moment."

The doorman, a silent mound of muscle, looked to the manager for permission. At her nod, he left his post and approached the desk.

Madeleine held up the zoomed-in image. "Who does this remind you of?"

Paul stared at the photo for a few long seconds. "That's René Bateau. Nice guy. Haven't seen him around in a while."

Triumphant, Madeleine turned back to her boss. "Don't you remember René? He didn't stay long. He filled in for Toby for two or three months after Toby's car accident."

The manager retook the phone, her expression unconvinced. "Are you sure? René had fair hair and a matching mustache."

"Dyed," Madeleine said with assurance. "It was pretty obvious."

"What did René do here? Was he a croupier?" I aimed for nonchalance, but my excitement seeped through each syllable.

"Yes," the manager said. "Mostly blackjack. Sometimes poker."

My heart rate kicked up a notch. Pierre Dubois had liked poker. What better place for him to seek a job than a casino?

"What did René tell you about his background?" Sidney addressed his question to the doorman.

The man shrugged. "Not much. I didn't know him well. Just to have a beer at the end of a shift. Talk about music and sport. He was a quiet bloke. He liked Formula One and poker."

"He was French," Madeleine supplied. "From Marseilles. Or so he said. I thought his accent was wrong for Marseilles, but what do I know? I'm Swiss, born and bred."

"He had a well-bred accent," Paul added. "Maybe he went to a fancy school."

"When did René stop working here?" I turned to the manager. "And do you know where he went when he left?"

The woman shifted her weight from one foot to the

other. "I can't give out information about our staff to strangers."

I brandished one of our glittery business cards and handed it to her. "We'd appreciate any information you can give us, now or later. We want to get our client answers. It's rough not knowing who your biological parents are."

The manager pinched the glittery card between her thumb and forefinger, her nose slightly upturned. "I suppose I could look at René's file. I'm not promising I'll share everything with you, though."

"That's fine," Sidney said, treating her to his most charming smile. "We'd appreciate any hint you can give us."

She sniffed again and commandeered Madeleine's keyboard. A few keystrokes later, she'd found what she was looking for. "René Bateau, age fifty-three, originally from Marseilles. Worked at several casinos in France and Italy before applying for the temporary position here."

"Could you give us a list of the places he worked?" I asked. "It'd be a great help."

The woman wavered for a moment and then shrugged. "All right. I'll print a copy."

Five minutes later, Sidney and I were back in the car, the printout safely scanned and saved onto my phone. I took the wheel this time, but I made no move to start the engine. "That was unexpected."

"I'll say," Sidney said, buckling his seat belt. "Do you think René Bateau's our man?"

"He could be. Pierre's father was called René, and *bateau* means boat in French. A reference to his fake boating accident?"

Sidney frowned. "Wouldn't he come up with a better pseudonym? This one is pretty obvious."

"Pierre's coworkers emphasized his lack of imagination." I started the car and reversed out of our space. "If we accept René Bateau as a lead in this case, we're accepting Ghiselle's story."

"Accepting the possibility that Pierre is still alive isn't synonymous with believing in Ghiselle's psychic powers. She may have heard a rumor he'd faked his death and made up that story to convince us to look for him."

"No, that makes little sense." I eased us back onto the main road and began the descent to Sierre and the motorway. "If Ghiselle had straight-up said she had info Pierre might still be alive, we'd have been more inclined to take her seriously right from the start. She might not be psychic, but she's clearly good at reading people. She had to have seen our skepticism that night at the café. Why did she stick with the story of the psychic visions?"

"I don't know, Angel. If Pierre is still alive, why is he working as a nomad casino dealer? None of this makes sense."

My gaze shifted to the dashboard clock. "At this rate, we'll be late getting to Charlotte's school."

The lousy weather curbed even my pedal-to-the-metal tendencies. I took it slowly on our way down the mountain. The snow fell steadily, but the route's popularity meant that snowplows were vigilant about clearing the road.

Once we reached the motorway, there was less snow. I hit the accelerator and made up some of our lost time. The drive to the school took thirty minutes. Thanks to our navigation system and efficient Swiss signposting, we had no trouble finding École Sainte-Marguerite. We arrived just ten minutes later than planned.

"Nice place," Sidney said as we drew up in front of the enormous limestone building, flanked by two smaller matching structures. "The boarding school I attended in St. Gallen was a gray mausoleum in comparison. This place looks more like a palace than a school."

"It's nothing like the convent school I attended in France," I said. "That was a spartan edifice with a few playing fields to offset the pervading sense of gloom."

Sidney cracked up laughing. "No way. *You* attended a convent school?"

"For my sins—literal and figurative. Having a porn star mother and a career criminal father made me a misfit. Although, to be fair, I found it hard to settle in at my previous schools. I don't deal well with institutionalized authority."

He grinned. "Major shocker."

I waited for a black BMW to pull out of a visitor parking space and then staked my claim. When Sidney and I got out of the car, the gravel courtyard was a hive of noise and activity. Parental vehicles pulled in and out, collecting offspring. Girls bid friends farewell with enough melodrama to give the impression they'd be parted forever rather than for the weekend.

A flight of stone steps swept up from the courtyard to the heavy front door. A woman with a neat chignon and a bad self-tan shook hands with parents and ticked names off a list on her tablet computer. Sidney and I made a beeline for her.

"Excuse me," I said, addressing her in French. "I'm Angel Doyle, and this is Sidney Foggington-Smythe. We're here to collect Charlotte Hauri."

The woman looked up from her tablet and peered at us through a pair of gold-rimmed spectacles, taking in Sidney's ultra-fashionable winter coat and my train wreck of a jacket. "I'm Sandrine Renaud, the headmistress. I think you're mistaken. Charlotte Hauri has already gone."

9

The gray sky, the falling snow, the glowing limestone buildings all receded into my subconscious. My heart performed a thump and roll, and my breath seemed wedged in my throat. "What do you mean, Charlotte's gone? You knew we were due to collect her."

Madame Renaud paled beneath her orange-tinged tan. "My assistant told me Charlotte had been collected. I assumed she meant by you."

"Obviously not." Fear clipped my words. "Can you ask her who collected Charlotte? As of ten minutes ago, we're responsible for the girl's welfare."

The headmistress's thin lips quivered. "I'm very sorry. I'll check. One moment, please." The woman fled back up the steps as fast as her high-heeled boots could carry her.

Sidney and I exchanged an anguished look. He

ran a hand through his hair, mussing his perfect blow-dry. "What now? She can't have gotten far, right?"

"Don't underestimate the ingenuity of a sixteen-year-old girl," I said grimly. "There'll be a love interest involved. I guarantee it. I knew this babysitting job would prove troublesome."

Sidney's eyes grew deer-in-headlights wide. "I didn't. I thought we'd spend the weekend at a luxurious Alpine chalet, eating Swiss chocolate and playing Monopoly with a kid."

"This 'kid' is almost an adult. Would you have welcomed the idea of weekend chaperones at her age?"

He gestured at the imposing buildings behind us. "The girl attends a convent school. She must be used to being chaperoned twenty-four seven."

"Precisely. *I* went to a convent school during my misspent youth. Look where that got me." I swallowed hard, fighting back a wave of nausea. Acid burned at the base of my throat. "I can't believe we've screwed up our first official assignment. Desirée will freak out when she hears about this."

Sidney squeezed my shoulder. "This isn't our fault, Angel. We showed up at the appointed time."

"More or less. We were ten minutes late."

"Mightn't have made a difference. We don't know when Charlotte flew the coop."

The headmistress's heels clicked back down the steps, followed at a more sedate pace by an efficient-looking nun wearing a traditional veil, black-rimmed glasses, and a severely tailored slate-gray suit.

Madame Renaud gestured at the newcomer. "This is Sister Céline, my assistant."

Sister Céline could have been any age between thirty-five and fifty. She gave Sidney and me the briefest nod of acknowledgment and didn't waste time on preliminaries. "Susi Heinz, one of Charlotte's classmates, informed me that Charlotte left at three thirty. I assumed the girl was telling the truth, so I checked Charlotte's name off my departure list."

"Aren't you supposed to monitor who leaves with whom? Isn't that your job?" Fear turned my delivery into a growl. "She's had forty-five minutes to get goodness knows where."

Madame Renaud took an instinctive step away from me, but Sister Céline was made of sterner stuff. "For the younger girls, we're stricter, of course. Charlotte Hauri is almost seventeen. She often catches the bus to the station and makes her own way to meet her parents on weekends."

"But this weekend, you were informed we'd collect her," Sidney reminded her. "Herr Hauri contacted you personally."

"How personal is an email?" Her terse tone softened a notch. "Yes, Herr Hauri wrote to us yesterday to say there'd been a change of plans. He mentioned you'd collect Charlotte in his place. But there was no sense of urgency in his email, and he certainly didn't ask us to watch her every move before you came."

"Exactly. We assumed it was a regular Friday pickup." Madame Renaud had found her voice again, even daring a glimmer of a smile. "The girls all mill around the courtyard, chatting and making plans to socialize. You know how teenagers are."

I knew the shenanigans Charlotte and her contemporaries could get up to all too well. Under the circumstances, it made my blood run cold. What if the threats against her father were genuine? What if we'd let her slip through our fingers and straight into a trap? A tremor of unease snaked over my skin, making me burrow into my ugly coat. "Can we speak to Susi? She might tell us where Charlotte planned to go."

Madame Renaud raised a questioning eyebrow at her assistant, but the other woman shook her head. "Susi Heinz left shortly after Charlotte. I can call her and ask, but you should try Charlotte's phone number first."

Muttering swear words in various languages, I found Charlotte's number on my phone and hit connect. The call went straight to voicemail. I left a brusque message, asking her to contact me. I had no expectation that she'd do so. Then I slipped the phone back into my pocket. "Please call the friend. We have no idea where to start looking for Charlotte."

"Of course." Sister Céline consulted her phone and dialed a number. She had more success than I'd had. After a quick call comprising brisk questions, she lowered the device. "According to Susi, Charlotte resented the idea of weekend babysitters and decided to make her own way to the chalet."

"See?" Madame Renaud's voice conveyed giddy relief. "Nothing to worry about. Charlotte often travels to Höllenberg on her own." Assured that she hadn't failed in her duty of care, she treated us to a patronizing smile that set my teeth on edge. "I know Swiss geography confuses foreigners. Just because we're in a French-speaking area here doesn't mean Höllenberg is far away. It takes less than an hour by car and not much more by public transport."

I met her patronizing look with one of steel-tipped determination. "Thanks for the advice, but I'm aware of the distance."

"We'd like Susi Heinz's phone number." Sidney infused his request with just the right mix of charm and resolution.

Madame Renaud flattened her lips. "We can't give out students' private information. I'm sure you can understand."

"This is a potential emergency," I pressed, not breaking eye contact. "Charlotte Hauri could be in danger. Why do you think her father wanted her to have bodyguards for the weekend?"

"Bodyguards?" Madame Renaud shot a panicked look at her assistant. "Herr Hauri didn't mention bodyguards in his email. Did he, Sister?"

The efficient Sister Céline ignored the question and focused on us. "We take data protection seriously, but I think we can make an exception on this occasion. I'll call Susi's father and get his permission to share her number with you."

Five minutes later, we were back in the car, driving through Sierre toward the motorway. Sidney had spoken to Susi Heinz on the phone, but he'd elicited no new information from her. We had to assume that Susi was telling the truth, and that Charlotte had made her own way to the chalet.

The snowfall was heavier than before, making it hard to see more than a few meters ahead. The weather matched my mood. My first task for the Omega Group had gone splat. Knowing teenage girls as I did, I'd expected a rough weekend. However, I hadn't anticipated the situation going south this quickly.

Sidney fiddled with the navigation system. "Should I input the chalet's address? Do you think Charlotte will be there by the time we arrive?"

"Can you check public transport connections from the school to the local train station? Maybe we can intercept her at the station. We have to stop there anyway to collect whatever goodies my mother packed for us."

Sidney checked his phone while I drove. "Assuming Charlotte went directly to the nearest train station when she left the school, she'll be pulling into

Höllental in ten minutes—that's the village at the foot of the Höllenberg mountain."

I swore under my breath. "Well, that foils my cunning plan. I assume she'll get a taxi to the chalet or call one of the staff to collect her."

"At least the chalet has a staff," Sidney pointed out. "She'll have two bodyguards and a housekeeper to keep her at home and out of trouble."

I snorted. "I wouldn't bet on it. She gave us the slip quite effectively."

"Should we call Desirée?" He looked at his phone as though it would bite him. "I'm dreading telling her the news. Even though Charlotte took off before we were officially on duty, Desirée's bound to blame us."

"Like you pointed out to me earlier, we followed Desirée's instructions. It's not our fault our charge did a bunk first. Let's hold off until we reach the chalet. If Charlotte isn't there, then we'll call my mother."

"After this debacle, Desirée's never going to let us train to be P.I.s," Sidney said forlornly. "Especially not if anything happens to the kid."

"Nothing will happen to Charlotte. Not before I find her and give her a piece of my mind." My words were more bluster than conviction. What if Charlotte's father wasn't overreacting? What if the girl was in genuine danger? Regardless of how I felt about babysitting her for the weekend, she was my responsibility for the next two days. Mine and Sidney's.

With tension in the car as taut as fraying elastic, I drove as fast as I dared in these weather conditions.

Sidney tried Charlotte's number again but shook his head. "No luck, I'm afraid. It goes straight to voicemail."

"Keep trying. We need to know she's okay." I increased my speed, skidded, and righted the car.

"Have you contacted your brother yet?" Sidney asked. "Today's his birthday, right?"

I grunted in assent. I was still in two minds about contacting Del. On the one hand, he was my brother, and I wanted to wish him a happy birthday. On the other, his rejection of me when I'd most needed his support still rankled. I didn't know if we could repair our relationship, and I wasn't sure I wanted to try. "I wrote him a message and saved it to draft. I might send it when we get to the chalet."

Sidney showed signs of wishing to pursue this conversation, so I switched on the radio and found an alternative metal station. He got the message. Giving me a rueful thumbs up, he put on his headphones, giving me the space to brood.

On our first road trip together, Sidney and I had learned there was no Venn diagram overlap between our musical tastes. Since then, whoever was driving chose the music, and the passenger wore noise-canceling headphones. It was a compromise that worked well for us.

The closer we got to our destination, the heavier

the snowfall. It was pounding down at such a rate that I had to slow to a crawl, making our journey take twice as long as it should have. By the time we pulled into the train station car park, flakes had given way to clumps, and the outdoor temperature had plummeted.

"Stay in the car," I told Sidney, "and keep the engine running. I'll check the locker and grab the bag."

"If they have a takeout coffee stand, can you bring me a cup?"

I opened my mouth to mention Charlotte and time being of the essence, but I shut it again. We had no concrete reason to believe the girl was in danger. And I needed to get the snow chains on the tires. We were stuck at the station for however long that took, like it or not. Why shouldn't Sidney drink a coffee? "Okay. If you watch the instructional video I found on mounting snow chains, I'll get you one. I'll forward it to you now."

He gave me a mock salute. "Yes, ma'am."

I stepped out of the car and immediately slid on a patch of ice, catching the side of the vehicle to break my fall.

Sidney rolled down his window. "Are you okay?"

"Yeah. Just not used to walking on ice and snow."

He wrinkled his nose. "I'm no pro, either. We don't get much snow in London."

"Nowhere I've lived gets harsh winters. Wind and rain, yes." I motioned for him to close the window. "Don't let the heat out." I pulled my hat over my ears and trudged toward the station building. The snow hit my face at a ninety-degree angle, momentarily blinding me. I shielded my eyes as best I could and staggered my way to the entrance.

I followed my mother's instructions to the ladies' toilets inside the small station building. The locker key was exactly where she'd said it would be: hidden in the cistern of the third toilet to the right. Feeling like a character in a spy film, I fished out the plastic bag and retrieved the key. After giving both the key and my hands a thorough washing, I proceeded to the public lockers.

Number 663 was in the top row. Ideally placed for a short person. I reached up on my tippy-toes. I could just about get the key into the lock. When I turned the key, it wouldn't budge. I pulled off my glove and tried again. And again.

I lowered my heels. Had Desirée given me the wrong locker number? I checked the key, but it didn't have the locker number. Then I checked the email she'd sent me. Yes, 663 was correct. According to my mother, Valentina had organized the bag drop-off with a Swiss contact. Had she deliberately sabotaged our locker? I breathed out hard. Tiredness and tension were making me paranoid. Valentina mightn't like me, but she was a pro. She wouldn't do anything to screw up an assignment.

So, what now? I scanned my surroundings. The security camera overlooking the lockers would be easy to eliminate, even if I had to resort to a tedious method. Without a strong LED flashlight or a camera jammer at my disposal, I'd have to go old-school.

I sidled away from the camera and pulled a mini can of spray paint out of my coat pocket. Having spray paint and a penknife on hand at all times was a remnant from my misspent youth. The spray paint had come in handy more than once as a legal alternative to pepper spray.

Angling the nozzle upward, I hit the camera full-blast, coating the lens with neon-green paint. The camera would've recorded me trying to open the locker, but it couldn't record me breaking into it. Later, I'd have to hack into the system and erase all of today's footage, but I'd deal with that when we were safely at the chalet.

I shoved the can back into my pocket and drew out two Swiss Army knives. Using one knife to bend the tweezers of the other to a ninety-degree angle, I created a makeshift tension wrench. I'd already filed the toothpick to a sharp point, so it slid neatly into the keyway. It had been a while since I'd last picked a lock, and my lack of practice showed. My first attempts failed. My feet ached from standing on my tippy-toes the whole time, but I refused to give up. The next wrench-and-twist was the winner. The locker door creaked open.

It was too dark to see the interior, so I stretched my

arm inside. My fingers closed around a fabric bag. I pulled the bag free and shut the locker.

Gingerly, I weighed the bag in my right hand. Too big to be a joke, too small to contain anything I considered valuable. Sidney and I could kiss goodbye to our dream of tasers and knuckle dusters. Taking a swift look around to make sure no one was paying attention to a foreigner dressed like an escaped Oompa Loompa, I risked a peek into the bag.

10

My mouth gaped wide enough to accommodate a tank. Lipstick? Perfume? And was that a powder compact? Was this a not-so-subtle swipe at my taste in makeup and scent? Confusion quickly morphed into active annoyance. Had I gone to all this trouble busting open the locker to be the butt of a joke?

I shoved the toiletry bag into my backpack and stomped back into the station. A train had just pulled in and disgorged its passengers. Dodging people and suitcases, I swung by the kiosk and ordered coffees for Sidney and me. I made mine a weapons-grade espresso. If my mother didn't see fit to provide me with usable self-defense paraphernalia, I'd take my shots where I could get them.

Back in the car, I tossed the bag onto Sidney's lap. "Unless Desirée is taking her cues from James Bond and those items are secret weapons, she gifted us makeup."

Sidney unzipped the bag and poked at the makeup. "This makes no sense. Who deposited our bag?"

"Some Swiss contact Valentina knows. He stashed the stuff in the locker late last night and let her know the locker number." I slammed my fist against my palm. "I bet this is Valentina's idea of a prank."

Sidney's face clouded. "I'm not Valentina's greatest fan. Would she risk screwing up an assignment, though? From what I hear, she's cocky about her P.I. abilities, but with good reason. However much she dislikes us, I doubt she'd obstruct an operation with a huge bonus at stake."

"No one regards our babysitting job as anything but a placebo for Crofton-Lowe's CEO." I left out the "including us" part. "Valentina wouldn't consider playing a joke on us as having any impact on retrieving the artifacts."

"Should we tell your mother?"

"I dunno. Assuming Valentina's responsible for the makeup bag, she's testing us. I'd rather tackle her personally than run to Desirée."

A muscle in his cheek flexed, reminding me that happy-go-lucky Sidney could be hard as granite when he chose to be. "There's a fine line between telling tales and standing up for ourselves. We can't allow Valentina to bully us."

"We won't. Valentina will regret messing with us,

believe me." I slid Sidney's cappuccino into his drink holder and popped a sugar sachet onto the lid. Then I took a sip of my drink. "One thing I love about the Swiss—even train station coffee tastes great. Did you have any luck understanding the instructions on attaching snow chains?"

He pulled a face. "I watched the video you sent me. It gave instructions. Whether we'll be able to follow them is another matter."

I washed down my sigh with a swig of espresso. "Come on, then. Let's give it our best shot."

Twenty minutes and much cursing later, we were back on the road and hauling up the mountain.

Sidney massaged his sore hands. "I hope the chalet has hand cream."

"I hope the chalet has good food and a hot bath." Most of all, I hoped the chalet had a stroppy teenage girl for us to babysit. With snow this deep, I wasn't eager to launch a search party. Besides, the chalet was our only lead. If Charlotte wasn't there, we'd have to contact my mother. Maybe even the police.

Like the way to Crans-Montana, the road wound past trees, houses, bus stops. Unlike Crans-Montana, there'd apparently been no snowplow to clear a path. It took us forty minutes to navigate our way through the ever-deepening snow. Our headlights were on full power, but visibility was down to the bare minimum. Halfway up the mountain, the navigation system gave up the ghost.

I hit the portable system's restart button. "No dice. This thing's dead. Can you use your phone to get us the rest of the way?"

Sidney fiddled with his phone. "That's weird. I don't have a signal. What about you?"

I tugged my phone free from my pocket and glanced at the screen. An icy foreboding formed a solid block in my stomach. "No signal. I don't get it. The Swiss pride themselves on having excellent mobile phone coverage. We should have service, even under these weather conditions."

"Should, but don't." Sidney's usual chipper demeanor was noticeably absent. "So far, Höllenberg is living down to its name."

"How do you mean?"

Sidney dropped his voice to a dramatic whisper. "The name translates as Hell Mountain."

"That's spooky." A tingle of uneasiness made me grip the steering wheel tighter. "Let's hope our adventurous drive is the only hellish incident we have on this mountain."

Sidney squinted through the windshield. "Any idea how we'll find our way to the chalet? I don't fancy getting lost in a snowstorm, especially with no functioning phone."

I shoved my phone onto his lap. "I downloaded all our routes last night. You'll find them in my files."

Sidney cast me a look of bemusement. "I thought you were confident in Swiss infrastructures."

"Cautiously confident. I'm tech-savvy enough to know never to trust in technology."

Sidney acted as our copilot for the next fifteen minutes, using my saved directions. Even with his help, I'd have driven right past the Hauris' property had it not been for the bright red-and-white Swiss flag painted on the gateposts, looking like an inverted Red Cross symbol.

"Finally." Sidney breathed an audible sigh of relief. "I was starting to think we were lost. It's been ages since we last passed a house."

The Hauris' chalet perched high on a slope, reached by a winding drive up from the gates. A crescent of snow-dipped pines loomed on the incline behind the house, lending the scene a picture-postcard quality. I didn't see any sign of a neighboring property through the snow-dark sky, leaving the impression that this house was totally isolated.

A shiver rippled across my shoulder blades. I didn't like the idea of being alone up here in the middle of a snowstorm.

Sidney peered through the windshield. "There are lights on in the chalet. Someone's home, even if it isn't Charlotte."

The gates had been left open, perhaps by a security guard. Maybe they'd done so because the entrance would be blocked once the snow grew deeper. At any rate, I was grateful to drive through with no drama.

I craned my neck and looked up the steep track

that ended at the generously proportioned, traditional Swiss chalet. The wooden house stood four stories tall. A wide veranda surrounded the second floor, decorated by now empty flower pots. All the third and fourth-floor rooms had balconies. The bottom floor was an exposed stone basement. Snow already hid a sizeable chunk of the basement wall. If the snowfall continued at this rate, it would be completely buried by morning.

Sidney happy-sighed. "Now that's what I call a chalet."

"As long as it has central heating and hot water, I don't care what the house is like." I pulled the car to the side of the track and parked beside a group of four tall pine trees. "I don't fancy sliding down that slope. Let's climb the rest of the way."

We grabbed our stuff from the boot and hauled ourselves up the hill. During our journey up the mountain, the temperature had plummeted. The strong wind blew snow in my face and froze my lips. Had I experienced temperatures this cold before? I didn't think so.

"I wonder if they'll let us borrow skis. If this storm lets up, I'd love to go skiing tomorrow."

"Rather you than me. My one and only skiing trip came to an ignominious conclusion when I collided with a children's ski class."

He regarded me with undisguised horror. "Was anyone injured?"

"Only my pride."

A flight of steps at the side of the house led up to the front door. Sidney and I took them two at a time. When we reached the door, I sat on the bell, anxious to get out of the driving cold.

The seconds turned into minutes. Just when I was at the point of whipping out my makeshift picklock, the door was opened by a sulky white girl with dreadlocks and a resting bitch face. She wore shapeless drawstring pants and a hideous handmade sweater that looked like something I'd knit.

It was hard to reconcile the smiling kid in the file photo my mother had sent me with this hostile creature. But despite the eco-warrior clothing and heavy eye makeup, a pair of yellow-flecked hazel eyes assured me we'd found our quarry.

Relief hit me like a sucker punch to the solar plexus. "Charlotte?"

She treated me and my orange jacket to a scathing once-over. "I believe you've mistaken my house for a homeless shelter."

"And I believe you're about to let me in." It's funny how being insulted helped me shed my reluctance to use my rusty German. I shoved the heavy door with all the strength I could muster, sending the girl staggering backward. I marched into the house and dumped my case next to the coatracks.

"I'm Sidney, and this is Angel." Sidney closed the front door and slid the locks back into place.

"Excellent. I see you have house shoes for guests. I packed my slippers just in case you didn't."

His remark startled me for a moment. And then I remembered that the Swiss didn't wear shoes at home. I hastily removed my snowy boots and put them on a waterproof tray by the door.

Sidney dug through a basket of sturdy-looking guest slippers and handed me a pair. "I think these are your size."

Having recovered her composure, Charlotte glowered at us through her smudgy eye makeup. "I suppose you're my so-called English teachers."

I dug myself out of my snow-encrusted jacket and slung it on a hook. "Why so-called?"

She rolled her heavily kohled eyes. "Puh-lease. Papa is paranoid. He thinks I'll run off if he's not here to monitor me."

"He's right," I reminded her. "You ran away from your school."

"I didn't run away. I simply left. Or is the difference too complex for your terrible German?"

"Ran, left, whatever." I wasn't about to let her rattle me. "If you have a problem with my German, we can speak French. You must speak it well if you attend a French-speaking school. Alternatively, we can make that English crash course a reality. It's up to you."

The girl glowered at me. "I don't see why I should accommodate your poor linguistic skills," she said in German. "I don't care whether you understand me."

Swallowing a sigh, I picked up my case. "Can you please show us our rooms and let the housekeeper know we've arrived? I'm starving."

Charlotte's smirk set off warning bells. "Then I hope you can cook. Frau Lenz quit last weekend."

"Quit?" An awful suspicion penetrated my brain fog. "The front gates are wide open. And you opened the door. Where are your guards?"

This time, no smirk, just a sulky shrug. "Dunno, don't care. They weren't here when I arrived, and they haven't shown up since."

Sidney and I exchanged a loaded look. "Does your father know you're here alone?" he asked in a gentler tone than mine.

"Probably not. Papa never concerns himself with the day-to-day running of his households. He always leaves that to his housekeepers or his PA."

My mother had sold Sidney and me this weekend assignment as an easy-peasy, no-danger job. The housekeeper quitting didn't concern me beyond the unwelcome prospect of cooking after a long day. However, the missing security guards worried me, especially in combination with our total lack of ammo.

I let the case fall and slid my phone out of my pocket. Still no signal. A tightness enveloped my chest, making it hard to breathe. Why had the staff deserted the chalet on the very weekend Charlotte's father was concerned for her safety? Was it connected with the theft at the auction house? "Is your mobile phone working, Charlotte?"

The girl wrinkled her nose. "It conked out an hour ago."

"What about Wi-Fi? Or a landline? Or any means of communication with the outside world?" My questions came as quick as bullets.

Charlotte's too-cool-for-school attitude dimmed a few watts. "The Wi-Fi's also out. We don't have a landline anymore. Who does these days?"

The cold foreboding I'd experienced earlier turned into full-fledged fear.

Sidney's expression mirrored my thoughts. "Can you show us the guards' rooms? Maybe they left a note or some indication of where they've gone."

Regaining her sullen attitude, the girl gave an exaggerated sigh. "Whatever. They both sleep on this floor, just down the hall." We followed her, and she pointed to two rooms next to each other. "Luigi's on the left, Guido's on the right."

Without consulting one another, Sidney and I instinctively took different rooms. Both doors were unlocked. Luigi's room was spotless and spartan. It was also empty. No clothes, no toiletries, no sign that anyone lived here.

I stuck my head into the hallway at the same time Sidney emerged from Guido's room.

He met my raised eyebrow with palms up. "No one

and nothing. The room's stripped of all personal belongings."

"Same for Luigi's. I don't like this." I turned to Charlotte. "They assured us you had a security team on the premises. Are you certain you don't know anything about the guards leaving?"

The girl blinked, her practiced sangfroid ebbing away. "No. Their things can't be gone. Did you check the drawers?"

"I checked the drawers, the wardrobe, and under the bed." I held open the door to Luigi's room. "Want to see for yourself?"

Charlotte took a cautious step toward the door. "I've never been in their rooms before."

"Screw Luigi's privacy. We're stuck in a blizzard with no way to contact the outside world, and all three of your household staff are missing. If you can get any clue about where he's gone and why, be my guest."

In the end, Charlotte searched both rooms. When she emerged from Guido's, she'd regained some of her composure. "Maybe the guys left when Frau Lenz quit. Neither of them can cook, and they certainly know how to eat. Yeah, that must be the explanation."

Sidney held his phone aloft. "Still no signal. What about you?"

"Nothing." A leaden feeling weighed on my empty stomach, unease warring with hunger. "Can you try your phone again, Charlotte? Maybe the Wi-Fi's come back on."

The girl checked her screen. Her fashionable caterpillar eyebrows formed an elaborate V. "No Wi-Fi, no phone. It's strange. We've had the Wi-Fi cut out before during a storm, but never our mobile phones."

The rising panic pushed bile into my throat. This scenario reeked. Had Sidney and I walked into a trap?

11

Until the moment Charlotte had told us the security guards were AWOL from the chalet, I'd shared my mother's opinion that the kid was in no danger. Now, all kinds of crazy thoughts tumbled through my mind like a psychedelic kaleidoscope. Had an outside influence interfered with the chalet's internet connection? Was the lack of a phone signal caused by a signal jammer?

I cast my mind back to the moment the navigation system had conked out. How far had we been from the chalet at that point? We'd moved at a snail's pace for the last couple of kilometers of our journey. A modern signal jammer could block signals for a radius of up to a kilometer. A couple of strategically placed signal jammers could extend that radius.

"The weather's too bad to drive back into town," Sidney said, correctly interpreting my panic, if not my precise thoughts. "The car's not suitable for these conditions, and neither you nor I have experience driving on snow and ice."

"Do you have a car here?" I asked Charlotte. "One that can get us out of here safely?"

The girl shook her dreadlocks. "Luigi and Guido have an SUV, but it's not in the garage. I checked when I couldn't find them."

And Charlotte wouldn't have a car of her own because sixteen was too young to have a driver's license in Switzerland. I bit back a groan. This day was getting worse and worse.

Sidney rested a hand on my shoulder. "Why don't you take a bath?" he suggested, switching to English. "In the meantime, I'll see what's in the fridge and rustle us up a meal."

"I don't have time for a bath. I must figure out a way to contact my mother."

"There is no way," he said gently. "Not at the moment. And you stressing about it won't solve the situation."

I blew out a breath. "This doesn't smell right to me. We need to get out of here."

"In this weather?" Charlotte's response was in German, but she'd clearly understood me. "We'd freeze to death."

"She's right," Sidney said. "I know you're worried, Angel, but worrying is what you do. True, the situation at the chalet isn't what we'd been led to expect.

However, there's no reason to assume the worst. Take a bath and chill out."

"The main bathroom has a tub with jets," Charlotte supplied grudgingly. "I suppose I can give you the bedroom next to it."

My stomach cramped. Any other day, I'd leap at the opportunity to soak in a jetted tub. This evening, all I wanted was a phone signal and a Glock.

Was Sidney right? Was I allowing my tendency to assume the worst to cloud my judgment? I stretched my neck from side to side, wincing at the tightness. "A bath would be nice."

Sidney checked his watch. "I'll try to have dinner ready in thirty minutes."

"Better make it an hour at least." Charlotte stuck her nose in the air as though I were an ignorant peasant. "We have the latest model in an exclusive range of tubs. It takes thirty minutes to fill, and that's considered fast for a tub of its size."

A half-hour would give me plenty of time to bolt every door and window in the house. "Can you show me your alarm system before you take me upstairs? I'd feel more comfortable knowing it was on."

Her lower lip protruded into a pout. "We only switch it on when we're out or at night."

"That's when you have armed security guards in the house," I pointed out. "The only arms Sidney and I have are attached to our bodies."

The girl rolled her eyes. "Whatever. The alarm panel's behind you, next to the door."

I checked out the alarm system. Unsurprisingly, it was state-of-the-art. "Can you please show me how to use it? And give us the code in case we need to switch it on or off?"

Charlotte didn't bother to conceal her impatience. She did, however, give Sidney and me a thorough run-through of the alarm system. Sidney punched the security code into his phone. I committed it to memory. I'd always found numbers easy to recall. Before I closed the panel, I made sure the alarm was active.

Sidney slipped his phone back into his pocket. "I'll investigate the fridge while Charlotte shows you to your room."

"And here was me thinking *you* were the hired staff." Sweeping us with a contemptuous glare, the girl tossed her scraggy hair over her shoulder and took off toward the stairs.

Sidney's eyebrows arched into his hairline. "The cheek."

"We're in for a fun weekend with that one. We'll need to add the social niceties to our nonexistent English lesson plans." I picked up my bag and followed her up the stairs.

On the way up, I noticed the chalet's wall decor for the first time. An impressive arsenal of historic weaponry punctuated the rows of twee country drawings.

"Is that medieval crossbow the real deal or a replica?" I asked.

Charlotte's over-the-shoulder look reeked of contempt. "My father's life revolves around antiques. Of course, it's genuine. He has a Tell complex."

"Tell?" I struggled to keep up with her rapid stream of German, and I wasn't sure I'd understood her correctly.

Her condescending smirk made me itch to deliver a withering put-down. "Wilhelm Tell? Swiss national hero?"

Enlightenment dawned. "*William* Tell? The dude who shot an apple off the top of his son's head with a bow and arrow and then took out his tyrannical overlord?"

"He's called Wilhelm around here. Why do you English need to Anglicize everything? And he used a crossbow, not a bow and arrow."

I bristled at her rudeness, but bit back the stinging retort that hovered on my tongue. "Actually, I'm not English. I'm—"

Before I could finish expanding on my dual national status, Charlotte swept over the landing and down a dimly lit hallway, pausing in front of the last door on the left. "You can use this bedroom. There's a connecting door to the main bathroom." She gave me another scornful head-to-toe. "I hope you're house-trained."

"I can guarantee I have better manners than you," I

said in a saccharine-sweet tone, "and my bar is set pretty low." With that parting shot, I entered the room and shut the door behind me.

The bedroom was the dictionary definition of "charming." It had gabled windows, a hand-carved wardrobe, and a queen-sized brass bed. Too quaint for my tastes, but it was a vast improvement over most of the crash pads I'd called home.

I tossed my bag on the bed and went straight to the wardrobe. Empty, apart from spare bedclothes and a purple silk kimono. I grabbed the kimono and laid it on the bed.

Now that I was on my own, my fear had ebbed slightly. Sidney was right. I was a born pessimist. And with my tendency to find trouble, I expected danger at every turn. Sure, the lack of phone and internet access was unusual. However, there was no justification for assuming malicious intent. I needed a bath, a meal, and maybe a glass of wine.

I checked my phone again, hoping the signal would have magically reappeared. It hadn't. At least the nonfunctioning phone and internet had solved the Del dilemma. I wouldn't be able to hit send on that birthday text.

I unlocked the connecting door and stepped into the bathroom. It was a gold-plated marble affair that veered too far into ornate. But the jetted tub? Simply awesome. The tub was a raised, circular whirlpool in the bathroom's center with a padded interior and a million settings.

I fiddled with the many dials. The taps gushed into action, and the tub began to fill with warm, steamy water. While the water ran, I locked the door that divided the bathroom from the hall and went back into the bedroom through the connecting door.

My main bedroom door didn't have a key in the lock. I scanned the room for one, and spotted it nestled on top of the doorframe. Weird place to keep it, but whatever. Grumbling about the disadvantages of being short, I dragged a chair over to the door, stood on it, and retrieved the key. I felt happier knowing I could lock my bedroom door.

After I unpacked my stuff, I embarked on my mission to ensure every single window in the chalet was locked. This floor consisted of six generous bedrooms, five of which boasted en suite bathrooms. Herr Hauri's room was stark and masculine and dominated by a velvet-curtained four-poster bed. His adjoining bathroom was almost as large as the main one and also contained a fancy whirlpool-style bathtub.

The guy clearly loved all things medieval. To the right of the bed, a complete suit of plate armor stood sentry. An Iron Chair occupied the opposite corner. I'd seen this medieval torture device in museums, but always behind glass. Repelled yet fascinated, I took a closer look. A hole was cut in the seat, allowing a torturer to light a fire under their victim. To add to the occupant's joy, sharp metal spikes covered the entire chair. I ran a fingertip over one and drew back. Still sharp, even after all these centuries.

Every centimeter of the spare wall was covered with an array of weapons, ranging from swords to daggers to lethal-looking devices I couldn't identify. A stacked collection of daggers sat on the dressing table, each hilt more exquisitely carved than the next. Even the bathroom contained a bow and arrow stored in a wall-mounted glass case. When I'd wished for a cool arsenal at my disposal, I'd had a more modern collection in mind. Why couldn't the guy have at least one twenty-first-century firearm?

Before leaving Herr Hauri's bedroom, I liberated a short sword from the wall. Despite my light-fingered past, I had no intention of keeping the weapon past the weekend. Sidney would think me crazy, but I felt more comfortable when my fingers closed around the grip. I had two Swiss Army knives in my pocket. However, they weren't ideal as self-defense tools. The sword would allow me to keep some distance from a potential assailant.

Sword at the ready, I moved through the other bedrooms at a swift pace, ensuring I bolted all the windows and balcony doors from the inside. Then I checked the upper floor. This must've been the former housekeeper's apartment. It was spartan in comparison to the floor I'd be sleeping on. Like the security guards' rooms, there was no sign that anyone had been here recently, save for a dust-free novel on the nightstand—the German translation of Agatha Christie's *The Body in the Library*. I approved of her reading tastes.

I went back downstairs and examined the windows and doors on the entrance level. The wide veranda that surrounded this floor of the house concerned me. It'd be easy to climb up and break in. I didn't breathe easy until I'd made sure all potential entry points were secured.

The open-plan living area boasted a roaring fire, complete with a neat stack of logs in a basket to the side of the fireplace. I added an extra log to the flames, warming my still-numb hands against the warmth. I'd have felt more comfortable knowing that the two security guards were on the premises, ready to ward off intruders, but at least we wouldn't freeze.

My next stop was the basement. Apart from one ventilation hatch too small for anyone to crawl through, this floor proved to be a window-free zone. In addition to a tiny entrance hall that contained the heating system and fuse box, the basement was divided into five sections. Two rooms were used to store sundry items, ranging from sports equipment to DIY tools to a spare first aid kit. One was clearly the laundry room, complete with two washing machines, a dryer, and an automatic ironing board.

An unlocked door led to a generous garage with enough space to accommodate four vehicles. At the moment, it was empty. I checked the garage door to make sure it was locked and then stepped into the final room. This housed nonperishable food items on one side and a fridge and a deep freeze on the other. A flimsy wooden stack of shelves was pushed against the far wall, each shelf piled high with random items. It was an eyesore in the otherwise pristine basement.

Satisfied that I'd done all I could to make sure no one could get into the chalet, I returned to my bedroom, locked the door, and stripped off my clothes. I rarely suffered from back pain, but the hours spent in a car with poorly sprung seats had taken their toll. A warm bath would be pure bliss.

I slipped on the kimono. It smelled comfortingly of washing detergent, and the silky material felt wonderful against my bare skin. I had no idea who owned it, but I figured they wouldn't mind me borrowing it for the weekend. It wasn't as though they had a choice.

A piercing sound attacked my ears with painful persistence, breaking my sensory bliss and skyrocketing my pulse. A fire alarm. I let out a long breath. No need to go into fight-or-flight mode. This had to be a drama in the kitchen.

Unhurried, I opened my bedroom door and stepped into the corridor. No smell of smoke, but plenty of shouting. Sidney and Charlotte were in the middle of a loud altercation. He'd reverted to English. She was screaming in German. The fire alarm's piercing cry continued for several painful seconds until someone shut it off. Clearly, dinner prep wasn't going smoothly. Grinning, I retreated to the peace of my room.

I put my toiletries and a fresh change of clothes in a pile and carried them through to the bathroom. The air was now thick with steam, making it hard to see. Had I set the temperature dial incorrectly? To create this much steam, the water must be close to boiling.

My heart beat faster as I deposited my clothes on an empty shelf. I'd had a niggling suspicion that something was wrong the instant Sidney and I had arrived at the chalet. That nagging doubt drove me back to the bedroom. I grabbed the sword off the bed. The feel of the rugged metal grip in my hand calmed me. Silly, I know. Maybe the bath would take the edge off my uneasiness. I couldn't lug a sword around all weekend. Charlotte was bound to tell her father. If that tidbit got back to my mother, she'd decide I was psychologically unfit to be a P.I. And I couldn't blame her.

Back in the bathroom, the heat was intense. Sweating under my robe, I edged closer to the tub, clutching the sword like a security blanket. The water was still running. The deco was still old-school chintz. But during the time I'd spent securing the premises, something in the bathroom had changed.

I squinted through the steam. And my heart froze.

A stranger sat in the tub—stark naked and totally dead.

12

The dead dude's fingers curled around the stem of a martini glass. He had a Freddie Mercury mustache, and his hair was Ronald McDonald red. A top hat was crammed over the curly wig, while a pair of gold-sequined sunglasses perched on his nose. From the nose down, he wore nothing but his birthday suit. Sitting in the tub's steamy water, the man looked alive—except for the dagger sticking out of his chest.

You know how fictional amateur sleuths always scream when they find a dead body? And then scan the scene of the crime, mid-scream, looking for clues?

That's not what I did.

I couldn't have screamed if I'd tried. Frigid fear slithered up my body from my feet to my throat, encasing me in an invisible sarcophagus. I couldn't move, I couldn't speak, I couldn't breathe. All I could hear was a roaring in my ears, like a thousand internal Klaxons.

I stood there for a full minute, maybe longer, staring under the water at the shimmering hilt of a dagger. Then the Klaxons died, my lungs filled, and I could feel my limbs again. The final jolt I needed came when my grip on the sword loosened and it hit the tiles with a clatter.

Breathing heavily, I took a step back from the Tub of Death. My foot slipped on a wet tile, and I careened across the bathroom like a cartoon character stuck on fast-forward. Think flailing arms, jelly legs, and ineffectual chicken squawks.

My stagger routine ended when I face-planted over the bidet. I slammed into the porcelain rim chest-first and bashed my nose against the tap. The impact deflated my lungs faster than a burst balloon. Shock gave me a five-second reprieve from the pain. But when it hit, it did so with a vengeance.

Raw agony spread through my face and chest. Had I busted my nose? Broken a rib? Punctured a lung? I slid to the floor, struggling to breathe. Black spots floated in front of my eyes, coalescing into dark silhouettes of the dead dude.

Who was that man? Who'd killed him? And why was he in this bathroom?

A pounding sounded on the main door. "Angel? You okay?" The thick wood muffled Sidney's raised voice.

"No. Not. Okay."

The door handle rattled. "This door's locked. Is the connecting door locked too?"

"No. But the bedroom door is." A viselike pain gripped my chest; I could barely get the words out.

Sidney muttered something inaudible and tried the handle again. "Stay away from this door. I'm going to break it down."

Skinny Sidney break down a door? I could imagine Luc shouldering a boulder into motion. But Sidney? His wiry frame was more likely to splinter before the door did.

He crashed against the door before I could stop him. The heavy frame shuddered, but didn't give way. Sidney's yowl told me all I needed to know.

Sidney hurled himself at the door five times before Charlotte's staccato German rose above his oh-so-English swearing. My German was rusty, but even I understood the gist. Poor Sidney was being called every type of idiot, using all manner of compound nouns.

A key turned in the lock, and the door opened a crack.

Charlotte batted her way through the thick steam and almost stumbled over me. My open robe revealed more of my body than I usually displayed before the third date. Blood trickled from my nose, adding to my train-wreck appearance.

The girl's gaze swept over my disheveled state and

rested on the fallen sword beside me. "Why do you have that sword in here?" Her upper lip curled in trademark teenage disdain. "First, your idiot friend tried to burn down the kitchen. Now you throw my dad's antiques around up here. And what have you done to the jetted tub? It shouldn't run this hot. Are you two trying to destroy my house?"

"Body," I gasped through the pain. "In the tub." My words came out in an unintelligible wheeze.

Charlotte turned to Sidney. "What's she trying to say?"

He emerged through the steam, clutching his right shoulder. At the sight of me spread-eagled on the floor, his eyes bugged out. He reached down with his good arm and hauled me to my feet. He tried to fix my robe. And failed. "What happened, Angel? Did you slip?"

"Dead. Guy." My words were clearer this time. "In the tub."

Sidney and Charlotte stared at me with matching expressions of horrified disbelief. In unintentional synchronized perfection, they whipped around and stared at the crime scene.

Charlotte's ultra-cool attitude evaporated faster than the hot water. Her high-pitched shriek reminded me of Mélisandre fighting with next door's tabby. The noise pierced my eardrums and added a headache to my list of woes.

Ignoring the girl's hysterics, Sidney rushed over to the tub and turned off the taps. Once he'd stopped the gushing water, he unlatched the bathroom window and threw it wide open. The freezing wind blasted snow into the room and dispersed the steam, making it easier to see.

I grabbed a wad of tissues from a box in the bathroom cabinet and clamped them over my still-bleeding nose. I prodded the bridge gingerly. Sore, but not broken. Thank goodness for small mercies.

While I tended to my injuries, Sidney examined the corpse. His skin grew ashen, his face more stunned than alarmed. "No way. Not again. Not another dead body."

"*Another* dead body?" Charlotte screeched. "Do you make a habit of finding dead people?"

"Not willingly," I said. "It just seems to happen."

"In my defense—" Sidney jerked a thumb at me, "—I only find them when I'm with her."

Charlotte's mouth opened and shut, carp-like.

Sidney went back to the window and leaned out. He muttered under his breath. "The Peugeot's stuck deep in snow, Angel, and the storm's turning into a blizzard. We're not going to be able to drive down to the village tonight."

A flutter of panic reignited my nausea. I didn't want to stay in the house with a dead body.

I massaged my sore ribs, willing my mind to focus. "That guy wasn't in the tub when I turned on the water. Someone put him there while I was touring the house, checking the windows and doors."

I sidled over to the tub, forcing myself to look inside. "Look at the water. It's clean. Our John Doe must've been dead a while before he went into the tub. A stab wound to the chest bleeds like crazy, but there's no blood in the water. Otherwise, you'd have thrown up by now. You know how you are about the sight of blood."

Sidney's pale face grew chalky white. "If the body wasn't in the tub before you filled it, then—"

"Then the killer could still be in the house." A wave of nausea rolled over me, making me gag. If a madman was on the loose, we were sitting ducks. A medieval sword wouldn't provide protection if the killer had a gun. And yet...

My gaze rested on the corpse, lingering on the dagger in his chest. The water distorted my vision, but it looked like an old-fashioned, carved hilt. Not a functional, modern knife. "Could that be a dagger from your dad's collection, Charlotte?"

"I don't know. I don't want to look." The girl backed away from the tub and wrapped her arms around herself.

Sidney followed my line of thought. "Yeah, it could be medieval. It's hard to tell while it's submerged. It'd make sense for the weapon to be an item the killer had close at hand."

That pointed to a crime of passion, not premeditation. The implication was more confusing than comforting. Regardless of why and how the murderer had dispatched his victim, a person who'd killed once was more likely to kill again.

Sidney checked both bathroom doors, locking the main one. If a murderer was on the loose in the chalet, neither door would keep them out for long, not with an arsenal of medieval weapons at their disposal.

I forced air into my sore chest. Breathing was agony. Moving was something worse. "Can you hand me the sword? I don't think I can bend."

"If you can't bend, I doubt you can hold a sword." Sidney picked up the weapon, tested the tip, and went through a series of professional-looking defensive postures.

This was my first time seeing Sidney armed and dangerous. "You wield that thing like a pro. Where did you learn to use a sword?"

"Don't sound so surprised. I had top marks in all my stage combat classes at drama school. Although I've never been in an actual sword fight, I can fake one with aplomb." His gaze dropped to our unexpected guest. "The way this weekend is going, I may have the opportunity to use a sword for real. Charlotte, are you sure no one was in the house when you arrived this afternoon?"

The girl shook her head, blinking back tears. "No one, I swear. I was surprised. I thought at least Frau Lenz would be home."

It took my still-addled brain a moment to place the name. "Your housekeeper? Didn't you say she quit last weekend? Why would you expect her to still be at the chalet?"

"I didn't know she'd quit until today. I found a note from her on the kitchen counter. She said she was sorry, but she could no longer work for us. No explanation, no notice."

I met Sidney's concerned look. The timing of the housekeeper's departure was mighty suspicious. No housekeeper, no security guards, no warning. And all on the very weekend Charlotte's father feared for her safety.

Charlotte looked as nauseated as I felt. All vestiges of bravado had deserted her. Brat or not, I felt bad for the kid.

"I'm sorry to have to ask you this." I touched her shoulder and made my voice sound like the nurturing parent I never had. "Would you please take a closer look at the dead guy? Maybe you'll recognize him."

After the initial shock of seeing a corpse in her bathroom, Charlotte had avoided looking at the dead man. She took a deep, heavy, shuddery breath. "Yeah, okay." She sidled past the tub, not eyeballing the corpse until she absolutely had to. When she did, her expression was rigid with fear. She took in the man, the costume, the dagger. Then she released a ragged breath. "I don't know this man. I don't know why he's dead in my house."

"You're positive he isn't one of the missing security guards?" I watched her expression closely. I couldn't put my finger on why, but I didn't trust Charlotte Hauri.

She kept her eyes on the dead man. "Even without the wig and the mustache, he looks nothing like Luigi or Guido. They're both typical southern Italians—dark tans, dark eyes. This man is too pale."

I refrained from pointing out that his pallor might've been exacerbated by blood loss. "Did you come into this bathroom at any point after you came home?"

"Yes. I needed to refill the soap dispenser in my bathroom. Frau Lenz keeps—kept—all the spares in here." Her voice was helium-high, verging on hysterical. "I swear that man wasn't in here earlier—dead or alive."

"And I would've noticed a dead dude when I switched on the taps," I added. "Half an hour ago, that tub was empty. What's more, I'm certain I put the water on a warm setting, not crazy hot."

A muscle in Sidney's jaw tensed. "The killer must've turned up the heat."

"But why? To ambush me in the steam?" Despite the heat, ice slid down my spine.

"Why would anyone leave a dead stranger in the chalet?" Charlotte cried. "It makes no sense."

Sidney lowered the sword and led Charlotte to a wicker chair in the corner of the bathroom. He diplomatically angled the chair away from the tub before urging her to sit. "Do you remember meeting a man named Colin Jones a few years ago? He paid a visit to you and your mother."

A frown line formed between her brows. "The name says nothing to me."

"Colin Jones and your father had a falling out, and Jones paid you and your mother a visit as a scare tactic." Sidney kept his tone calm, courting her confidence. "Are you sure you don't remember an Englishman visiting you out of the blue?"

Charlotte considered the question. "When I was around ten or eleven, a man came to my mother's house. He spoke German with a funny accent. It might've been an English accent. I'm not sure. My mother didn't seem to know him at all, but he knew us. My father was furious when he found out. I assumed he was annoyed because the man was interested in my mother. At the time, they'd only recently separated, and they were always fighting."

My eyes met Sidney's. "That might've been Colin Jones." I focused on Charlotte. "I know it's a long shot, but is there any chance you'd recognize him if you saw him again? The only photo we've seen of him was poor quality."

"I doubt it." Charlotte looked at Sidney, then at me. "Is Colin Jones the reason my father wanted you to be with me this weekend? I never believed the English lessons excuse. My father is a lousy liar. I figured he'd sent you to keep an eye on me."

Sidney nodded. "You're right. We're not here to give you a crash course on English phrasal verbs."

"Just as well," I added, trying to lighten the mood. "I doubt I could identify a phrasal verb in a lineup."

"It's possible that Colin Jones caused the situation your dad is dealing with at work this weekend," Sidney said. "Angel and I were supposed to be extra protection for you in case Jones showed up here and caused trouble. However, we were sent on the understanding that you had two armed security guards in residence."

"Two security guards *and* a housekeeper—all of whom have disappeared." I turned to Sidney and voiced the fact that neither of us wanted to face. "We need to search the chalet."

13

After my moment of bravado, neither Sidney nor I moved, each waiting for the other to take the initiative. In my injured state, I needed pain meds and a good night's sleep. Not an encounter with a killer. I inhaled deeply, wincing at the pain in my ribs but needing the air to think through the pain. "If we don't search the chalet, we'll be stuck in this bathroom until morning. Sidney might not be able to break down the door with his shoulder, but our mystery man has access to a veritable arsenal of medieval weapons, including a mean-looking ax. We can't stay in here with just one sword between us."

Sidney slid his phone from his pocket. "Still no signal."

"Did you expect there to be?" Charlotte demanded, her snotty attitude back in full force. "And why do you want to search the house again, Angel?

You said you'd checked all the windows to make sure they were bolted."

I sucked air through my teeth. "Yes, I did. And during that time, someone snuck a dead body into this bathroom. I was in every room in the house, but not simultaneously. Also, I was concentrating on keeping people out of the house. It never occurred to me to worry about danger from within."

"You had plenty of time while I was stopping that fool from burning down the kitchen." Two spots of color formed on her cheeks. "How do I know *you* didn't put the body in here?"

"Steady on," Sidney said, sounding annoyed. "Angel didn't kill anyone. And it's not my fault the toaster is broken. A bit of smoke set the alarm off, not a raging inferno."

"Maybe you deliberately set off the smoke alarm to distract me and give your friend a chance to kill that man and put him in the tub."

The accusation burned. On top of everything that had happened since I'd arrived at the chalet, it took all my self-control not to lash out at the girl. Only the fact that I was charged with her welfare kept my temper in check. Besides, I'd be asking the same question if our positions were reversed. What did Charlotte Hauri know about Sidney and me? And what did we know about her beyond the trite facts in the file my mother had compiled?

I unfurled my fists and unclenched my jaw. "I

didn't kill that man. And I didn't stage the scene in the tub."

"Before you accuse me of murder as well as attempted arson, *I* didn't kill him, either." Sidney picked up the sword again and gave it an experimental swish. "Angel's right. We need to search the house. I suggest we leave this sword with you while we're gone."

"A sword? What good is a sword I can barely lift?" Charlotte's voice rose to a whine.

"It's not that heavy—maybe a kilo? If it's too much for you to handle, you can always pull the dagger out of the corpse." Mean, but I wasn't feeling the warm fuzzies toward her. She'd just accused me of murder.

Charlotte stared at the dagger, then at me. "You're insane."

I shrugged. "Maybe. Still not a killer."

She squared her shoulders as though steeling herself and took a cautious step closer to the tub. "Maybe that's not a real corpse. Maybe it's a dummy. Maybe this whole thing is my dad trying to teach me a lesson."

Sidney's eyebrows arched. "You think your dad would fake a *murder victim* just to shock you into behaving?"

Her defiant eyes met his shocked gaze. "Have you met my father? No? Then you have no idea what sort of person he is. He'd do anything to keep me in line."

It took a supreme effort not to roll my eyes at her melodramatic teenage tirade. "Unless you two want to see me naked, look away now. I refuse to face a potential killer wearing nothing but a kimono."

"It might be a dummy," Charlotte persisted, paying no attention to my impromptu strip show. "And someone played a mean trick on us. I bet the wig's part of my father's carnival costume collection. He has an entire wardrobe full of costumes stored in one of the guest rooms."

I took my clean clothes from the shelf where I'd left them. Getting dressed was a slow and painful affair. After my first attempt to close my bra sent sharp shafts of agony through my chest, I gave up on the idea of wearing one. While I struggled into my sweater, I distracted myself from the pain by replaying what Charlotte had said.

Her dad's costume collection intrigued me. I'd concentrated on windows and balcony doors during my search of the house. It hadn't occurred to me to look in wardrobes. The dead man's top hat and gold-sequined sunglasses screamed bad taste. And his hair was synthetic. Maybe the mustache too. They fit my idea of Mardi Gras costume accessories. "We should check what the dead guy looks like without the bling."

Sidney's headshake was emphatic. "Absolutely not. This is a crime scene. We can't touch anything until the police get here."

"News flash, friend. No phone, no internet, no cops." I opened the cabinet over the sink and pulled out a pack of disposable rubber gloves, presumably left by the former housekeeper. "We'll wear these."

It was soon apparent that the others interpreted my "we" as the royal plural. Neither one made a move to touch the gloves or the corpse.

Sighing, I pulled the tight rubber over my hands. "Can you at least snap a few photos of the body before I touch him? I left my phone in the bedroom."

Sidney's face developed a greenish tinge. Despite his tangible distaste, he squared his shoulders and took several photos from various angles. When he was finished, he pulled on a pair of disposable gloves. "Let's get this over with."

I stepped closer to the tub. Forced myself to look at the dead guy, his chest, the dagger. I had to appear calm, cool, semi-together, not like a frenetic freak-out machine. Swallowing past the rock in my throat, I removed the man's top hat and examined the inside for labels. "This says, '*Fasnachtsladen Fritz.*'"

"Fritz's Carnival Shop," Sidney translated. "Charlotte's right. These must be from her father's collection."

Next, I removed the wig and revealed a clean-shaven head. A light tug at the corners was all it took to peel the mustache off the man's upper lip. He looked different without the fake hair—more human and more dead.

The sequined sunglasses were the last to go. Until now, I'd been careful to avoid contact with his skin. I wasn't concerned about contaminating the crime scene. I simply had a natural disinclination to touch a corpse. When I removed the glasses, my fingers brushed against his cheek. Even through the rubber gloves, the skin felt ice cold.

I leaped back, breathing hard. "Something's wrong."

"Understatement much?" Charlotte drawled. "I'd say several somethings are wrong, starting with the dead stranger and ending with your ineptitude."

Ignoring her barbs, I braved another feel of the man's skin. "This man wasn't merely dead before he went into the water. He'd been dead for some time. His body's been frozen."

Sidney's eyes grew flying-saucer wide. "Are you sure?"

I gestured to the box of rubber gloves. "Feel for yourself."

With palpable reluctance, he drew on a pair of gloves and felt the man's shoulder. His eyes met mine. "You're right. And look at the way he's holding the martini glass." Sidney poked the knuckles and made a moue of distaste. "At least one finger is broken. Someone forced his fingers around the stem, probably after death."

I took a closer look at the hand. Now that Sidney mentioned it, the fingers curled around the glass at an unnatural angle. "Let's say we're right and he's been dead for a while. Maybe that's why whoever put his body in the tub ran the water so hot. They wanted to thaw him to cause confusion."

Charlotte shuddered. "That's gross."

"Yeah, and it has important implications." I turned the idea over in my mind. "If the man was kept on ice, we have no idea how long he's been dead."

"But we do know how long he's been in the tub," Sidney said. "You raised the alarm less than fifteen minutes ago."

"It feels much longer, but that's about right."

"And you let the tub fill while you checked the windows and undressed. That took you, what? Thirty minutes?"

I nodded. "About half an hour, yeah."

"In that case, the body's been in hot water for a maximum of forty-five minutes. I don't know how long it takes to thaw a frozen corpse."

"Unfortunately, we can't use the internet to find out. And I'm not convinced that info is even relevant. For whatever reason, someone used the thirty minutes I was absent from the bathroom to sneak a frozen dead guy into the tub." I looked at Charlotte. "I assume you two were together the whole time I was doing my security round?"

"You think I need an alibi?" Charlotte's eyes flashed. "I have no reason to kill anyone or put a dead body in the bathroom."

"We were together the whole time." Sidney's smile was wry. "Fighting, mostly."

"You're the one with no alibi," Charlotte pointed out. "How do we know you're not the killer?"

"You've already accused me of that. Take a moment and chew on that thought some more." I indicated the difference in my height compared to hers and Sidney's. "I'm no weakling, but I'm short. I'd have a hard time hauling a non-frozen corpse around the house, never mind one straight out of a deep freeze."

Charlotte's face went through a variety of contortions. "The deep freeze we use to store food?"

"Do you have another variety?" I turned to Sidney. "I saw a deep freeze down in the basement. We'll have to check it out."

He nodded and looked at the window. "It's pretty cold outside. It's possible that the man was killed outside and left there until the murderer brought him back into the house. Regardless of where the body was stored between his death and bringing him up to the tub, whoever put him in here was strong."

I frowned and took another look at the tub. "You're assuming the killer and the person who staged the tub scene are one and the same."

"Probably wishful thinking on my part. I prefer the prospect of a face-off with one crazed individual rather than two." Sidney pushed the body forward and leaned in to look at his back. "This is odd. See this mark on his back? It looks like he was lying on a sharp object. Not sharp enough to pierce the skin, but it left a dent."

I took a look at the small round mark. "Are you sure it's not skin discoloration? I've heard that happens to dead bodies. Not rigor mortis, but similar."

"Livor mortis," Charlotte said in a bored drawl. "It's the settling of the blood after death."

Her unexpected contribution startled me. "You're well informed."

She twirled a dreadlock around her index finger. "I like true crime shows."

"We need to search the house before our own crime story gets a second episode." Sidney pushed away from the tub, stripped off his gloves, and picked up the sword. "Lock the bathroom door after us, Charlotte. Don't let anyone in unless they knock five times—two long, three short."

She backed against the wall. "I don't want to stay in here with the corpse. Can't we leave the house? Maybe get a room down in the village for the night?"

"I'd love to, but the snow's terrible, Charlotte. We don't have a four-wheel drive, and it's too dangerous to ski."

"I don't want to stay in this house. I don't want to be anywhere near that body."

"You can stay in my bedroom," I said. "I locked the door to the hallway from the inside, and you can lock the connecting door behind you when you go through.

Just let me do a quick check first, okay? I'll make absolutely sure it's empty."

Without waiting for her to agree, I took the sword from Sidney's outstretched hand. Now that my ribs were compromised, it felt heavier than before. Despite the weight, no way was I venturing out of the bathroom without a way to defend myself.

I unlocked the door to the bedroom. The room looked exactly as I'd left it, right down to the open wardrobe doors. Nevertheless, I checked inside for lurking lunatics. To my relief, it was a person-free zone. So was under the bed.

"It's safe to come in," I called. "No strangers, dead or alive."

Charlotte slouched into the room. "You have a warped sense of humor."

"You've accused me of worse." I handed her the sword. "Take this. Does your father keep any twenty-first-century weapons in the house?"

She stared at me with wide, frightened eyes. "No. Only Luigi and Guido had guns."

But the security guards weren't here. They, like the housekeeper, had done a Houdini. "We'll have to grab weapons off the walls."

Charlotte perched on the edge of the bed, clutching the sword in a white-knuckled grip. "My father will freak when he finds out you've been messing with his medieval paraphernalia."

"Your father will freak out more if you come to any

harm. Seeing as his weapons collection is our only option, he'll have to deal."

Sidney checked that the door from the bedroom to the hallway was still locked. "Don't forget what I said, Charlotte. Five knocks—two long, three short. Otherwise, don't react."

She inclined her head slowly. "Okay." A pause. "Don't be gone too long."

My irritation with her softened. "We won't. Stay here and don't move."

Back in the hallway, Sidney locked the bathroom door behind us. "What happened to our safe, boring weekend assignment? If Valentina really stole the self-defense gear Desirée intended us to have, I'll make it my mission to get her demoted."

"You're kinder than I am. If she's responsible for us having to scavenge for thousand-year-old swords, I'll make it my mission to hack every device she owns from now to infinity."

"Where did you get that sword, by the way? I've only seen larger weapons on the walls."

"In what I presume is Herr Hauri's room. It's an ode to medieval torture, complete with an Iron Chair." I pointed down the hallway. "Follow me, and I'll show you."

When we stepped inside the room, Sidney shivered. "It's a veritable chamber of horrors in here. Fitting for a house on Hell Mountain." While I scoured the walls for likely self-defense tools, he explored the room. "What kind of man sleeps with a ball and chain on the wall behind his bed? This is no sex toy. Those spikes are lethal."

"The kind of man with an inferiority complex and too much disposable income." I removed a short sword from a hook on the wall and weighed it in my hand. It was lighter than the one I'd left with Charlotte. Ideal for a woman with sore ribs. "If you see anything that strikes your fancy, grab it."

Sidney's hand hovered over the ball and chain. "Perhaps this will prove useful to more than Herr Hauri's ego."

"Sure. And make sure you take a backup weapon." I paused in front of a stacked display of daggers, each with an elaborately engraved hilt. One space was empty. The implication took a moment to crystallize. When it did, a ripple of revulsion ran through my body. "Sidney, we have a problem."

He swung around, his fingers clenched around the handle of the ball and chain. "Another problem? Don't tell me you've found a second corpse."

"No dead body, but a clue about the first one." I indicated the display stand. "I'm certain all the daggers were present and correct when I came in here earlier. Now there's an empty space. That means whoever put the body in the bath got the dagger from this room."

He stared at me, his eyes clouded with confusion. "Well, we knew that. We figured he'd been killed with one of Herr Hauri's knives."

"Right. But when we talked about the source of the dagger, we hadn't yet realized the man had been dead for a while. Could he have been stabbed, then frozen, then moved to the tub within thirty minutes? That doesn't seem possible."

"The whole situation is improbable." Sidney frowned at the ball and chain, as though willing it to provide answers. "Why would anyone move the dead body to the bath and put him in a costume, right down to the detail of forcing his fingers around a martini glass?"

"No clue. To scare us? Let's say we're right and the body was frozen, either in the deep freeze or out in the snow. Did the killer freeze the body with the weapon still sticking out of the wound? Why would he do that? Apart from being a waste of a weapon, wouldn't moving a body with a knife attached be super awkward?"

Sidney arched an eyebrow. "Would it? I defer to your expert knowledge of moving dead bodies."

"You're so funny, I forgot to laugh. My point is, did the killer add the dagger as a finishing touch to scare us? Did the man actually die of a stab wound? We didn't examine the body. We don't know his cause of death."

Sidney's face developed a greenish tinge. "Are you suggesting he was stabbed post mortem?"

I spread my palms wide. "It's a possibility. It'd explain the total lack of bleeding."

"Even if that's true, where does that information get us? We still don't know who the dead man is or who killed him. All we know is that we're stuck in this house with a lunatic on the loose."

"I don't know if the corpse being stabbed before or after death has any relevance to our current situation. It's another strange detail to add to our growing collection of things that don't add up." I fingered one of the daggers on the display stand, then slipped it into my pocket. "We need to get moving. We can't leave Charlotte on her own for much longer. I'll take the next floor. You can finish searching this floor."

It didn't take me long to check the housekeeper's apartment. The rooms were as empty as they had been when I'd been up here earlier. I met Sidney at the foot of the attic stairs. "Any luck?"

He shook his head. "No one's on this floor, but someone's been in the room to the right of the landing. Herr Hauri's carnival costume wardrobe has been ransacked. When I opened the wardrobe, a pile of costumes tumbled out."

"Another theory proved correct." The sinking sensation in my stomach went down faster than the *Titanic*. "I don't feel comfortable splitting up downstairs. There are too many places for someone to hide in the open plan living space. And the basement gives me the creeps. It's a series of small rooms with no visible means of escape."

"I agree. We should stick together." Sidney made for the main stairs, gesturing for me to follow.

The instant I stepped onto the landing, two things occurred in ominous succession. First, the lights died, plunging us into darkness. And then the front door swung open, revealing two dark figures silhouetted against the moonlight.

14

When I'd agreed to take on this weekend babysitting gig, dealing with armed intruders hadn't been part of the job description. Sidney and I hunkered down on the landing and peered through the banisters. My eyes struggled to become accustomed to the dark. Once our unwanted visitors had closed the front door, we were reliant on the light cast by the fire to monitor their progress.

From the intruders' size and the way they moved, I guessed both were men. Unlike us, they appeared to have no trouble seeing their way. *Night-vision goggles.* My breath froze mid-inhale. These people were pros.

One guy snuck into the open-plan living area, handgun poised. The other man fiddled with the alarm system, disabling it with discomforting ease. Whoever these guys were, they knew the alarm code. I strained to get a better look. I dared not use the light on my phone or my Swiss Army knife flashlight in case the beam drew their attention up to our precarious hiding place.

The intruders moved from room to room with ninja stealth, like they were searching for someone—searching for Charlotte.

Fear held me in its death grip. If I didn't want death to become my reality, I needed to pull myself together. I released a shaky breath. "First, the dead dude. Now, these creeps in balaclavas. What the blazes is going on?"

"Nothing I signed up for." Sidney's whisper was Grim Reaper gloomy. "What are we going to do?"

"That's the million-euro question." I fingered the hilt of the dagger I'd filched from Herr Hauri's bedroom. "One thing's certain: we need to rethink our self-defense strategy. How good are your archery skills?"

"I'm better with a crossbow." As though he sensed my surprised reaction even if he couldn't see it, he added, "I was an extra on a fantasy TV series."

"And I thought my past was questionable."

Downstairs, our uninvited guests were still on the prowl. One nudged the other and gestured to the ceiling. Any moment now, they'd come upstairs.

My stomach cramped, and my throat felt like a noose was tightening around my neck. I pushed away from the banisters, keeping my head low. Sidney followed suit. We crawled on all fours until we were past the exposed landing. Once we were no longer sitting ducks, I got to my feet and tugged off my slippers. "Follow me."

I groped my way along the hallway until I located the patch of wall between the main bathroom and my bedroom. Then I slipped my penknife out of my pocket and shone the flashlight at an object hanging on the wall. "A crossbow," I whispered, "complete with arrows. Time for you to put your dubious TV career to good use."

"They're called quarrels, not arrows." Sidney removed the crossbow from the wall and snatched the two quarrels from the hooks above. "I hope I can hold this with my sore shoulder."

As if in sympathy, a spasm of pain shot through my ribs. "All you can do is try your best. We're up against professionals—or people with an intimate knowledge of the chalet."

He reeled around and stared at me. "You think this is an inside job?"

"Didn't you notice how quickly that dude disabled the alarm system?"

Sidney fiddled with the crossbow and inserted a quarrel. "I assume they cut the power in order to disable the alarm system."

I shook my head. "The alarm system wasn't affected by the power cut. They're equipped with backup batteries. One of the men switched it off when he came into the house."

"By hacking it?" He sounded hopeful.

"Much simpler than that. He knew the code." I unlocked the bathroom door, and we slipped inside, armed with our motley assortment of Swiss Army knives and historical weapons.

Sidney locked the door behind us. "You can't be sure they knew the code, Angel. We could barely see what they were doing in the dark."

"True, but I have experience disabling alarm systems. He was too fast for it to have been a hack. I'm telling you, whoever these guys are, they know the security code." Buoyed by pure adrenaline, I threw bath towels onto the still-damp floor. The last thing I needed was a second close encounter with the bidet. Then I dropped to my knees and opened the cabinet under the sink. "You'd better get Charlotte in here. It's safer for us all to be in the same room."

He nodded and rapped on the connecting door, using the code he'd given Charlotte. She appeared in the doorway, sword in one hand, phone in the other. In the glow of her phone's light, she looked wide-eyed and terrified. "What happened to the lights? Did you find anyone? Was the dead guy really in the deep freeze?"

Sidney pulled her into the bathroom and locked the door. "I need you to stay calm. Two armed intruders are heading our way."

Charlotte's face crumpled, and she began to sob. "That's not possible. The alarm would've gone off if anyone had broken in."

"Angel thinks the intruders knew the security code. How well do you know Luigi and Guido? Or Frau Lenz, the housekeeper?"

"What? You think they'd break into my house and threaten me?" Terror made the girl sound younger than her sixteen years. "No. I don't believe it. I've known them for years. They'd never hurt me."

But would they be willing to sell information to people who might? "Someone gave our unexpected guests the security code. If they lived here, they must've known the code."

Breathing through the pain in my nose and chest, I rifled through the shelves and cabinets, selecting toilet rolls and bottles of cleaning fluids. Lightning quick, I pulled the cardboard tubes out of several toilet paper rolls. I unscrewed the lids from a bleach bottle and a liquid hand sanitizer. After I'd scrunched the cardboard rolls to fit, I stuck them into the bottle openings.

"Please tell me you're not planning to chuck homemade bombs at them." Sidney's voice sounded strained.

Charlotte wound a fuzzy chunk of hair so tight around her finger, the skin turned white. "Are you crazy? You can't blow up my house."

I winced. "Jeez, say that a little louder, why don't you? Instead of moaning, help me. Look through the shelves and cabinets for anything you can use against an assailant. Hair spray, for example. Any kind of canister spray that'll sting their eyes."

The girl let go of her hair with a snap of her fingers. "That's your plan? We try to fight them? In what world do you think we can win?"

"We'll win because it's either that or give up. I'm not a quitter." I dug in my pocket and tossed Sidney one of my Swiss Army knives. "Unscrew the towel rail. That'll make an excellent weapon. I'll tackle the toilet lid."

While I removed the screws from the toilet lid, Charlotte laid down her sword and found two cans of hairspray. "What will a toilet lid do against a bullet?"

I held the lid against my chest. "Shield me. Instead of complaining, get creative. Look in the drawers and cabinets and find something—anything—we can use against these guys. Shampoo, for example. Spread it all over the floor in front of the doors."

"How do you expect us to get out with the floor covered in shampoo?"

I jerked a thumb at the window. "We'll climb out. My bedroom's balcony extends past the bathroom window. Now hurry. They'll try this room any second."

While Sidney and Charlotte spread shampoo and hand soap in front of both bathroom doors, I pooled our little arsenal. We'd amassed three short swords, two Swiss Army knives, two daggers, and one crossbow. Add the towel rail, the toilet lid, and my improvised

Molotov cocktails to the list, and we were in a better position to defend ourselves than I'd feared five minutes ago. Not bad for amateurs.

Sidney and Charlotte backed away from the doors, carefully avoiding the mess they'd created. The next moment, the handle of the main door rattled. My breath caught mid gasp. Any second, and they'd be through.

"What now?" the girl whispered. "We run?"

"No. We stay and fight. There are only two of them. I'm confident we'll get the upper hand." It was a bald-faced lie. I wasn't any type of confident. In fact, I wasn't convinced I'd make it through the encounter without puking.

"Take a sword and a can of hair spray and hide out on the balcony. We've got this." Sidney's voice resonated with reassurance. I envied his ability to slip into whatever role was convenient to play. Right now, he was the brave knight, gearing up to face the enemy at the castle gates. He opened the window and helped her to climb out. "Keep low and out of sight."

After he closed the window, Sidney helped me remove the towels I'd placed on the floor. Once we'd ensured we had a direct escape route to the window, we smeared hand soap over as much of the tiles as we could manage.

The door shook violently. My heart leaped, and my sharp intake of breath sent a spasm of pain through my chest. I piled our little arsenal behind the tub and crouched down. The dead man's back loomed over me, an unwelcome reminder of our fate if we couldn't ward off our attackers.

I picked up a sword and tested my penknife's firelighter. My hands were surprisingly steady, my breathing was calm. Who knew? Maybe I was getting the hang of having my life threatened every few months.

The door shook for the second time. I was banking on the men not shooting their way into the bathroom. Charlotte was their target, and they'd want her alive. Plus, everything I'd read about Colin Jones implied he was ruthless, but not violent.

Ruthless but not violent...

The words nagged at me, burrowing deep despite my nervous distraction. Why would a smooth mover like Jones perform a tactical U-turn and send armed intruders after a sixteen-year-old girl? He'd successfully smuggled the cache of Egyptian artifacts out of the Crofton-Lowe auction house. Losing a major client's property to thieves had the potential to torpedo the auction house's reputation and its CEO's career. Wasn't that sufficient payback for Hauri getting Jones into hot water with the police? And why wait years to exact his revenge?

Sidney squatted on the floor beside me and balanced the crossbow on the edge of the tub. "I'll only get one shot. I can't miss."

"You have two quarrels, don't you?"

"Yeah, but it'll take too long to cock the second one. If these blokes have guns, they'll shoot me before I can get it ready." He grabbed my arm and held it tight enough to hurt. "Join Charlotte on the balcony. I'm serious, Angel. Take her and run."

Sidney was willing to put himself in danger to protect us? Tears stung my eyes. I blinked them into submission. "Absolutely not. We're a team. What kind of friend would I be if I left you to tackle two thugs on your own?"

15

Our assailants' door-breaking skills were superior to Sidney's. The wood splintered on the third battering, and the handle gave way on the fourth. They burst into the bathroom, guns raised.

The shampoo booby trap worked its slippery magic. One second, the men loomed in front of us, pistols pointed straight at Sidney and me. The next, two hundred kilos of muscle hit the tiles. One guy retained control of his handgun and let off a shot that took out a chunk of the ceiling. The other dude let go of his weapon when he smashed into the toilet.

Sidney seized his chance. He fired the crossbow at the guy with the gun. Judging by the yowl fest that followed, he'd hit his mark. I threw a towel onto the floor to prevent myself from being the next toilet-smash victim. Toilet lid held high, I scooted out from behind the tub. The dude who'd crashed into the toilet moaned and groped for his pistol.

I whacked him across the face with the lid. He grunted, crumpled, and collapsed onto the floor, trapping his pistol beneath his meaty frame. I swore aloud. The guy weighed a ton. How could I get him off the pistol? I whipped around and grabbed the towel rail Sidney had unscrewed from the bathroom wall. Then I inserted the rail under the unconscious thug and nudged the pistol to freedom.

Sidney claimed the other man's gun, giving us a decided upper hand. He pulled a stray strand of blond hair out of his mouth. "What now?"

I didn't know what role Sidney had slipped into, but it was a badass character. I approved.

Sidney's dude moaned, stirred, and tried to get up.

"Oh, no, you don't." I brought the toilet lid down on his head with a satisfying *thunk*. The man swayed, his eyes rolled back in his head, and he hit the tiles face first. The crossbow bolt remained stuck in his right arm. "Now we strip these bozos and tie them up. And check the fuse box. I bet they set a timer to switch off the lights. If so, it'll be an easy override."

I leaned over and removed the men's night-vision goggles. I tossed a pair to Sidney and strapped on the other pair. It took me a moment for my eyes to adjust. "Keep your gun trained on them. I'll rescue Charlotte from the cold."

I picked myself up off the floor and navigated a

soap-free path to the window. I opened it and poked my head out into the icy air. "Charlotte? You can come in now."

She huddled in the corner of the balcony, hugging herself for warmth. "Finally. I thought you'd leave me out here for the night." She climbed through the open window, panting for breath.

I examined her flushed cheeks and heaving chest. "Are you okay? You look like you've run a marathon."

Her cheeks grew redder, and her eyes flashed. "I feel like it. I had to run up and down the balcony to keep from freezing to death."

"I'm sorry you had to wait out in the cold, but surely it was a better option than getting kidnapped?"

Charlotte's only response was a grunt. Ungrateful little minx. Even the wildcat Sidney and I had rescued last summer had been friendlier than this girl. Sidney and I had risked life and limb to keep her safe, and all she could do was complain? "Help us remove their weapons."

She gave her head an emphatic shake. "No way. I'm not touching them. What if they wake up and attack me?"

"They're both out cold. Besides, Sidney and I have their guns."

Charlotte backed against the door, trembling with fear. "Please don't make me go near those men. Can't I stay in my room? I promise I'll lock the door."

"We need to stick together. What if these fools have friends lurking in the chalet?"

"I'll take something to defend myself. A dagger. Or maybe one of the pistols. I just want to get out of this bathroom." Her voice broke on a sob. "I don't want to be in the same room as a dead body."

I blew out my cheeks. "Yeah, okay. Take a weapon with you, but not a pistol. We'll need those in case the thugs wake before we finish tying them up. And don't just lock your bedroom door. Put something up against it to buy yourself time. Your room has a balcony, right?"

She nodded. "Yeah. All the rooms on this floor do."

"I inspected all the windows before I found the dead guy, but recheck yours again, just in case."

"I'll do that." She snatched up a dagger from the pile at my feet and scrambled out of the bathroom, deftly avoiding the slippery sections.

After she'd gone, Sidney and I stripped the intruders of their weapons, amassing an impressive selection of knives and backup ammo for the two pistols. When I went to remove their balaclavas, one man moaned. My blood pressure shot up. I groped for the toilet lid and gave him another whack. The guy grunted and went limp.

I mopped sweat from my forehead. "The grand unveiling can wait until they're hog-tied."

"It's not as if we're likely to recognize them," Sidney said, "although Charlotte might if one of them is Colin Jones."

"Maybe. She didn't remember much about meeting him." I sorted through the pile of stuff we'd found on the thugs. Even with the night-vision goggles, it was hard to see clearly. "No car key. I was sure they'd have a car key. Did you find one?"

"Unfortunately, no." Sidney got to his feet, holding his pistol at an awkward angle. "We'll take another look after we tie them up. I spotted handcuffs and leg shackles in Herr Hauri's room. We've just got to hope they come with keys."

"If not, we can secure them with padlocks. I saw a box of them in the basement. When you come back with the shackles, I'll go down and deal with the electricity. If we need padlocks, I'll grab a few while I'm down there."

Sidney finished securing a roll of bandages around the men's wrists. He eyed the bolt sticking out of the dude he'd shot. "Can you deal with this while I get the gear from Herr Hauri's room? I'm not great at patching up people."

I aimed my pistol at the prone men. "If you want me to play nurse, you'd better get those shackles. I'm not touching him until I'm sure he can't touch me."

"Point taken." He weighed his pistol in his hand, hesitating. "Should I give this to Charlotte? I don't feel comfortable leaving her alone in her room."

"We can't hand a loaded firearm to a kid. She has a dagger and she'll have locked her bedroom door. The best thing we can do for her is to tie these guys up and then find a way off this mountain. Even without a car key, I'll figure out a way to get the engine started."

"Okay. I'll raid Herr Hauri's room." He was back within five minutes, armed with medieval leg shackles and handcuffs. "I could only find one set of each. What'll we do about Thug Number Two?"

I didn't miss a beat. "He can spend the night on the Iron Chair."

Sidney quirked an eyebrow. "I'm happy to hog-tie them, but I draw the line at torture."

"We won't torture anyone. We'll put cushions on the seat and back. Once we're done pimping it out, it'll be a throne—a throne with inbuilt shackles." I slipped a spare magazine into my pocket. "I'll be as fast as I can. We'll all feel better when we can see again."

Finding my way down to the basement was awkward, even with the night-vision goggles. To my intense relief, my suspicion that the lights had been disabled with a timer proved to be correct. It didn't take me long to unset it, and welcome light flooded the room.

I grabbed the first aid kit I'd spotted earlier. It was as heavy as a toolbox and larger than any first aid kit I'd ever encountered. Before heading back upstairs, I filled my pockets with sturdy twenty-first-century padlocks to make absolutely sure the thugs couldn't escape their medieval shackles.

When I got back to the bathroom, Sidney had

secured the handcuffs and leg shackles on the guy he'd crossbowed.

"Here you go." I dropped a handful of padlocks, complete with keys, onto his lap. "I hope he's up-to-date on his tetanus shots. Those handcuffs have a touch of rust."

"Seeing as he just tried to kill us, I wouldn't shed tears if he wound up with lockjaw."

Once Sidney had made double-sure the man couldn't escape, he guarded the toilet-crash thug while I attended to the crossbow injury. When I pulled the bolt out of the man's arm, I wasn't too gentle. I must've struck him hard with the toilet lid because he didn't stir, not even when I cut through the fabric of his jacket and poured antiseptic into the wound. I finished my slapdash emergency treatment by placing a dressing over the cut and securing it tightly with bandages.

I sat back on my heels and admired my work. "He'll live—unless he tries to attack us again."

Sidney nudged the unconscious toilet-crash victim. "Let's deal with this one first. I'll breathe easier when they're both under lock and key."

I helped him drag the man across to Herr Hauri's room. I was sorely tempted to make the guy sit on the pins unprotected, but basic humanity triumphed over my animal instinct for revenge. I picked the most hideous cushions I could find and placed them on the Iron Chair. Then we hauled the thug into the chair and secured the bolts.

Crossbow Dude came next. By the time we'd finished tying him to the mattress using the ropes from the four-poster bed, my back was slick with sweat.

Sidney wiped a damp strand of blond hair out of his face. "Remind me never to believe your mother again. Cushy weekend job? What a joke that's turned out to be."

"With a lightning bolt of luck, these clowns will provide us with a way off this mountain. If they got up here in this blizzard, they must have a better ride than we do. Probably an SUV. Definitely a four-wheel drive."

"Did you see skis in the basement?" Sidney asked. "Or snowshoes? I could ski down and look for help."

"In this storm?" I shook my head. "However good you are on skis, you'd break your neck. If we're still stuck with no transport in the morning, and the storm's calmed down, then absolutely try to ski to civilization. Our best chance of getting off this mountain is a weather-appropriate vehicle, and even then, we may end up sleeping in it. Key or no key, I'm going outside to check if these goons parked near the chalet."

"What if they have a getaway driver? Or a backup team somewhere around the property?"

I raised the pistol. "Then I'll use this." I grabbed one of our homemade bombs. "And this."

Sidney regarded the bleach bottle and its toilet roll fuse. "Won't a homemade bomb do more harm than good?"

"I don't intend to set it off," I said, "but it'll act as an effective deterrent to any would-be assassin. What would you do if someone held this in one hand and a firelighter in the other?"

"Wish I'd worn incontinence pants?"

"I rest my case." Despite the stress rolling off me, Sidney's horrified expression made me laugh. "I promise I won't blow anything up, dude. Pinky swear. And I'll check on Charlotte before I venture outside." When I knocked on her bedroom door, her response was a muffled, "Who's there?"

"It's Angel. Just wanted to let you know we've tied up the thugs. I'm about to go out and search for their car. Do you want to stay in your room while I'm gone? Or would you prefer to join Sidney in your dad's room?"

The door opened a crack. Charlotte peered out at me with deer-in-headlights eyes. "I'll stay here. I don't want to be anywhere near those men."

"Fair enough. I'll knock on your door again when I get back. We need to find something to eat."

She lowered her clumpy lashes, and her gaze rested on the bleach bottle. "You're taking that outside with you? You're insane. How do you even know how to make homemade bombs? The dark web?"

"I'm confident that info can be found through a regular search engine," I said dryly. "However, I came by my knowledge closer to home." Jimmy the Rat, my dad's best mate and a former IRA bomb-maker, had never been much of a godfather. Making and defusing homemade bombs was one life skill he'd made sure I knew. Unsurprisingly, Jimmy spent a lot of time behind bars.

Charlotte's expression hovered between intrigued and appalled.

"Keep that door locked. Any trouble, yell for Sidney. He's down the hall keeping watch over the bad guys."

Leaving her to barricade herself in her bedroom, I bounded down the stairs and put on my horrible orange coat and winter boots. I pulled my hat low and braced myself to face the cold and whatever—or whomever—lay in wait outside the chalet. The prospect made me shiver.

It was easy to be brave in front of an audience. Yes, Jimmy'd shown me how to make a bomb out of household supplies. Didn't mean I'd actually *lit* one. As for the pistol, I knew how to use it, but I had hardly any shooting practice. If another armed villain attacked me in the darkness, would I be able to defend myself?

I tugged on my gloves and opened the front door. Outside the house, the strong wind blew snow into my eyes. I didn't make it halfway down the steps before I regretted my decision to leave the chalet. It was hard to see anything through the blinding snow. Even if the thugs had arrived in a snowplow, no way could Sidney or I drive in these conditions.

By some miracle, I made it down the steps without incident. My good fortune didn't last long.

I staggered down the slope, falling several times. Each stumble sent sharp shafts of pain through my sore ribs. When I reached the gates of the Hauri property, the Peugeot was almost entirely covered with snow. I shielded my eyes with my hands and shone my penknife flashlight over my surroundings. I almost wished I'd worn the flaming night-vision goggles again.

Everywhere I looked, all I saw was snow. There was no sign of a vehicle, snow-worthy or otherwise. After floundering about for fifteen minutes, I gave up the search as a lost cause. On the plus side, no car meant no getaway driver to tackle. I kept my eyes peeled for lurking thugs, but no one appeared on the snowy horizon.

Despite my gloves, my fingers were too frozen to keep hold of the pistol and the flashlight. I pocketed the gun and carried my bathroom bomb under the crook of my arm. Gripping my flashlight with both hands, I staggered back up the slope. The wind was ferocious and kept pushing me back. Before now, I'd found the storm more irritating than scary, but not being able to walk in a straight line was developing a nightmarish repetitiveness. After what seemed like an age, I reached the steps that led up to the front door.

A dark figure emerged from behind a snow-laden tree, radiating menace.

I didn't hesitate. I whipped out my pistol and fired

a shot into the air. The answering hail of fire had me hitting the deck. The impact sent shafts of pain shooting through my injured ribs. Facedown in the snow, I flailed about in my too-big coat, making unintentional snow angels. My flashlight went flying. And where was my gun? I'd had it a moment ago. I groped around on the snow, each breath a war between my body's need for air and my impulse to throw up.

The dark shape was on the move again, looming closer. It signaled with its hands, probably communicating with yet another vicious villain. My fingers made contact with something. My bathroom bomb. I tried to grab it, but it rolled out of reach. I pushed myself onto my elbows and crawled forward.

Almost there...

I stretched out a hand, lost my balance, and landed face-first in the snow. Until this point, my nose had avoided further injury. Now, pain blasted through my face. I lost the battle against nausea.

When I'd finished hurling, I looked around for the bleach. It had rolled down the slope, coming to rest at the foot of a tree. I'd never reach it. And there was no sign of the pistol. My heart beat so fast it hurt.

The man with the gun was almost upon me. He yelled something—either at an unseen companion or at me—but the wind whipped away his words.

I pulled off my gloves and dug in the snow with my bare hands. It was like taking a skinny-dip in liquid nitrogen. The cold burned my skin but I kept searching. Finally, my fingers felt a hard object. I pulled with all my strength and freed the pistol. When I raised the gun, my hands shook with cold. My first shot went wide, pinging off something in the distance.

The man was running now—running toward me. Any second, he'd be on me. I raised the gun and fired. He gave a bearlike growl, grabbed his left leg, and collapsed in front of me. Despite its battering by the bidet and the snow, my nose picked up the familiar scent of the man's spicy aftershave.

My breath caught in my throat. Frantic, I rolled him over and stared into a familiar pair of electric blue eyes. "Luc?" I croaked. "What are you doing here?"

16

I'm sure I would've hyperventilated and stammered something incomprehensible had the Peugeot not chosen that moment to blow up. One second, I was kneeling in the snow, gawking at the man I'd just shot. The next, an almighty explosion rocked my world.

The force of the detonation sent a tremor rippling up the slope, upending Luc and me and burying us under an avalanche of snow. My ears rang with head-splitting force, and my face and chest rode continuous waves of pain. What had just happened? And had I really shot Luc?

I tried to breathe and wound up with a mouthful of snow. It invaded my mouth and nose and jolted me out of my shocked stupor with the power of an electric cattle prod. After I'd cleared a space around my face to breathe, I punched up a couple of times. Each punch was a stab in the ribs, but I didn't give up. Finding myself in an ice-cold coffin had blasted me into fight-or-flight mode.

When my frozen fist felt the cutting wind, a wave of hysterical relief washed over me. Snow enveloped me, but it wasn't too deep. Inhaling a lungful of air, I continued to punch through the snow until I could stick my head out into the biting wind. In the battle between windburn and asphyxiation, I'd take a chapped face any day.

Once my head was free, it didn't take me long to dig out of the snow. When I hauled myself out, I surveyed the scene. All that was left of the car was a ball of fire. One of the gateposts had been reduced to rubble, and the trees down by the gates were in flames. How and why the car had blown up was a question I'd explore as soon as Luc and I were snow-free and indoors.

A figure in a ski jacket stumbled down the slope from the chalet. The light from the blaze lit up his fair hair and frightened face. "You pinky swore you wouldn't blow anything up."

"Sidney." I sounded more like Kermit than me. "Luc's still under the snow. We have to find him."

He floundered down the slope, landing on his behind beside me. "Luc? But he's off chasing stolen artifacts."

"He's here." I dropped to my knees and began to dig. "I shot him, and then the Peugeot exploded, burying us both in snow."

Sidney's jaw descended in stages like a broken elevator. "You shot him? No way."

"Yes way. Help me find him."

Sidney didn't need to be told a third time. He rolled over and plunged his hands into the snow. "Did you blow up the car, too? What in the blazes happened out here?"

"I mistook Luc for another thug and shot him. I have no idea why the car blew up. It can't have been my bleach bomb. That rolled down the slope in the opposite direction."

"It can't be a case of spontaneous combustion." Sidney dumped an armful of snow onto the ever-growing pile behind him. "Are you sure we're digging in the right place?"

His question sent an acid infusion into my stomach. "I don't know. This is close to where I was, and Luc was right next to me when the car blew up."

We dug at a frantic pace, clearing snow, searching for a hand, a foot, an elbow, an ear. Time passed in a vacuum, leaving me with no sense of how long we'd been digging. And then a fist punched through a mound of snow to my left.

My heart flipped, rolled, and landed somewhere in my throat. "Luc's over here."

We scrambled to the mound and grabbed armfuls of snow. Luc continued to box his way out. Between our efforts and his, he was soon free from his icy prison.

He hacked up snow, tried to stand, and fell back, clutching his injured leg.

Hot tears burned a path down my frozen cheeks. "You're alive."

Luc's bright blue eyes rested on my face, and the corners of his mouth quivered. "Angel. What a misnomer. You're more like an angel of death. First, you shoot me. Then you try to blow me up."

His voice was a deep rasp, like he'd gargled with whiskey, but he spoke in complete, clear sentences. The tension in my neck eased. Luc was going to be okay. "I shot you, but I wasn't responsible for the explosion."

Or was I? Could someone have used my bleach bomb? A vision of my homemade bomb rolling down the slope had my poor, beleaguered heart once again performing leapfrogs. I scanned the area and spotted my bomb still resting at the foot of the tree.

I staggered over to it, pulled out the now-frozen toilet paper fuse, and emptied the bleach into the snow. I'd had enough explosions for one night. Down by the gates, the car still burned. The strong wind whipped through the flaming trees, thankfully blowing in the opposite direction from the house. There was nothing else nearby for the flames to consume. My expertise on fires was limited, and I hoped this meant they'd soon burn out independently.

When I got back to the men, Sidney helped Luc stand. "We must get him up to the chalet. Can you take his other arm?"

"What about the fire? I'm worried it'll spread."

Luc cast an eye over the scene of the disaster. "Call emergency services. It should extinguish itself before long, but best to be safe."

"No one can get a phone signal. And the Wi-Fi's out."

Luc swore beneath his breath. "We'll need to keep an eye on the fire, but it looks like Mother Nature is already taking care of it."

He was right. The snow was falling so fast it was already coating pieces of the car that were no longer burning.

Still feeling unsettled by the prospect of an impending inferno at the chalet to add to our trauma, I grabbed onto Luc's waist. With Sidney on one side and me on the other, Luc lurched up the slope, one groan at a time. When we were halfway up the steps to the front door, he slipped, almost pulling Sidney and me down with him. I clung to the railing, and Sidney managed to break Luc's fall.

A few painful minutes later, Luc lay on a sofa in front of the fireplace, pale and panting. My ribs ached, and my lungs still hadn't recovered from their forced deflation under the snow. Sidney ran back out to check the progress of the fire.

"It's already going out. I think we're good."

"We're anything but good," I countered. "Look at the state of Luc."

Sidney and I stripped off our outdoor clothes whip-fast, dumping them in a pile by the fire. "We need to get Luc to the hospital," he said. "He needs medical treatment."

"How? The Peugeot is toast, and we have no way of calling an ambulance. We'll have to treat him as best we can." I reached for Sidney's belt buckle, but he swatted my hands away.

"Hey, what are you doing?"

"We've got to put pressure on his wound. We'll use your belt as a tourniquet. Do you know where to find clean dishcloths?"

"Yeah. In the kitchen. I'll get some now." He whipped off his belt and handed it to me.

He was back with a stack of clean cloths before I'd finished looping the belt around Luc's leg. Keeping his head turned away from the injury, Sidney neatly dropped the pile onto Luc's belly.

Despite the gravity of the situation, I almost laughed. Sidney and blood didn't make a good combo. To do him justice, he didn't throw up this time, but any first aid would have to fall to me.

I placed two cloths over the torn patch of Luc's pants. Blood seeped through the white fabric at a heart-thumping rate. I pulled the belt tight enough to make Luc cry out. "Sorry, dude, but we have to slow the bleeding." I turned to Sidney. "The first aid kit is still in the bathroom. Stay with Luc while I get it."

Up in the bathroom, I avoided looking at the dead man. I found the kit and managed not to fall on the soap. Then I jogged down to the basement and grabbed a sleeping bag, a bottle of mineral water, and an unopened set of variously sized scissors.

When I got back to the living room, Sidney had put cushions behind Luc and removed his boots. To my relief, the cloths over Luc's wound were red but not oozing. My makeshift tourniquet was doing its job.

I deposited my loot on the coffee table. "I've got this, Sidney. You'd better go upstairs and ensure our guests haven't done a moonlight flit. If they're awake and want to know what happened, leave out any mention of Luc."

"Makes sense. The less they know, the better." His attention moved to the window. "Good news is the fire's almost out. I can try skiing down for help."

"No way," Luc and I said in unison.

Luc fixed Sidney with a stern stare. "Visibility is poor, and the snow hides tree stumps and other objects. Even if you didn't fall and break your neck, you'd freeze to death if you got lost. It'd be dangerous to ski in these conditions during the day. At night, it'd be suicidal."

Sidney pulled a face but nodded. "Okay. At first

light, I'll survey the lay of the land and plan to go then. We need the police and an ambulance."

"I'll live." A wicked grin broke through Luc's pain. "Angel put the bullet in me. Now she gets to take it out."

Sidney made for the stairs. I called after him. "Hey, can you tell Charlotte to come down? None of us has eaten. She can help me fix food. This place has to have packages of soup, at the very least."

The grin on Sidney's face looked like it came from a chimpanzee. "Even you can't screw up soup."

I batted him with my snow-caked scarf. "Don't be so cocky. You're the one who set off the smoke alarm, remember?"

His chimp-grin faded. "Yeah, that was strange. I still can't figure out how that happened. Toasters shouldn't catch on fire like that."

"In an evening of strange events, a smoking toaster is the least of my concerns." I squared my shoulders. "Okaaaay. It's time to put my first aid skills to the test."

Sidney went upstairs, and I focused on Luc. I'd never been this close to him. Never touched his skin.

The reaction deep in my belly redefined the butterfly effect. Heat torched my face. Great. I was a hot mess when I needed to be a cool surgeon.

He'd pushed himself into a sitting position and struggled to remove the backpack slung over his left shoulder. His skin looked gray beneath his tan.

"Here, let me help you." I removed the backpack and pulled his left arm out of its sleeve.

"Watch the other side." He delivered each word between gritted teeth. Beads of sweat had formed on his forehead.

When I reached for his right sleeve, I saw why. "Your arm is in a sling? Why didn't you tell me?"

"You were too busy trying to kill me." His teasing smile doused my spike of temper.

I ripped open the package of scissors and selected the largest of the bunch. "Is this why you're here instead of with the rest of the team? Because you got injured?"

"Yeah. Dario, one of Rocco Casetti's guys, jumped me when Valentina and I were checking out a warehouse outside Brig. During the struggle, he managed to dislocate my shoulder."

"Mega ouch."

"That quarter-million-euro bonus has nuked any chance of fair play between our agency and theirs. Desirée ordered me to drive here to recuperate."

I raised an eyebrow. "She ordered a man with one functioning arm to drive all the way here in a snowstorm? How far away is Brig?"

"An hour...in good weather."

"In other words, Desirée had used your injury as an excuse to get you here to keep an eye on Sidney and me." I didn't bother to hide my bitterness.

Luc's megawatt smile dimmed. "What's going on

here, Angel? Where are the security guards? And where'd you get that gun? It wasn't in the bag we arranged for you to pick up at the station."

I scowled at him. "I know it wasn't. What was the big idea? Did you know that all the bag contained was makeup? Did Valentina prank us?"

"What?" Luc's surprise rang true. "Valentina wouldn't do that. She was responsible for making sure her Swiss contact delivered the bag, but I took care of the packing. Your bag contained pepper spray and tasers." He tried to sit straighter, but collapsed against the cushions. "What's happening here? Why didn't the security guards react to you shooting up the place? And where were they after the explosion?"

"I didn't shoot up the place. I'm sorry I mistook you for an intruder." I checked out his pants situation and held up the scissors. "Should I try pulling off your pants, or will I need to resort to using these bad boys?"

Luc undid the buttons. And the temperature in the room rose by a few degrees. Oh, boy. *Don't think, don't react, don't lose focus.*

He tried to pull the pants over his hips. "It's no good," he said between gasps. "You'll have to cut them off. I'd take too long getting them off for it to be safe without the tourniquet. And I think the bullet's still in my leg. I don't want to risk it going in any deeper."

I slapped my forehead. "And we forced you to walk up to the chalet. I'm sorry, dude. After the explosion and getting buried in snow, I couldn't think straight."

"Looks like you've had a lot going on. Like missing security guards and exploding cars. Care to share?" He pointed to his injured arm and leg. "It's not like I'm going anywhere for a while. I'll hazard a guess that your simple and safe babysitting job hasn't gone as planned."

Even to my still-ringing ears, my laughter held more than a tinge of hysteria. "That's the understatement of the millennium. Charlotte wasn't at her school when we swung by to collect her. We tracked her down to the chalet and discovered the entire staff was AWOL. I don't suppose you can get a phone signal up here?"

Luc pulled out his phone and frowned at the screen. "Still nothing. It stopped working halfway up the mountain. I called you and Sidney, but it always went straight to voicemail."

"Our phones stopped working on the road up here. And the Wi-Fi's dead. I was about to check the modem, but that plan was derailed when our uneventful weekend took a dramatic U-turn. Since then, I've been busy fighting bad guys." I cut up the side of his pants, stopping a few inches above the bullet hole.

"What bad guys? Are they the guests you mentioned to Sidney?"

"And that's why they pay you the big bucks. Two masked guys snuck into the chalet and attacked us. They're chained upstairs—literally. Charlotte's father has a penchant for medieval weapons and torture devices. Having none of the twenty-first-century variety at our disposal forced Sidney and me to improvise."

Luc let out a low whistle. "And we all thought Herr Hauri was paranoid about his daughter's safety. Where did you get your pistol? From the guys who broke in?"

"Yeah—a pistol I lost in the snow."

"You and me both. I dropped mine when you shot me. I must've lost my taser when we got hit by the snow." He shook his head. "And to think I arrived at the chalet assuming the worst part of my day was over. Imagine my joy when you greeted me with a bullet."

"Please tell me that backpack contains more ammo?" I asked, lining up the items I'd need to close Luc's wound. I hadn't helped stitch an injury in years, but the steps were imprinted into my memory.

"Spare bullets for a pistol I no longer possess and two grenades. I don't know about you, but I'm kind of over explosions." A smile cracked through his white-faced pain. "I hope you sew better than you knit. I have a feeling I'll need stitches."

"Spoiler alert—I don't. My stitches won't be pretty, but I can get the job done."

Luc pointed at the ceiling. "Ask Sidney to deal with the sewing part. Francine said he's excellent at repairing costumes."

"I'd gladly hand him the task, but for one salient

fact. Sidney feels faint at the sight of blood. Do you remember when he nicked his finger chopping vegetables for ratatouille?"

Luc's wince practically shook his whole body. "Oh, yeah. I thought we'd need to resort to smelling salts to revive him. Okay, I'll allow you to attack me with a needle and thread. If I don't like the way you're doing it, I reserve the right to take over."

"With your left hand?"

His grin was back and more potent than ever. "Desperation always finds a way."

Shaking off the hot-guy effect Luc was having on me, I applied myself to the task of treating his leg. I removed the belt and blood-stained cloths, and once I'd cut off the left side of his pants, I got a proper look at the bullet hole. It was small and neat and scary.

"The bullet's still in there. There's no exit wound. You're going to have to dig it out." Luc's bravado shoved out the words, but I could hear the fear in his tone.

An image popped into my mind. My father slumped on the sofa. My godfather, Jimmy the Rat, digging a bullet out of Dad's shoulder.

Yet another life lesson courtesy of jailbird Jimmy. If he could do it, so could I.

I swallowed past the boulder in my throat and searched for the tweezers in the first aid box. This wasn't your typical household first aid kit. Its collection of surgical tools looked like something a medic would use on a battlefield.

Using antiseptic, I cleaned the wound as best I could. Then I took a deep breath and picked up the tweezers. "You know digging for the bullet is going to hurt, but I need you to stay still."

Luc pulled up his black T-shirt, exposing an expanse of tanned, toned chest. With the hem of the shirt clamped between his teeth, he gave me a thumbs-up.

I had to tear my eyes away from those taut abs. *Wow*. I needed a fan in here. I breathed out and flexed my shoulders. Time to concentrate on the wound, not the abs.

I'm not sure how I got through the next few minutes. Luc stayed statue-still. Only an occasional hiss communicated his pain. Fortunately for both of us, the bullet wasn't lodged too deep. At first, I had trouble grabbing hold of it. Once I got the tweezers clamped around the bullet, it was easy to extract.

Pressing a fresh wad of cloths over the wound, I held the bullet up to the light. "Did I get it all out?"

Luc reached for the bullet, and I let it drop into his palm.

He examined it with an expert eye. "Yeah, this is intact. Good job. Good shot, too. You took me down like a pro."

His praise made me smile, but just a little. I still had to get through the sewing part. What if my hands shook so much I couldn't get the needle in? I took a long breath, held it, felt my belly expand. I exhaled slow, and steady, then looked at Luc. "Can you apply pressure while I thread the needle?"

I'm proud to say that my hands didn't shake. My saving grace was that Luc only needed a few stitches to close the wound. I wouldn't win awards for my needlework, but the hole was closed. I tied double knots for good measure. When I finally cut the thread, all my nervous energy was spent, and waves of pain made it hard to breathe. I cleaned the wound again and applied a gauze dressing and bandages on top.

He watched me as I worked. "You were just as cool and proficient as any doctor. Where'd you learn to do that?"

The memory of my dad and Jimmy played on repeat. How could I explain my childhood to a man like Luc? He'd served in the military and trained as a lawyer before becoming a hotshot private investigator. His grandfather was one of the most respected lawyers in France. I was the daughter of a career criminal and a porn-star-turned-P.I.

"Television makes us all medical pros." I doled out two painkillers for him and two for me. Then I closed the kit and stood. "I'll see about making soup. We could all do with something warm."

"Oh, no, you don't." Luc grabbed my wrist. "Sit your butt down and tell me exactly what's going on. I want to know everything, starting with the guys upstairs."

I was too tired to protest. I sank into the armchair and fixed Luc with an ironic stare. "Which guy do you want me to start with? The two bozos we chained and shackled in Herr Hauri's bedroom? Or the dead dude in the bath?"

17

One thing I'd learned about Luc during the short time I'd known him: the guy wasn't easy to shock. His default reaction to every outrage was sardonic sangfroid. When under physical attack, he coolly pulled a pistol. When faced with a verbal battering, his response was deadpan sarcasm. The pain and blood loss must've lowered his natural resilience. My casual reference to the dead dude shattered his equilibrium with sledgehammer efficiency.

He gawked at me, goggle-eyed. "Who's the corpse? Another intruder?"

"Your guess is as good as mine. I wanted to chillax in the jetted tub. You can imagine my joy when I found a corpse instead."

"Was this before or after the break-in?"

"Before. Strictly speaking, it wasn't a break-in. The intruders knew the alarm code."

Luc whistled. "Sounds like an inside job."

"That's my guess." I raised my eyes to the ceiling. "It wouldn't surprise me if the thugs upstairs are none other than Luigi and Guido, the missing security guards. I'd have asked them, but when they pulled guns on us, Sidney and I took the 'hit first, ask questions later' approach. They're currently shackled and chained in Herr Hauri's bedroom."

"And the body? How long had he been there?"

"In the tub? Thirty minutes, max. Dead? Your guess is as good as mine."

"Whoa." Luc tried to lean forward and groaned when he strained his sore leg. "Are you saying the man was already dead when he was dumped in the water?"

"Yeah. My command of forensics is courtesy of bad TV, but I'd say he'd been frozen before he was placed in the bathroom for me to find. When the other two clowns broke in, Sidney and I were heading downstairs to discover if his killer had stored him outdoors or in the deep freeze."

I recounted the events of the evening as faithfully as possible, starting with our arrival at the chalet and ending with me mistaking Luc for another intruder.

When I'd finished, Luc reached for the mineral water and took a long swig. "Even by your low standards, this is a wild tale."

"It's been a wild night. But then we are on Hell Mountain."

Luc looked a question at me. "What do you mean?"

"Sidney tells me Höllenberg means Hell Mountain. Appropriate, wouldn't you say?"

"Crushingly so." He stared into the open fire, lost in thought. "Who would go to the trouble of accessorizing a dead body?"

"Someone with a flair for the dramatic?"

"Or a lunatic. How was the man killed?"

"A stab wound to the chest." I paused for a moment, rewatching the scene on my mental monitor. "At least, I think so."

His inky-black eyebrows shot into his hairline. "But you're not sure?"

"Well..." I rubbed my temples, trying to think past the pain in my ribs and nose. "The body has a dagger sticking out of his chest—part of Herr Hauri's medieval collection. However, I'm one hundred percent certain that the dagger was still in Herr Hauri's bedroom thirty minutes before I found the body. Given our supposition that the guy was dead long before he wound up in the tub, I don't see how that particular dagger could've been the murder weapon. Or if it was used to kill him, then his killer removed it, cleaned it, and put it back on its stand."

A line etched across Luc's forehead. "And then returned and reinserted it into the wound? That seems unlikely."

"No more unlikely than putting a wig and a fake

mustache on a corpse. The scene in the bathroom was staged, presumably for our benefit."

"Why, though? To scare you into leaving the chalet?" He stared into the fire, unseeing, his face screwed up in an expression of deep contemplation. "If the intruders broke in to kidnap Charlotte, which is what Herr Hauri feared, then scaring you and Sidney into leaving the chalet makes no sense. You wouldn't have left without the girl."

This thought had already crossed my mind. "It's possible the men wanted to lure us outside. We'd have been more vulnerable away from the house, floundering about in the snow. Even before the Peugeot blew up, I knew I couldn't drive it through snow this deep. I had a heck of a time getting the car up the mountain, even with snow chains, and we've had heavy snowfall ever since. The whole reason I was outside when I shot you was because I was looking for the thugs' car. I hoped we could use it as our getaway vehicle."

Luc nodded. "Makes sense. A Range Rover was parked near where I abandoned my car. Seeing it in a field at the side of the road gave me the idea to leave mine at that spot and walk the rest of the way. I bet that's their vehicle."

"Probably. If you give me the keys, I'll walk down and collect your SUV. It's our only way to get off this mountain before morning."

His headshake was vehement. "It's a better car in

snow than the Peugeot, but you won't make it. I have experience driving in these conditions, and I struggled to get the Merc as far as I did. And not just because I was driving one-handed. Even in top form, I couldn't have driven it all the way to the chalet."

"I'm sure I could get it far enough for a phone signal." I sounded about as convincing as my little brother Kev when he'd insisted my goldfish had asked to swim in the toilet.

"Driving in this storm would be madness, Angel." Luc's frown returned. "Why do you think there'd be phone service farther down? Don't you think the storm caused the signal issue?"

"I did at first. Now I'm not so sure. Before all the craziness at the chalet, I assumed the Swiss had overestimated the reliability of their mobile phone coverage. But with a dead body, two thugs, and an exploding car, I'm less inclined to blame the weather."

"So what's causing the outage? A signal jammer?"

"That's my guess. Or, rather, a strategically placed series of signal jammers. That would account for the lack of phone signal over a large area. Someone doesn't want us to communicate with the outside world. If my signal jammer theory is correct, I should be able to place a call close to where you abandoned your car."

His headshake was vehement. "The storm's getting worse. Driving's not an option, however eager we are to get away from here. I have an emergency flare in the kit box I left in my car. I suggest you and Sidney make sure the guys upstairs are securely locked up. Then try walking down together to get the flare."

"A flare?" Relief made me giddy. "That's brilliant. We can use it to alert emergency services."

His expression wasn't as ecstatic as I'd expected. "Only if it's safe for you and Sidney to go outside. If the weather's too bad, don't risk it."

"I'd risk a lot to get off this mountain tonight, Luc. It gives me the creeps.

"I get that, but it's not worth putting your lives in danger. At least you've caught the killers. With them locked up, the chalet is probably the safest place for us to be, even with two bad guys and a corpse." Luc's gaze turned to the ceiling. "If I could walk, I'd check out the crime scene. And our unwanted houseguests—dead and alive. Can you describe them to me? I've crossed paths with many villains in my time. Maybe I've run across these three."

"I can do better than that." Forgetting my injured chest, I bounced to my feet. My reward was a pain so sharp my eyes stung. "I took photos of the crime scene on Sidney's phone. I'll go up and ask him to give it to me. While I'm there, I'll take mug shots of our pet thugs."

"Good idea." Luc looked around the ample downstairs living space. "Where's the kid? I thought Sidney was sending her down to us."

"Charlotte brings teenage truculence to a whole new level. She probably didn't listen to him. I'll try to persuade her to come downstairs." I unzipped the sleeping bag I'd snagged from the basement and used it as a blanket to cover Luc. "Before I go upstairs, do you have everything you need?"

He conducted a rueful inspection of his injured limbs. "Except for the ability to move, yeah. Hand me a magazine from that pile on the coffee table. And the pack of pain meds. The combo will help distract me."

I selected a current affairs journal and tossed it onto his lap. "Unless you want to keep up with celeb gossip, this is your only option. Don't overdo the painkillers."

I checked on the progress of the fire before I went upstairs. As Luc had predicted, it had burned itself out. At the rate the snow was falling, it would soon coat the wreckage. Thank goodness we'd avoided another disaster on the aptly named Hell Mountain.

When I entered Herr Hauri's bedroom, Sidney sat on the one semi-comfortable seat in the room, a high-backed wooden chair that wouldn't have looked out of place at a medieval banquet. He'd propped the crossbow against the wall beside him, and held his pistol in one hand and the remaining crossbow quarrel in the other. The two thugs were still bound and chained, balaclavas in place. There was no sign of Charlotte.

I surveyed the intruders. "Why haven't you removed their masks? And where's Charlotte?"

Sidney blinked owlishly. "I knocked on her door and asked her to go down to you."

"Well, she didn't." A prick of annoyance lent a sharpness to my tone. Charlotte was a brat, and I was responsible for this brat until Sunday evening.

"As for the masks, removing them would involve me getting close to the crooks. Not happening. Shackled or not, I've had enough close contact with that pair for one evening. I'm dreading what we'll do when they need to use the facilities."

"They should've thought about that before they attacked us. They can pee their pants for all I care."

"My sentiments exactly." He cracked a smile. "It seems Ghiselle was right about us facing danger this weekend. Not sure where the bears come in, though. Can we expect them to come knocking at any moment?"

"Given our run of bad luck, probably. Hey, Luc says he has an emergency flare back in his car. If we can walk as far as the car, we'll be able to send up a distress signal."

Sidney's face cracked into a smile. "That's the first good news I've heard since we arrived. We should set out immediately."

"Not so fast. We need to coax Charlotte into coming downstairs to stay with Luc. But first, I need your phone. Luc wants to see the crime scene photos." I jerked a thumb at the thugs. "And glamor shots of these two beauties."

Sidney pulled out his phone. "Rather you than me. I'm pretty sure they bite."

I lowered my voice so only he could hear. "We need to persuade Charlotte to look at these guys. Maybe she can identify them."

His eyes twinkled with ironic amusement. "Good luck with that request."

"Oh, I won't ask her to come in person. I'll show her the photographs. Surely she can't object to looking at a few photos?"

Sidney's snort told a thousand words. "I doubt there's anything Charlotte Hauri can't object to doing."

I took his phone and approached the bound thugs. I poked at their chains, making sure they were secure. Once I was confident they couldn't pounce, I yanked off their balaclavas, revealing two hirsute men of southern European origin. By now, they'd both regained consciousness. They greeted me with matching growls.

I snapped a few pictures of their snarling snouts and then stood back and beamed at them with radioactive glee. "Hello, boys," I said in German. "Enjoying your evening?" I switched to Italian. "Would you prefer to continue this conversation in your native language? I gotta admit my Italian's better than my German."

The guys exchanged startled looks. Good. I wanted to keep them off-balance, shock them into revealing what they knew.

I toyed with the dagger display and selected a particularly sharp-tipped specimen. "If subterfuge was part of your plan, tapping in the alarm code with zero hesitation kind of gave the game away. And the trick with the lights? Easy to do—especially when you're familiar with the house's power box. So what's the big idea, Luigi and Guido?"

The men gaped at me, spluttered, and looked to one another for support that neither was in a position to give.

The dude in the Iron Chair was the first to find his voice. "How do you know our names?"

His horror at me figuring out their identities made me roll my eyes. "Puh-lease. Charlotte told us the names of the chalet's mysteriously missing security guards. When you two punched in the alarm code without hesitation, we figured it was an inside job. The most obvious suspects were the three AWOL members of staff." I made an exaggerated examination of Iron Chair Dude's beard. "I'll wager the housekeeper is less hairy than either of you clowns."

"So if you're the security guards," Sidney said, proving he could add proficient Italian to his list of linguistic accomplishments, "then who's the dead man in the bathroom?"

Their shutters slammed down blitz-quick. They pressed their lips into tight lines and scowled at us. The dude tied to the bed rattled his chains. "I'm saying nothing. You won't get anything out of me."

In his defiant, jutted jaw, I read the complete opposite. Given a little prompting, this bird would sing.

"It seems your definition of saying nothing and mine differ," I replied in a tone as dry as sandpaper. "What about your pal in the chair? Is he equally determined to maintain a steadfast silence?"

Iron Chair Dude's black-eyed, wild-haired, scowling face reminded me of a pantomime pirate. "Yeah. You won't get anything out of me, lady. I can keep my trap shut."

My response was an oh-so-sweet smile. "Okay. So while you're both keeping your mouths shut, care to share who hired you? Clearly, neither of you is the brains behind this operation. Was it by any chance a man named Colin Jones?"

Iron Chair Dude snorted. "You don't know nothing."

It seemed this thug was even slower-witted than his hairy companion. "That's not quite true. I now know Colin Jones didn't hire you to attack us."

The man spluttered a denial, but his friend on the bed butted in. "Shut up, Guido. You'll give the entire show away."

"And you won't, *Luigi?* Thanks for giving me a heads-up about which of you idiots is which. Luigi's on the bed, Guido's on the chair. Good to know. Seeing as we're getting friendly, I'm Angel, and this is my friend Sidney."

Sidney waved from the safety of his seat. "Under

different circumstances, I'd say nice to meet you, but seeing as you tried to kill me, I'm not feeling hospitable."

In Guido's efforts to get out of the Iron Chair, he dislodged his cushions. He howled when the metal pins pierced through his clothing.

Sighing, I shoved the cushion back into place. "You are tiresome. I made a special effort to protect your back and buttocks."

"You aren't supposed to be here," Guido muttered. "We tried to get you to leave. It's not our fault if you couldn't take a hint."

Luigi rattled his chains. "Seriously, man? Stop talking."

"I assume the hint you're referring to is the dead man in the bathtub," I said, weighing the dagger in my hand.

"And we assumed you were pros." Sidney shook his head. "If you hadn't been so quick to cut the power and attack us right after Angel found the dead man, we'd have granted your wish. Do you think we wanted to stay in a house with no phone, no internet, and a corpse?"

"You took too long to find him," Guido whined. "How were we supposed to know she'd take ages checking windows?"

"Pardon me for being suspicious when the entire staff disappears," I said. "Why did you want us to leave the chalet, anyway? To make it easier to ambush us?"

"No. We didn't want to hurt you. We just wanted you to mind your own business and drive back to town." He glared at me and his lower lip stuck out ever so slightly, reminding me of a sulky toddler. "Why didn't you just turn around and leave? Then none of this would've happened."

"When I get out of these chains, I'm gonna break your face," Luigi snapped at his partner in crime. "Why do you keep talking to these people? You're gonna get us both killed."

"Lemme get this straight," I said. "You prize idiots wanted us to leave the chalet and drive back to the village. So why did you blow up our only ride?"

I failed to mention the possibility of using Luc's car to skedaddle the instant the weather improved. Given Luc's injuries, I didn't want these thugs to know he was in the house.

Guido strained against his shackles. "Was that what blew up? That piece-of-junk car down by the gates?"

"Yes. Now that piece-of-junk car is literally in pieces." I slow-clapped. "Well done, boys. If your goal was to scare us away from the chalet, destroying our only mode of transport wasn't a smart move."

Luigi stared at us, slack-jawed. "That wasn't us. How could it be? We were out cold until the blast woke us."

I judged Luigi to be the smarter of the two, but Guido had set the bar pretty low. "You could've set a timer before you came into the house. You used a timer to control the lights."

"Well, yeah, but that's easy. I don't know how to set a bomb. Look, lady. We work security in a low-risk setting. We're not hired assassins."

I snorted. "You could've fooled me. You attacked us, and you killed that man."

"That wasn't us." His outrage sounded oddly genuine. "He was dead already. Our only mistake was agreeing to take this stupid job in the first place."

Sidney stretched his neck from side to side. "Are you referring to your posts as security guards for the Hauris or your nefarious side gig? It seems to me you're not suited to either job."

"What were you hired to do?" I asked. "Why did you ambush us with guns if all you wanted was to intimidate us into leaving the chalet? Were you planning to kidnap Charlotte?"

Luigi's scowl was back in place. "You ask way too many questions, lady."

"And I'll keep asking them until you give me answers. You attacked us within minutes of me finding a dead body. Soon after, our car blew up. You say you had nothing to do with the corpse or the explosion. Why should we believe you?"

"That wasn't— We just—" Guido struggled to get his story straight, shooting agonized glances at his pal on the bed.

Luigi grunted and glowered at me. "Look, lady—

and whatever your friend identifies as—we don't care what you believe. We're not killers, and we didn't blow up your car, okay?"

The man's swipe at Sidney's gender identity made me want to bash him with the toilet lid all over again. Not having one to hand, I settled for the dagger. One wrist-flick later, the blade soared across the room and embedded itself in the headboard right above Luigi's head.

Luigi gave an inhuman roar. He babbled in Italian too rapidly for me to catch every word, but his diatribe began and ended with *mamma mia*. "You're insane," he shouted. "First, he shoots me with an arrow—"

"A quarrel," Sidney said, deadpan. "Or a bolt if you insist."

"—and then you throw knives at me," Luigi continued. "What sort of people are you?"

"The sort who object to being threatened." I selected another dagger and held it aloft. "Ready for another round?"

Luigi issued a spew of invective.

"This trip is doing wonders for my language skills," Sidney mused. "I must make a note of those curse words."

I opened my mouth to ask Luigi to repeat the last couple of swear words. At that precise moment, a monumental *bang* ripped through the night.

18

At the sound of the explosion, the pulse in my neck throbbed, and numbness crept over my limbs. Sidney leaped out of his seat, got his foot stuck in the crossbow, and stagger-tripped across to the balcony door. The thugs shouted obscenities and shook their shackles.

I'd had enough of this house of horrors. Sadly, it seemed it hadn't had enough of me. I forced my leaden feet into motion and joined Sidney on the balcony. A blaze crackled farther down the mountain slope, illuminating the night sky with orange flames. Wordlessly, we stepped back into the room and closed the door.

Luc's shout from downstairs brought me back to my senses. I grabbed Sidney and dragged him into the hallway, ignoring our prisoners' protests. "I'll get Charlotte. Wait for me in the hallway."

When he turned left in the direction of the stairs, I swung right—and collided with the wide-eyed and shaking girl.

"What happened?" she demanded. "Was that another bomb?"

"We think so." I grabbed her arm and propelled her toward the landing. "You can stay with our friend in the living room while Sidney and I check this out."

Her lower lip protruded, giving her a sulky look. "What friend? I don't want to stay with someone I don't know. Not after all that's happened tonight."

I couldn't blame her for being wary. In her shoes, I'd probably feel the same.

Sidney stopped mid-step and looked at me. "You should stay in the chalet. There's no point in both of us going outside. I'll see what's happened while you stand guard here. Do you still have your pistol?"

"I lost mine in the snow when the Peugeot exploded. Luc lost his too." My chest rose and fell, the implications hitting me with renewed force. "Which means we only have one gun."

He swore under his breath, something I'd rarely heard him do. "Then you keep mine while I'm gone. You'll need a weapon in case the thugs break free."

I shook my head. "It's smarter if you take it with you. We have no idea who's outside. If the guys get unruly, I'll threaten them with the crossbow."

Sidney's lips twitched. "Do you have any idea how to use it?"

"Absolutely none, but I'm excellent at bluffing. And if I aim a few knives at them, they'll fall into line."

"Before I go, can I have my phone back? I'll take photos of whatever I find out there. And maybe I'll get lucky and get a phone signal."

"Sure." I handed him the phone. "Come on, Charlotte. You'd better stick with me."

"Even if you're staying in the house, I'm still not hanging out with your friend. You can't make me."

Charlotte's scowling pout emphasized lips that looked artificially plump. Her sculpted eyebrows were reminiscent of social media stars—another fashionably incongruous contrast to her choice of clothing and hairstyle. But then, what did I know about teen fashion these days? Perhaps eco-warrior chic was all the rage.

"You don't have to be alone with Luc if you don't want to. I'd appreciate your help finding something to eat. I don't know my way around your kitchen." Any kitchen, actually. Domestic talents weren't exactly my forte.

She sneered. "And you think I do? When I don't dine out, I have a staff to cook for me."

I shot her a sidelong glance. "I doubt you dine out much at boarding school—unless convent schools have changed since my day."

She lowered her hot-mess mascaraed lashes. "The nuns are dying out. Convent schools aren't as strict as they used to be."

This was true. I'd mainly had lay teachers when I

was at school, but they'd been just as strict as the nuns. However, Charlotte's school was a lot fancier than mine had been. And given her hairstyle, they were lax on both conformity and cultural appropriation.

Luc stood by the front door when we reached the hallway, leaning on an umbrella and clutching a pair of binoculars. His skin was a sickly shade and slick with sweat. "You two are death on cars. First the Peugeot, now the Merc. I'll have no vehicles left after this trip."

I was torn between reprimanding him for getting off the sofa and lamenting the loss of the emergency flare. I settled on a more pertinent question. "Why do you think your SUV blew up? It might've been something else."

Unlikely, but we couldn't rule out the possibility before we'd checked out the scene of the explosion.

"Whoever's responsible for tonight's shenanigans is determined to prevent us from leaving the chalet. Blowing up our cars is a good way to ensure we stay put until morning." Luc limped to the door and reached for the handle. "I need to gauge the lay of the land."

Sidney stepped forward and stopped him. "What you need to do is rest and heal. I'll see what's happened. You won't get down to the gate in your state, never mind all the way to the fire. Plus, you have ripped pants. You'll freeze out there."

"And tear the stitches I worked so hard to sew." Pushing past my reticence to be physically close to

Luc, I slipped my arm around his waist. "Let me help you back to the sofa."

Anger and frustration flashed across Luc's face. He tensed, making his muscles taut. After a moment's hesitation, he relaxed and grunted his assent. "Okay, you win. But I want you to draw me a map of the house and the surrounding area. Someone is out there. We need to make sure they can't get in."

In the end, it took the combined efforts of Sidney, Charlotte, and me to get Luc back on the sofa and settled with cushions and his makeshift blanket. An embarrassed flush stained his cheeks. For a man who prided himself on his physical strength and mental agility, being reliant on others sucked. Luc wasn't used to being helpless. And he didn't like it one bit.

Sidney retrieved his outdoor gear from the pile in front of the fireplace and pulled on his snow pants and jacket. "Will you be okay holding the fort, Angel? You'll have to stay upstairs with Guido and Luigi."

"Guido and Luigi?" Charlotte's gasp reminded me we hadn't had the chance to tell her the intruders' identities.

"Yeah, I'm sorry," I said. "Turns out they're the guys in the masks."

"But...why?" Her eyes grew wide. "Why would they try to hurt me?"

Sidney zipped and fastened his coat and put my remaining Swiss Army knife in his pocket, alongside the pistol. "We're not sure that they wanted to hurt you. I suspect they were paid to kidnap you, probably by the man we mentioned earlier, Colin Jones."

Charlotte drew back, trembling. "How awful. I trusted them."

Luc handed Sidney his car key. "Just in case the Mercedes is still intact. If it is, get that emergency flare."

Sidney took the key and gave us a mock salute. "I'll report back soon. In the meantime, stay safe."

"You, too." A lump formed in my throat. "If you see anyone lurking about, don't try to be brave. Head right back here."

He forced a smile. "You know me. I'm a born coward. All my bravery is an act."

If it was an act, he was convincing. I watched him leave with the sinking realization that I was now the only able-bodied adult in the house.

After Sidney left, Charlotte and I searched the kitchen. We found the fridge and cupboards stuffed with food, including ready-made soup, fresh bread, sliced meat, and an array of cheeses. My heart sang a little when I found a stash of premium Swiss chocolate. I popped a piece into my mouth, relishing its rich, sweet goodness.

And then a thought struck me, marring my enjoyment of the chocolate. Who had filled the fridge? The housekeeper had been gone for a week. Had Guido and Luigi gone shopping? They must've done. They'd have wanted to eat. But hadn't Charlotte said they couldn't cook? Perhaps she'd simply assumed they were useless in the kitchen. The fresh meat and vegetables in the fridge couldn't be consumed raw, showing at least one man had some cooking skills.

While I arranged sliced meat and cheese on a plate, Charlotte made a half-hearted attempt to cut bread. She appeared to be wholly ignorant of how to heat soup.

She threw the bread knife onto the counter with a clatter. "This is stupid. I'm not even hungry."

"Well, I am." I glanced at the ceiling, acutely aware that I couldn't risk leaving Guido and Luigi alone for much longer. On the other hand, I was starving. We all needed to eat, especially if we faced any more unpleasant surprises before morning. "Arrange the sliced meat on a plate and cut some cheese to go with that bread. I'll check on the men upstairs, and then I'll deal with the soup."

Charlotte glared at me but made no protest. I ran upstairs as fast as my sore ribs and short legs allowed me. The guys were still tied up and greeted me with a cacophony of protests and abuse. In a blow-by-blow repeat of my search earlier, I scanned the room for a key. I couldn't see one at the top of the doorframe, but it might be laying flat.

Without responding to the insults hurled at me by the thugs, I dragged Sidney's chair over to the door and stood on it, thus solving my short girl dilemma. I ran a finger over the top of the doorframe and felt a wave of relief when my fingers closed around a key. I'd feel safer with this pair locked in, as well as chained up.

When I got back to the kitchen, Charlotte had done a hatchet job on the cheese. She hadn't been joking when she'd said she had no experience cooking for herself. Feeling like a domestic goddess in comparison, I found a bowl for the soup and popped it into the microwave.

I served Luc on a small tray. "I put your soup in a mug. I thought it'd be easier for you to consume with one hand. Do you want me to fix you a sandwich?"

"Just put some bread and cheese on a plate, and I'll serve myself." His voice sounded gritty, and his skin still had the sickly tinge. His determination to drag himself to the hall had cost him whatever sliver of strength he'd had left.

A pang of guilt gnawed at my conscience. I was the reason Luc was in such pain.

Charlotte sat in an armchair and picked at her food, maintaining a moody silence, refusing to respond to any of Luc's attempts to make conversation. I wolfed down my meal, more out of fear than out of hunger. Even with the bedroom door locked, I didn't want to leave the thugs unattended for long.

I was loading the dishwasher when Sidney returned. I rushed into the hall the moment I heard the door.

The icy wind had turned his pale cheeks pink. He shook the snow from his clothes. "It was Luc's

SUV that blew up. I didn't see anyone else around. And before you ask, the fire can't spread. The car was all on its own in an open field. It'll burn itself out."

"What about a Range Rover? Luc said one was parked close to where he left his car."

"There isn't one there now." Sidney's expression grew dark. "But there were tire tracks. The snow's dumping down. Those tracks had to be recent."

I swore under my breath. No car and no emergency flare. And the tire tracks meant we had to entertain the possibility that Luigi and Guido weren't alone.

I followed Sidney into the living room, where he helped himself to soup and bread and repeated his findings to Luc.

"I'm sorry I couldn't be more helpful," he said between mouthfuls of bread. "I've never had to scope out potential enemy territory before. All I could do was look around and hope I met no more bad guys."

"You did good," Luc assured him. "Even I couldn't search the entire area on my own in this weather. How were you sure the exploded car was mine?"

"Your reg number. I found the number in the snow and recognized it instantly." Sidney swallowed a spoonful of soup and grinned at me. "I don't have Angel's knack for memorizing numbers, but we've parked the Peugeot next to that car every day for the last four months."

Luc nodded in approval. "Well done. We'll make a private investigator out of you yet."

"After today, my mother will have to stump up for our P.I. training." My jaw tightened. "She put our lives at risk by sending us on this job unprepared and unarmed. Not cool."

"To be fair to Desirée, she didn't know this would happen. None of us expected a plot of this sort to unfold at the chalet." Luc regarded Charlotte, who was still moodily picking at a slice of bread. "Apart from Colin Jones, can you think of anyone who'd want to hurt you or your family?"

Charlotte gave a one-shoulder shrug. "We're rich. Isn't that motivation enough? Maybe someone wanted to kidnap me and extract a ransom payment from my father."

"Is that why your father hired security guards?" I asked. "We were given to understand that he was worried about Colin Jones targeting you, but that threat is connected to something that happened this week at the auction house. It doesn't explain your father's decision to hire a full-time security team for the chalet."

Her eyes locked onto mine, and I read the scorn in them. "You wouldn't notice, but we have a lot of valuable antiques in this house. Paintings, too. Art thieves would love to get their hands on Papa's collection."

She was correct in her assessment of my antiques

expertise, but I wasn't sold on this theory. "The Swiss Alps are dotted with wealthy families, many of whom have a mini-museum's worth of art and antiques. And yet the crime stats are low. Why was your father so concerned about this house? Does he employ security guards for his other residences? He has several, right?"

"A few, but most have tenants. He only has four that he uses regularly."

Only four? How the other half lived… "And do any of those residences include a security team?"

"A man lives at our apartment in Monaco. He has security training. Papa has a personal bodyguard too, and a chauffeur." She pushed her plate onto the coffee table and stood. "I'm going back to my bedroom. I'm locking myself in, and I'm not coming out until Papa arrives."

I got to my feet. "Okay. I'll come up with you."

Charlotte swept out of the room without waiting for me or looking at either of the men. Clearly, we were all unworthy of her attention.

I jogged after her, catching up with her on the landing. "If you need anything, call out. And if we need you, we'll use the knocking code Sidney suggested earlier. Five knocks—two long, three short. Got it?"

"Whatever." She swept past me and into her room.

I was half annoyed, half relieved, when I heard the key turn in her lock. She was a handful, but this evening had been horrific. I had to remind myself that she was still a kid. If I was having a hard time processing all that had happened, how must she feel?

I walked back along the corridor, intending to check on the Italian stallions. I was reaching for the key in my pocket when Sidney crested the stairs. "Finished eating already?"

He pulled a face. "I ate fast. I'm uneasy having those two up here on their own, especially in a house covered with weapons and surrounded by balconies."

"I know how you feel. So now what? Do you want to take shifts guarding Heckle and Jeckle?"

"Yeah, that's a smart idea. I'll take the first shift." He nodded at the key in my hand. "Did you lock them in while I was gone?"

"I thought it was the smart thing to do."

"Where'd you find the key? I looked everywhere for one."

"On top of the doorframe." I handed him the key and glanced at my watch. "How in the world is it only ten-thirty? This day feels never-ending. When should I take over from you? Midnight?"

"Make it three a.m. You need sleep, and a couple of hours won't cut it."

"Okay. I'll be back here at three. If you need anything, shout down, and I'll come. I'll make up a bed on the sofa opposite Luc's."

Sidney inserted the key in the lock. "Before you get your beauty sleep, Luc wants you to draw him a plan of the house."

"Oh, that's right." I looked at a door farther down the hallway. "I saw office materials in that room. I'll grab a notepad and pen."

I hadn't gone more than a few steps when Sidney uttered a yelp. I whipped around, instantly on the alert. "What's wrong?"

He staggered back from the door. "Angel, we have a problem."

"Dude, you just stole my line." Even as I uttered the words, I knew I'd need more than black humor to defend myself against whatever was in that room. Sidney's haggard expression was eloquent.

I stepped inside and surveyed the scene with heart-thumping resignation.

Guido and Luigi were still shackled and chained, but with one key difference. The hilt of an elaborately carved dagger protruded from each man's chest.

19

I experienced no thudding heart, no shortness of breath, nor any other signs of panic. In the last couple of hours, I'd discovered a corpse, endured an ambush, shot my housemate, and survived two exploding cars. Adding two more dead bodies to the list felt disturbingly like my new normal.

I went over to the Iron Chair and examined Guido. To my uneducated eye, the death blow had been clean and professional. There was just one stab wound, and the man had bled profusely. I straightened, went over to the bed, and turned my scrutiny onto Luigi's mortal remains. Same deal—a single stab wound to the chest and plenty of blood. The fancy hilts hinted the weapons used were from Herr Hauri's collection. A quick count of the daggers on the display stand confirmed my suspicion—two more were missing.

"I don't have the bandwidth to deal with this." Sidney slumped in the doorframe, clutching his pistol in a shaky hand. "What have we walked into? When we had all the action in July, at least we could jump in the car and drive."

"The killer must be in the house." I surprised myself at how calm I sounded. "I have to check on Charlotte."

I pushed past Sidney and ran down the hall to her bedroom. I rapped on her door using our coded knock. "Charlotte? We need you to come downstairs again. Something's happened."

A rustling sounded in the room, but she didn't open the door. I flexed my jaw and rapped again, this time louder.

Finally, her muffled voice came through the door. "I don't care what's happened. I'm not leaving my room until my father or the police get here."

I sucked in a breath and willed myself to remain patient. "Look, I know you're scared. So am I. And I believe it's safer for us to stick together."

"I don't care what you believe. How do I even know you are who you say you are? You and your weird friend showed up at the chalet and introduced yourselves as my weekend English teachers. How do I know you're the people my father hired? He didn't send me your pictures."

All valid points. But we had a killer in the house—

or lurking outside with a handy-dandy means of access. "Charlotte, you need to—"

"Leave her, Angel. I'll keep guard outside her room."

I whipped around to see Sidney marching toward me, lugging the chair he'd been using in Herr Hauri's bedroom, and wearing a distinctly green-about-the-gills expression.

"Are you sure?"

"No. But if Charlotte refuses to come downstairs, we have no choice." He positioned the chair in front of Charlotte's door and held up the pistol. "We can take turns like we'd planned to do for the thugs." A flicker of revulsion crossed his face. "Speaking of the thugs, I took photos of them before I locked the room. I also inspected the place. The windows and balcony door were bolted from the inside. The connecting bathroom was still locked and proved to be empty when I peeked inside. There were no visible footprints on the polished wood floor. Apart from the daggers in the dead men's chests, everything in the room looked just as it did before the second explosion."

Whoa. Sidney couldn't abide the sight of blood. Yet he'd pushed past his fears and not only examined the bodies but also taken photographs. Respect. "I...well, thank you."

He handed me his phone. "We forgot to show Luc the photos you snapped in the bathroom with all the commotion. Now you can show him the whole gory picture gallery."

I took the phone but made no move to return downstairs. "Whoever the killer is, they like a splash of the theatrical. Why else use two separate daggers to kill Guido and Luigi? And then leave the daggers in their bodies for us to find?"

"It's the same over-the-top gesture as dressing up the man in the tub." His forehead creased. "How is the killer evading us? I mean, they must be hiding in the house, right? It's too cold to stay outside and break in whenever they feel the urge to kill someone."

"Yeah. Either the killer is an unseen mystery person who's been hiding in the house this whole time, or it's one of us." Simply voicing that thought out loud sent a shiver slithering down my spine.

Sidney's gaze fixed on Charlotte's door. "We have an obvious candidate." He dropped his voice to a whisper. "Whoever killed the men had a key to that room."

"Or a picklock," I said. "How much do we know about Charlotte?"

"Not a lot. However, casting a sixteen-year-old as the villain seems far-fetched. Why would Charlotte be involved in this plot?"

"Money? Revenge? Who knows? The only snag in this theory is that she's too slight to haul a frozen corpse into the bathtub."

"Guido and Luigi took care of the corpse. Perhaps Charlotte was in league with them."

I blew out my cheeks. "And then killed them? Why?"

"To stop them talking. The second explosion was a distraction to get us to leave the room and give her the chance to go in and stab them."

"I agree that the second explosion was a ploy to get us to leave Guido and Luigi alone, but the timing doesn't work for Charlotte to be their killer. I was with Charlotte the entire time you were gone, and she was with us in the living room after you got back. She didn't go upstairs until I escorted her to her room."

"Are you certain she had no opportunity to slip upstairs while you were getting the food ready?" he asked.

"I'm positive. Charlotte was in the kitchen alone for all of thirty seconds while I brought Luc's tray into the living room. She came in with her food while I was still getting his set up. That's not enough time to run upstairs, kill two men, and get back before I noticed her absence."

"Yeah, you're right. That's not enough time." He sounded disappointed. "Are you sure she wasn't alone at any other point?"

"Only when I came upstairs to check on the guys and search for a key. They were alive when I locked them in. Plus, there's the not insignificant matter of the blood," I added. "We've established our mystery man in the tub didn't bleed because he'd been dead a while. That wasn't the case with Guido and Luigi. Whoever stabbed them can't have escaped getting blood on themselves. Even if Charlotte was a super sprinter and made it upstairs and back in less than a minute, she'd never have had the time to clean up after the murders."

Sidney made a gagging sound but pulled himself together. "Okay. We can rule her out for the thugs' murders, but she could have planted both car bombs. She was out on the bathroom balcony when we were fighting Guido and Luigi."

"True. She might have had enough time to set a bomb in the Peugeot, but could she have got down to the second car, too? How far from the house was it?"

Sidney grimaced. "Too far. You're right. I just wanted a neat solution and an obvious suspect."

"I'm not ruling out the possibility that Charlotte's somehow involved. So far, though, her reactions have been typical under the circumstances. She wants to barricade herself in her room and stay away from us. If our roles were reversed, I'd do the same. She doesn't know for certain who we are. She does know that since our arrival, her house has turned into a morgue."

"All true." Sidney scratched the back of his neck. "Okay. Changing of the guards at four a.m.?"

"I thought we'd settled on three."

"Yeah, but that was before we discovered the thugs had been murdered. It's close to midnight now. You should try to get some sleep."

I doubted I'd sleep with a killer on the prowl, but I didn't argue the point. "All right. Before I go down to Luc, I'd like you to take another look at Charlotte Hauri's file. Maybe we missed something. I just need to get my phone from my room."

It didn't take me long to grab my phone, some blankets, and a few toiletries from my room. I returned to the hallway and handed Sidney my phone, Charlotte's photo open on the screen.

He examined the photo and her file for a couple of minutes. "This looks like her. Just younger and with straight brown hair. The same photo's downstairs on the mantlepiece, and the other family photos are of the same girl. Younger than she is now, but definitely her."

"Yeah." The word came out with a long sigh. "I'd half-hoped we'd discover she'd been posing as Charlotte. The other half of me is relieved to find she is who she says she is. Otherwise, we'd once again find ourselves missing a minor. I'll grab that notepad and pen and get back to Luc."

Sidney handed me back my phone. "Did we ever find out why he showed up at the chalet?"

"A tussle with a member of the rival P.I. agency. Turns out that a quarter-million bonus brings out the worst in all of them."

Sidney frowned. "Thanks to said tussle, Luc is now out of commission. You don't think Rocco Casetti's agency is behind what's been happening here? Isn't Rocco supposed to be dodgy?"

"Unscrupulous and not afraid to venture into the legal gray zone. Would that include murder?"

He shrugged. "Probably not. Still, it's worth asking Luc."

The niggling doubt that had been at the back of my mind since I'd discovered I'd shot Luc wriggled to the surface. I took a deep breath and blurted it out. "Could Luc be the killer? He has the skills to plant car bombs and the strength to lug a dead body into the tub. And we only have his word that he arrived at the chalet just before I shot him. For all we know, he might've been here the whole time."

Shock suffused Sidney's face. "No way. Not Luc. Not our housemate."

"I don't want to think it, either." And not only because I found him hot. "Luc's barely been home in the four months we've lived in the villa. How well do we know him?"

Sidney scratched his chin. "Not particularly well, but he's not a sharing sort of bloke. He was kind enough to get us the Ghiselle job."

"Which he admits he did as a joke. How do we know he didn't pay Ghiselle to come up with her mad story and send us on a wild goose chase to Swiss casinos?"

"But to what end? How would our detour have any bearing on what's happening at the chalet?"

"I have no idea. I only have questions at this point, not answers. We have to add Luc to our list of suspects.

He had the means and the opportunity to kill the man in the tub and set those car bombs."

"He has a busted shoulder." Every word signaled Sidney's relief. "He can't be the killer. He'd never be able to drag a dead body with his arm in a sling."

The thoughts tumbling through my mind triggered a wave of nausea. Is this what P.I. work would be like? Not be able to trust anyone? I liked Luc. More than liked him. But I had a track record for falling for bad men—*really* bad men. That was the whole reason I'd stopped dating. I didn't trust myself to choose a boyfriend who'd be good for me.

"We don't know Luc's injury is the real deal, Sidney. He might have made up that story as an excuse in case one of us discovered him on the premises. Look, I don't want him to be a cold-blooded murderer, but we can't rule him out at this stage."

"Fair enough, but you can't accuse him of being involved with Guido and Luigi's deaths. Even if he's faking his shoulder injury, the bullet hole you put in him is genuine."

I massaged my temples, thinking hard. "Valentina? Could they be partners in crime? We said before that we wouldn't put anything past Valentina."

Sidney breathed a groan. "Okay. We'll keep Luc on the list. Regardless of who's responsible for the three murders, try to get some rest."

Rest on a sofa opposite a potential killer? Not likely. I looked up and down the hallway, relieved to find no skulking villains. "If you need me, shout. In the meantime, I'll pump Luc for info. Even if he's innocent, I bet he has a more detailed file on this case than we do. Perhaps there's a clue in that file. If there is, I intend to find it."

20

When I rejoined Luc in the living room, he'd finished the current affairs journal and flicked through a glossy celebrity gossip magazine. His complexion looked healthier than earlier—less pinched and pale. The pain medication was having an effect.

He glanced up when I walked in. His hooded gaze skimmed my body, halting at boob level. He rapid-blinked, turned an adorable shade of pink, and buried his nose in the magazine.

Luc's agitation brought a secret smile to my lips. However much I'd love to think he had a crush on me, I didn't flatter myself. He was a solid ten on the looks scale, whereas I was merely average. Still, it was fun to see the perpetually unfazed Luc flustered.

"You can drag your nose out of that magazine, dude. Sore ribs equal no bra, even for big-boobed me."

He lowered his magazine with a sheepish grin. "Sorry to stare. I hadn't paid attention before, but aren't you usually more...upholstered?"

"Extra-support sports bras. A close encounter with a bidet means no bra for me until I can fasten one without an impromptu opera performance." I leaned over and peeked at the two-page photo spread he'd been examining with forensic fascination. "Moving on from the riveting topic of my underwear, let's talk about your choice of reading matter. I didn't have you pegged as a gossip fan."

"It's called desperation. I read the journal cover to cover and ran out of options. I don't know who most of these so-called celebs are, but they all look alike to me— same self-tan, identikit eyebrows, blindingly white teeth."

I examined the photos. They'd been snapped at a red carpet event. For what, I neither knew nor cared. That would've required reading the captions. "Charlotte has those eyebrows."

"Yeah, but at least she hasn't overdone the tooth bleach."

I dumped my pile of blankets on the sofa opposite Luc's and took out Sidney's phone. I'd appreciated our moment of levity. It had lightened my mood, albeit temporarily, but I couldn't procrastinate any longer. "I come with bad tidings. Our dead body count has risen."

Luc's electric blue eyes widened, then narrowed to wary slits. "Who's dead this time?"

"Guido and Luigi. They were stabbed with two of Herr Hauri's medieval daggers."

He released a ragged breath. "Whoever killed them has to be in the house."

Hopefully not in this room. The hairs on the nape of my neck prickled. Luc couldn't be responsible for the security guards' deaths. As Sidney had pointed out, the leg injury was real. And I should know—I'd caused it. But if Luc had a partner in crime—a partner like Valentina—he could be complicit.

"Sidney's keeping guard outside Charlotte's room," I said. "I came down to show you the photos we took of both crime scenes. While you're flipping through those, I'd like to see the file my mother sent you on the Crofton-Lowe case."

Luc dug his phone out of his pocket and swiped the screen several times. "I'm not supposed to share this info with anyone who's not an official part of the team. However, I'll make an exception. We've landed you and Sidney in an appalling situation, and you're handling yourselves like pros. I don't know that it'll help us figure out what's going on, but you deserve to see the full case file."

His faith in me produced a mixed reaction. While I was grateful that he trusted me with confidential info, I wasn't sure how far I could trust him. Not knowing where I stood set me off balance. I liked certainty. Nagging doubts made me feel rudderless.

We traded phones. For the next few minutes, he looked at photos while I read the file on the Crofton-Lowe case. My mother had given us the gist during yesterday's meeting. Luc's file filled holes such as the precise time of Wednesday night's theft, an itemized list of the stolen artifacts, the low-down on Urs Hauri, and information on Bernard Roulez's heirs.

Hauri was a clean-shaven, blandly handsome man who'd been born into a prominent Zürich banking family. He'd started his career in the financial sector, branching out to auction houses fifteen years ago. There was no known dirt on him. He had a reputation as a playboy, which had cost him his marriage to Charlotte's mother. Had his ex-wife cooked up this plot in revenge? Unlikely. The couple had divorced several years ago. Why would she risk her daughter's life?

I turned my attention to Bernard Roulez. The arms billionaire had left a vast fortune, of which the Egyptian artifacts were merely a part. His six heirs comprised his third wife, Clothilde; his children from his first marriage, Séverin, Claude, Bernice, Nancy; and his step-daughter, Margot. They'd been at loggerheads since the reading of the will, each claiming they were entitled to a more significant portion of the estate. Besides the named heirs, two court cases were pending, involving family members who felt unfairly excluded from the will. One involved Patrice Sablé, a son from an extramarital relationship whom Bernard had refused to acknowledge. The other concerned his late daughter Jeanne's daughters, Jeanne-Ursine and Marianne Monet-Roulez.

"The Roulez heirs sound like a cheerful bunch," I said dryly. "Who says money buys happiness?"

Luc raised his magazine. "It appears to buy self-tan, identikit eyebrows, and tooth bleach. They're all over these celeb magazines, either in their own right, or because of who they're dating. Intrigue and backstabbing appear to be a Roulez family sport."

"I can imagine one of them being involved in the Crofton-Lowe robbery. However, I don't see a motive for them killing people at the chalet."

"Nor do I, but there has to be a connection." Luc slid Sidney's phone onto the coffee table, his expression grim. "At least I can identify the corpse in the bath."

My heart leaped. "You can? Who is he?"

Luc's lips twisted into an ironic smile. "None other than our prime suspect for the Crofton-Lowe robbery, Colin Jones."

I sucked in a breath. "Wow. I didn't see that coming. So there is a connection between the robbery and the chalet. Did Jones come here intending to kidnap Charlotte?"

"Either that or he used the chalet to hide the stolen artifacts. He got rid of the housekeeper and paid the security guards to cooperate. Then he hid the cache in the most unlikely place for any of us to search. Having the goods here allowed him to plant a couple of items to implicate Hauri in the robbery and thus get his revenge."

Made sense. My distrust barometer sank by a couple of bars. "It's also possible that Hauri and Jones are in this together. Although Hauri would hardly have wanted us to come here if that was the case."

"I considered that, and I have to agree. I can't see why he'd have wanted extra protection for his daughter if he planned to hide the goods at the same place she was due to spend the weekend."

"Unless the plan went wrong and Jones wasn't supposed to die?" I ran the scenario through my mind. "Could there be two parties at work? The thugs were adamant that they just wanted to scare us off, and they denied killing Jones. Although I gathered from what they said that they put his body into the tub. They insisted their actions were designed to get us to leave the chalet. Yet whoever blew up our cars wanted us to stay."

The idea of two entities being behind the incidents at the chalet left me discombobulated. How could we defend ourselves if we were dealing with two different foes, each with a separate motive?

Luc frowned into space, visibly thinking. "I'm not ruling out the possibility that two groups are at work here. However, I'm more inclined to think that this is a case of dishonor among thieves. Someone involved in the plot betrayed the others."

I hadn't struck Luc off my list of suspects, but I was willing to work with him for the moment. I picked up the notepad and pen. "Do you still want me to draw you a map of the house?"

"Yes, please. If the artifacts are hidden on the property, we need to find them."

I drew a map of the entrance level. My drawing skills were mediocre, but I was capable of getting the basics down, even though my proportions weren't accurate. "Sidney and I combed the house. I can't imagine us missing a crate's worth of Egyptian artifacts."

"All the same, I'd like a look at that map." Luc's eyes wandered around the room. "How many medieval weapons are in this house?"

I glanced up from my sketch of the uppers floors and snorted. "Too many to count. The place is covered in them."

"Could you and Sidney round them up and bring them all here? I don't like the idea of a killer having easy access to this much metal."

I blew a stray curl from my face, buying myself time to think. Would it be a mistake to have all the weapons in close proximity to Luc? On the other hand, having them in one place meant I could keep an eye on them—and on him. "I can gather up the knives and swords, but some items are too heavy to carry."

"Do your best. The killer is likely to have modern weapons at their disposal. Still, we should try to reduce the number of easily accessible knives."

I finished my sketch of each house floor and handed it to Luc. "You can check out my map while I round up swords."

The rounding up business took longer than I'd anticipated, eating into my allotted time to rest. As I doubted I'd be able to sleep, I didn't mind. I visited every room on the entrance floor and created a pile of loot on the living room floor. I took what I could carry —swords of varying lengths and weight, daggers, spears, and lethal-looking contraptions I couldn't identify. The pile soon included several crossbows and accompanying quarrels. Charlotte hadn't exaggerated when she'd said her father had a William Tell complex.

When I ventured into the small bathroom off the hallway, I discovered yet another crossbow and a spear. "For goodness' sake. How many crossbows does one man need?" I lifted the weapon off its hook, wincing at the pain spiraling through my ribs.

Then I reached for the spear.

And froze.

The white paint where the crossbow had hung had a tiny reddish-brown smear. My heart hammered as I took a closer look. Was this rust? Or dried blood? I examined the crossbow, running my fingers over the smooth wood. My fingers came away sticky with the same substance. Blood.

Heart thumping, I hurried back to Luc. "I think this crossbow was fired recently. There's blood on it."

Luc scrutinized the weapon. "If it was fired, I'd expect to find blood on the bolt, not the weapon itself."

"Unless it was fired at short range." I glanced at the basement door. "There are a few weapons downstairs. I'd better get them."

"Wait." For the first time, I read something akin to fear in Luc's expression. "Shouldn't you ask Sidney to go down with you?"

"He has to guard Charlotte. We can't leave her unprotected." I picked up a spear. "This'll do nicely. No one will mess with me when they see this rusty spear."

My words were strong, but I felt anything but brave. The last place I wanted to go was the basement. Still, we needed to make sure we'd taken all available weapons away from the killer.

I unlocked the basement door and took cautious steps down the stairs. Thankfully, no one leaped out at me, and there were no obvious lurking occupants in any of the four sections. I gathered all the lethal weapons I could find, mostly broken spears.

I was about to go back upstairs when my gaze rested on the deep freeze. It was massive—easily double the size of any I'd seen outside the restaurant industry. Sidney and I had meant to check it out earlier to see if it had once stored the frozen corpse I now knew was Colin Jones. I put the weapons on the ground and eased up the lid of the deep freeze.

Unseeing frozen eyes stared back at me. A middle-aged woman lay on her back, fully dressed in a plain black dress and stockings. A broken bolt stuck out of her chest, its diameter an excellent match for the dent on Dead Dude Number One's back.

I wobbled, staggered, and collided painfully with a food shelf.

For some reason, this dead body scared me more than the other three combined. Perhaps because my gut told me that, unlike the other three, this woman was no crook.

I must have screamed. I have no memory of doing so. But within a couple of minutes of me finding the body, Sidney thundered down the stairs, caught his foot in the pile of broken spears, and hit the floor with an ominous crunch. His pistol skidded across the floor and came to rest at my foot.

My stomach flip-flopped. I dropped to my knees by Sidney's side and assessed the damage. Thank goodness he hadn't fallen on the spearheads, but his ankle was twisted at a funny angle. I touched the ankle.

Sidney yelped in pain and pulled back. "That hurts."

"I know it does. Hold still. I need to check if it's broken." After subjecting his ankle to my amateur poking and prodding, I sat back on my heels. "I don't think it's broken, but you have a nasty sprain."

"Fabulous," Sidney groaned. "Just what I need when I'm likely to be chased by a killer at any moment."

This was the second injury I'd caused in one evening. At the rate I was going, I'd have no able-bodied helpers left. "I'm sorry, mate. I didn't expect you to come thundering down the stairs. But then, I didn't expect to find a dead body in the deep freeze."

"What's happened?" Luc's boomed down from the top of the steps. "Are you two okay?"

"Are you off the sofa again?" I yelled. "I don't want to have to stitch you up again."

"And I don't want you two battling killers on your own. What's going on down there? If you don't tell me now, I'll come down, and that'll definitely bust open my stitches."

"Keep what's left of your hair on," I shouted. "We're coming up."

I stuck the pistol in my back pocket and helped Sidney stand. I reached up to close the lid of the deep freeze. My movement wasn't fast enough. He caught sight of the body and let out a wheeze. "Who's that?"

"The explanation for the bathtub murder victim's mark. Look at the size of the broken bolt? I bet that caused the indentation on his back. He must have lain on top of her in the deep freeze." I let out a ragged breath. "This has to be Frau Lenz, the missing housekeeper."

I thought of the book on her nightstand, a mystery

she'd never finish. A wave of sadness flowed through me for this unknown woman who'd shared my love of crime fiction. Who had killed her, and why? Had she been an inconvenient obstacle to the killer's plans? Or had she merely been in the wrong place at the wrong time?

Sidney bent over and examined his ankle. "I don't think I can walk on this foot."

"I can't carry you. You'll have to lean on me and hop."

Unsurprisingly, this method of ascending the stairs took several torturous minutes. Luc was waiting for us when we reached the top, brandishing a sword in his only functional arm.

His lips pressed into a hard line when he saw the state of Sidney. "What happened?"

"He fell over the pile of weapons I'd gathered in the basement," I said. "Now, get out of my way and let me help Sidney to a sofa."

Luc stepped aside and limped after us. "Why did you scream, Angel? Was someone down in the basement with you?"

I shivered at the memory of those frozen, frightened eyes. "In a manner of speaking. The good news is that I found the housekeeper—that's one mystery solved. The bad news is that she's dead, probably due to that bloodstained crossbow. The even worse news, at least from our point of view, is that Sidney won't be able to walk on that ankle. He can lie on my sofa, and I'll get him an icepack. Then I'll take his place outside Charlotte's door. You two will have to fend for yourselves."

Wordlessly, Luc reclaimed his sofa, his brow furrowed in concentration. "I don't like this. We have to get out of here."

"How? Did you notice any hidden escape routes on the map I drew?"

His jaw tilted at a belligerent angle. "No, but we can't stay in this house."

"If you can come up with a way for me to get one terrified teenager and two large men down the mountain, I'm all ears. You guys have two working legs between you. My ribs are shot, and Charlotte refuses to budge from her room."

I went into the kitchen to fetch an icepack for Sidney. When I returned, the men reclined on their respective sofas, armed with celebrity magazines and an assortment of weapons.

Luc examined a dagger with a curious I-shaped hilt.

"It's a baselard," Sidney informed me. "A traditional Swiss dagger. I had to use one in a play once."

Luc lowered the weapon. "If we're staying here overnight, we need to stick together." His face and tone were hard as granite. "That means everyone in the living room, no exceptions, and a buddy system when one of us needs to use the bathroom. You'll have to get

Charlotte down here, even if it means breaking into her room."

"Okay. I'll get forceful. Frankly, I don't fancy spending the night alone in the upstairs hallway. Too many doors for people to hide behind. Charlotte and I will get bedding from our rooms and set up camp in here with you." I opened the first aid kit, found a compression bandage, and handed it to Sidney. "Do you need my help getting this around your ankle?"

"I'll manage. I want to let the ice do its job before I touch it." He propped himself up on cushions and placed one under his sore ankle. "What do we do in the morning? Send out smoke signals? The snow won't magically melt and clear the road.

I sighed and pushed a loose strand of hair out of my face. "Look, it's only a few hours until first light. Regardless of the weather, I'll go out first thing. There are snowshoes in the basement. I can use those to get down to the valley and call for help."

Luc eyed me with suspicion. "Have you ever walked downhill in snowshoes?"

"Sure. I've done it plenty of times." Make that once when I was a teenager. On that memorable occasion, I'd landed on my backside and broken my tailbone. I forced a smile. "We've got this. All we have to do is survive until morning."

21

Persuading Charlotte to spend the night downstairs required a combination of cajolery, bribery, and straight-up threats. In the end, she agreed to join us in the living room, but on the proviso that it was only for the night. In the morning, she'd return to her self-proclaimed sanctuary and barricade the door until her father arrived to rescue her.

I wasn't thrilled with this arrangement. Sticking together was the safest option for all of us. However, I conceded to Charlotte's terms, figuring I'd use our shared sleeping arrangement to build bridges. We trooped downstairs with an assortment of bedding, two inflatable mattresses, and a veritable army of anime plush.

When she caught me eyeing her stuffed toy

collection, Charlotte bristled, instantly on the defensive. "So I like anime characters. Big deal."

"I didn't say anything. I'm all for people following their passions. If you enjoy collecting them, go for it." I picked up a toy that looked like a cross between a pig and a cartoon girl. "She's cute."

Her eyes flashed, and she snatched it out of my grasp. "That's my favorite."

Stung by her rudeness, I took an involuntary step back. "Sorry. I didn't think you'd mind me taking a look."

"Well, I do mind. Keep your paws off my stuff."

The cheek of her. She'd had no objection to me helping carry the collection. So much for building bridges. Dealing with Charlotte was akin to throwing a lit match onto a petrol-soaked rope bridge.

While Charlotte and I pumped our mattresses and made our beds, Sidney fashioned a spear into a crutch and fixed a pot of steaming hot chocolate. He filled four mugs and decorated each with a piece of melting chocolate surrounded by marshmallow hearts.

I accepted mine gratefully, savoring the comforting aroma and the warmth of the mug in my still-cold hands. I'd never fully warmed up after my adventure in the snow.

"Mmm." Luc took an appreciative sip. "This is delicious."

"One thing the Swiss know how to do well is chocolate." Sidney settled back onto his sofa and elevated his ankle. "While you ladies were sorting your bedding, I unearthed a couple of games. Want to play *Monopoly*? Or *Truth, Lie, Bare*?"

"*Monopoly* gets a hard pass," I said, eyeing the pile of games on the coffee table. "What's *Truth, Lie, Bare*? An X-rated card game?"

"Yeah. It's a card version of *Truth or Dare*? But for adults. I filtered all the not suitable for work cards. Never fear. No garments will be removed."

"Seeing as we're currently responsible for a minor, I'm relieved. Are you game, Luc?"

He shrugged his one good shoulder. "Sure. But I reserve the right to skip a question."

"That's included in the rules." Sidney handed him the fold-up instructions. "Everyone gets a set of joker cards to play when we want to skip a question."

Charlotte wrinkled her nose. "I'm not playing. It sounds silly."

"Yeah, but silly's what I need right now. We've had so much drama here tonight. I'm feeling kinda drained, yet too keyed up to sleep." I looked at Sidney. "Want me to shuffle the cards?"

He handed me the pack. During our time as housemates, we'd discovered that while he excelled at cooking, my talents lay elsewhere. We'd fallen into the habit of dining together once a week and playing a game from the villa's collection. I was the designated card-shuffler. I performed this task now, expertly mixing the cards with rapid hand movements.

"You're fast," Luc said, impressed. "Where'd you learn to shuffle like that?"

"When we spent rainy summers with our Irish grandmother, the only games she had in the house were *Monopoly* and a pack of playing cards. My brothers and I soon learned to play a mean game of poker using *Monopoly* money. Shuffling became a competitive sport."

Luc's brow puckered. "I forget you have siblings. I guess it's because I associate you solely with Desirée."

"And she's the least likely maternal figure you can imagine," I said dryly. "Yeah, I have half brothers. Let's just say my dad likes to think of himself as a ladies' man. He tends to wind up with the kids when his relationships implode."

I laid the cards in four neat piles on the table and pushed one toward each player. Charlotte ignored hers but didn't reject it. She was probably biding her time, deciding if she wanted to admit to interest.

The game was exactly what Sidney described—a spiced-up version of *Truth or Dare?* With the spicy parts neutered. The questions were inane, and we responded accordingly, earning laughs from our fellow players. As the game progressed, Charlotte joined in the fun, and we pitted ourselves against the men. We learned Luc had an older sister, a secret penchant for K-dramas, and had once dated a B-list TV actress who'd starred in a crime series Sidney enjoyed.

I shared the story behind several of my tattoos,

omitting those in locations not suitable for polite company, and described my childhood summers spent on Whisper Island, the small Irish island where my father had grown up.

As we were now playing as a team, Charlotte was also asked to describe her favorite summer holidays. She screwed up her nose. "Hmm...hard to say. Probably camping in Brittany. We'd spend all day scouring the beach for special shells to make shell necklaces and sometimes not get back to the caravan until after dark. My mother never scolded me, though. She was always calm, never cross."

"I imagine a camping holiday was fun for you," I said, "especially when you've always lived in such nice homes. All kids love sand, regardless of their background."

"What?" I'd startled her out of her reverie. Her gaze shot to the mantelpiece. "Yeah. All kids like the beach."

I ran my eyes over the row of perfectly posed photographs of Charlotte and her father, most taken on expensive trips abroad. "Is your mother the more down-to-earth parent?"

"I guess." She fiddled with the bow tie on her pig-girl plush.

"How long has she been living in New York?" Sidney asked. "It must be rough for you with her so far away."

Charlotte sniffed, her emotional shutters sliding

back into place. "It's not that far away. All I have to do is hop on a plane." She plumped up her pillow. "I'm going to sleep. Try not to wreck my house before morning."

Luc's struggle not to laugh wasn't successful. "I'll make sure Sidney and Angel behave."

Sidney checked the score sheet. "Okay, we're down to our last question. Which of us do you want to ask first?"

"You went first last time, so I vote for Luc." I picked up the final question card in my pile. "Oooh... looks like Sidney missed a dirty card. Never fear. I can make it family-friendly. The original refers to an item you've removed from your person over the course of the game. I'll just pick something you're wearing. The question is as follows: 'Tell us the story behind your... watch. Why did you pick it, and what does it mean to you?'"

Luc glanced at the enormous smartwatch on his left wrist. His smile was smug. "Wrong thing to pick. The short answer is, your mother picked it, and it's part of my P.I. kit. No sentimental value, no stories connected with it that I'm allowed to share. But I'll be nice and give you another shot."

I checked him out, my gaze resting on the scar on his ear. "Okay, this is cheating, but is that an earring hole? I've never seen you wear an earring."

Luc's smirk didn't slip. He reached down to his pile of cards and pulled the only joker he'd played all night. "Sorry, Angel. That's a mind your own beeswax."

"It is?" My curiosity was well and truly piqued. "You don't want to talk about an *earring hole?*"

"You found it significant enough to remark upon," he pointed out.

"I'm so going to find out about the story behind that hole. I'll make it my mission."

"You do that, but you won't succeed tonight." Luc tossed the joker back onto the table. "Over to you, Sidney. What's the deal with your vintage watch? Everything else you wear is ultra-modern. Does it have sentimental value?"

Sidney didn't look at the watch and betrayed not so much as wrist-twitch of a reaction to Luc's question. "This is a Rolex Submariner 1680, purchased in nineteen seventy-two. It's a collector's item." After an infinitesimal pause, he added, "It was my grandfather's."

"Ah." Luc drew the word out, nodding as though Sidney's response clarified everything. "So you wear it to honor his memory."

"Right." Sidney's face adopted a bland expression I recognized from our card games when he didn't want me to read his reactions.

Curious. He'd often spoken of his domineering grandmother, but only mentioned his grandfather in passing. I wondered what it was about the watch that had triggered his nonreaction. Luc was correct. The old-fashioned watch was at variance with the rest of Sidney's wardrobe.

Sidney yawned and gathered up the cards. "I don't know about you, but I'm exhausted, killer, or no killer. It's past one o'clock. We need to sleep."

I looked out at the hallway, still brightly lit. "We should take turns keeping watch."

"I'll go first." Luc's tone brooked no argument. "I've just taken my medication, and I'll be awake for a while until it kicks in. Makes sense for me to take the first shift."

"Wake me at two?" Sidney smothered another yawn. "Then Angel can take the last watch before she heads out to get help."

"Nah. Sleep. You'll need to be wide awake once Angel leaves in the morning. I'm used to pulling all-nighters." Luc looked at me. "I'll wake you at four, okay?"

I nodded, thinking hard. Did I want Luc awake all night with access to the pistol? Did I still consider him a suspect? I wanted to strike him off the list, but I'd been burned too often to trust my instincts when feelings were involved.

"Okay, but I keep the pistol." He opened his mouth to protest, but I cut him off. "Sorry, Luc, but look where I'll be sleeping. Charlotte and I are nearest the hallway and more vulnerably positioned than either you or Sidney. Besides, you only have one working hand."

He narrowed his eyes and studied me from beneath dark lashes. "I don't think that's why you want to keep the gun. You don't trust me, do you?"

"It's not a matter of—" I began, but stopped myself. Why prevaricate? My reaction was nothing to be ashamed of and understandable under the circumstances. "You're right. You're on my suspect list. You had the means and the opportunity to murder the first two victims and set the car bombs."

Luc's bitter crack of laughter flayed me like a lash. "Unbelievable. You know me. We share a house. I work for your mother. Why would I want to kill a bunch of random strangers?"

The hurt and anger on his face triggered the guilt that never lingered far beneath the surface. I blamed the nuns. "I'm not saying you killed anyone. My assignment is to look out for Charlotte's welfare, and that's what I'm doing, regardless of my personal opinions or your feelings. There are four dead bodies in this house. I must consider all angles to keep her safe."

He drew in a shuddery breath. "I was a good sport about you shooting me, Angel, but I draw the line at being cast as your number one suspect. If you want to join the team, you'll need to become a team player. That means trusting your partners implicitly."

I punched my pillow into shape with more force than was strictly necessary. Charlotte pretended not to listen in to our conversation, but I was aware of her following our every word. I didn't need to turn around to know Sidney was doing the same. Right now, I didn't care if we had an audience.

"I've never been a team player, Luc. And I don't believe I should be expected to trust people blindly simply because we have the same employer. In the line of work we—*you*—do, I'd have thought keeping a reserve of wariness was part of the package."

I got under my covers before he could respond, pointedly turning away. Childish, perhaps, but I'd been through an emotional wringer today, and I was all out of cares to give. Luc and his bruised ego could wait until we escaped Hell Mountain.

With the clamorous exception of Sidney's snoring, the rest of the night passed quietly and without incident. No more accidents. No more exploding cars. No more dead bodies. I'd like to say the quiet came as a relief, but it felt more like the calm before the category-five hurricane.

Armed with the pistol, a thermos of black coffee, and the housekeeper's copy of *The Body in the Library*, I relieved Luc at 4 a.m. and took the last watch. Since the book was in German, I didn't understand every word. Seeing as I'd read the Miss Marple story in English several times, I was able to get the gist.

The hours crept by in an adrenaline-spiked haze. My heart leaped at every creak. My breath caught at every shadow. Why was sunrise so late this time of year? Typically, the seasonal differences didn't bother me, but I needed the light. By the time the orange glow of dawn seeped through the windows, it was close to seven thirty, and I was jittery from nerves and caffeine.

When I judged the light outside to be sufficient to see my way, I crept over to Charlotte and shook her gently. "I'm going outside to see if I can get help. Do you want to come with me? We can snowshoe down to the village. Or try skiing if the conditions look good."

Her response was a string of German invective. It seemed the camaraderie we'd established last night was at an end. "Are you crazy? I'm not going out in that snow."

"Please come with me, Charlotte. We don't know where the killer is. They might still be in the house."

"Or they might be waiting for me outside." She rolled over and began gathering her things. "Now that I'm awake, I'm going back to my room. I'll stay there until the police arrive."

I sighed. This kid was a royal pain, but she was probably right. We'd be mighty exposed outside, especially on skis. I'd dance an Irish jig for joy once Charlotte was no longer my responsibility. "Why won't you stay here with Sidney and Luc? You're safer as a group."

"How do I know one of them isn't the killer?"

"Because you're still alive? If they wanted you dead, they could have done it while you were asleep."

She pouted. "I don't care. I'm not staying down here with men I don't know."

I threw my arms up in the air. "Okay. You win. Go back to your room. But take a weapon with you. And don't open the door for anyone, even if they know the knock."

With a *harrumph* worthy of my granny, Charlotte stomped up the stairs. I hurried after her, quickly checked to make sure her room and bathroom were murderer-free zones, and left her to sulk in solitude.

The instant I stepped into the hallway, Charlotte slammed the door. I bit back the sharp retort I wanted to make. The sooner I got down to the village and fetched help, the sooner I'd be rid of my truculent charge.

I massaged my neck and examined my injuries. My nose felt better this morning, but my ribs ached, making my movements slow and stiff. I tip-toed downstairs, not wanting to wake the guys in the living room if Charlotte's antics hadn't already, and opened the front door.

A crisp wind greeted me with a flurry of snowflakes. I shielded my eyes and surveyed the landscape. The snowfall had eased but not stopped. A smooth blanket of white covered every surface. The trees were so laden with snow that they blended into the background. It'd take me hours to walk to the village, even in snowshoes. Skiing down would be faster, assuming I didn't break a leg in the attempt.

I took another look at the smooth, white slope. Was I confident I could ski in these conditions? No. Was I going to try? You bet. Anything to get off this mountain.

I closed the door and crept down to the basement, careful to avoid the mess on the floor. After the dual commotions of finding the body in the deep freeze and Sidney twisting his ankle, tidying the pile of broken weapons hadn't featured high on last night's list of priorities. Wishing to avoid a future accident, I shoved the stack away from the foot of the stairs and into the room with the deep freeze. When the cops got here and wanted to check out the body, they'd just have to deal.

Once I'd dealt with the mess, I investigated the Hauris' impressive collection of winter sports equipment. They had everything from skis, to snowboards, to snowshoes, to sleds. I selected the shortest pair of skis I could find, but I suspected they were still too big for me. I found a helmet that fit me well and added goggles, poles, and a pair of snowshoes to my haul.

Luc was awake when I returned to the living room and deposited my equipment in a heap. His face was pale and drawn. I suspected he'd slept with one eye open. "You heading out already? Are you sure it's safe to ski out there?"

There was a reserve in his tone that hadn't been there before our disagreement. It stung, but I accepted it as my due. It wasn't nice to be suspected of something you hadn't done. I should know. Yet I had to keep an open mind about this case, however much I doubted Luc was a criminal.

"The slope looks smooth. I'll pack snowshoes as my backup plan." I disinfected my hands and lined up everything I'd need to apply a fresh dressing to Luc's wound.

He eyed my preparations with a wary look. "Shouldn't we wait for a medical professional?"

"We don't know how long it'll take to reach the village. It could take hours to find help. We don't have antibiotics, and I don't want to risk your wound getting infected."

Luc grumbled, but allowed me to remove last night's dressing and apply a new one. That he trusted me to treat his injury after I'd kept him on my suspect list twanged my guilt strings.

He looked up at the ceiling. "I heard Charlotte return to her room."

"Kind of hard not to hear. She wasn't quiet. I tried to persuade her to come with me, but she was having none of it. Says she feels safer in her room."

"With all of us awake, it probably doesn't make much difference if she's there or here, as long as she keeps her doors and windows locked."

"She will. She's scared." I opened the bottle of antiseptic.

Luc tapped the drawing I'd made for him yesterday evening. "I stared at your map of the chalet until it was burned into my brain. Assuming the map is accurate, I don't see any potential secret hiding places."

"It's as accurate as my poor drawing skills could manage. I can't rule out a secret room, but I don't know where we'd find one."

When I poured antiseptic into his wound, Luc's loud hiss woke Sidney.

My friend sat up and blinked at us through a haze of sleep. He took slow, silent stock of his surroundings. As Sidney usually bounced out of bed mid-sentence, he must be feeling rough.

"How's the ankle?" I asked, placing clean cloths over Luc's bullet hole. "Do you need to swallow another painkiller before I go?"

Sidney made an involuntary shudder at my mention of his sprained ankle. "Give me all the meds. I'm in absolute agony."

"I'll refrain from making derogatory remarks about males and their pain tolerance. How many have you had so far?"

"Not nearly enough. We're not tough like you. Right, Luc? We stub our toes, and it's a national tragedy."

Luc's lips twitched, but he made no reply, probably because I chose this moment to tighten the bandages around his leg.

Sidney's doped-up gaze came to rest on the heap of ski equipment. "Don't tell me you're planning to ski down the mountain, Angel?"

I pointedly regarded his swollen ankle. "Are you volunteering to take my place?"

"I'd gladly go, but for this stupid injury." He screwed up his face in a comical effort of concentration. "I seem to recall you saying you couldn't ski."

Luc wagged a finger at me. "Angel the Intrepid. Didn't you say you'd snowshoe down?"

I read a mix of amusement and exasperation in his lively, blue eyes. "I will if I have to, but it'd take hours. I'll be faster on skis. Despite what Sidney says, I know the basics." I tried to channel confidence I didn't feel. "It's just been a while." Make that ten years, give or take.

All traces of humor vanished from his expression. "Can you make it down the mountain without breaking your neck?"

I shrugged and forced a confident smile. "I guess we'll find out."

Two fine lines snaked across his forehead, marring its smooth perfection. "I don't like this plan, Angel. What if you have an accident? Unless you take a tumble in an area with phone service, you'll have no way to call for help."

"Do you have a better idea?" I gestured to his bandaged leg and then to Sidney's visibly swollen ankle. "Neither of you is in a position to take my place."

"Couldn't we send Charlotte down the slope?"

Sidney suggested. "Have you seen all the skiing trophies in her bedroom? I noticed them when we searched the house yesterday."

"I was too bowled over by her father's medieval killing implements to notice," I said, my tone bone-dry.

"Well, she has a lot of them."

"Good for her. I wanted her to come with me, but she was disinclined to listen. And honestly? She's probably as safe barricaded in her bedroom as she would be outdoors. The situation outside is still precarious. We'd be sitting ducks for anyone wishing to take a pot-shot at us."

Luc frowned out at the snowy landscape. "You don't know the terrain. You'll get lost."

My irritation was growing. Here I was, trying to be solution-oriented, and the two people who wouldn't be taking any action kept shooting down my ideas. "Do you have a better suggestion, Luc? We're responsible for Charlotte's welfare. We don't know who's targeting us, nor why, and we have no way to contact emergency services. Our priority must be to alert the police. If it doesn't work out with the skis, I'll stash them behind a tree and walk the rest of the way."

"If you insist on doing this, you'll need supplies." Ignoring our protests, Luc heaved himself off the sofa, picked up his backpack, and limped into the kitchen. He returned a few minutes later. "I've removed the grenades but left my first aid blanket in case you get stranded in the snow. I've added a coffee thermos, water bottle, energy bars, and some chocolate."

I took the backpack without looking at him. His kindness made me feel awful for doubting him, and I suspected the awkwardness between us would linger long after we escaped off this mountain. "Thank you. Now all I need are some badass weapons. You sure I can't take one of your grenades?"

He cocked an eyebrow. "Do you know how to use them?"

"I've watched enough movies to know how it works."

His mouth curved into a smile. "I'll take that as a 'no.'"

Sidney swept an arm at the pile of weapons I'd created last night. "Take your pick from this lot. Does a medieval spear strike your fancy? What about a morning star?"

"What is a morning star?"

"It's like a mace but with spikes."

"I'd prefer something more modern. Seeing as that's not an option, the morning star isn't a bad idea." I strode to the heap of weapons and picked up the one Sidney had described. It was heavier than it looked, and the spikes on its head were mighty sharp. I crammed it into the backpack and scanned the pile for other likely candidates. I settled on a mean-looking dagger and added it to my collection, along with a can of hair spray I'd found in the downstairs bathroom.

"That's quite the motley collection of would-be weapons," Luc remarked. "Aren't you taking the pistol with you?"

"No." I pulled it out of my pocket and handed it to Sidney.

He took it, his brow creasing. "Why not give this to Luc? I guarantee he's a better shot than I am, even using his left hand."

I gave him a significant stare, but his pain-fuddled brain wasn't picking up on my hints. "You're no worse a shot than I am."

Luc snorted, drawing my attention. His eyes glinted with a mix of anger and amusement. "You did a pretty good job shooting me, Angel."

"You're lucky I didn't hit an artery," I said frankly. "I don't have much experience with guns."

I went over to the fireplace and retrieved my snow gear from the still-soggy pile on the floor. I should've hung up my pants and jacket to dry last night, but I'd had other things on my mind—like the bullet hole in Luc's leg.

"Don't wear damp ski gear," Luc said. "It's a recipe for a nasty cold. Did you see any ski suits down in the basement? Preferably ones from this millennium?"

I wrinkled my nose, remembering the hot-pink monstrosity I'd guessed was Charlotte's. "None I'd want to wear."

Sidney snorted with laughter. "Because that orange suit looks so good on you?"

I shot him a death-ray glance. "Careful, or I'll accidentally on purpose trip over your sore ankle."

"Seriously, get a dry suit." Luc's tone brooked no argument. "Apart from catching a cold, a wet outfit will weigh you down, impede your range of motion, and increase your risk of falling."

I let a long sigh. "Okay. Hot-pink it is."

A few minutes later, I checked out my reflection in the hallway mirror. In Charlotte's too-tight, too-long, too-hot-pink outfit, I looked like a beach ball stuffed into a ski suit. When you're five-foot-nothing and a few kilos over the norm, it's hard to pull off wearing a willowy sixteen-year-old's ski gear.

When the men saw me, Luc gave a cough that sounded suspiciously like a laugh. Sidney didn't bother to hold back his mirth. "That's even worse than that powder pink maternity outfit you were wearing when we first met."

"Hey, I was in disguise then. This morning, it's a choice between being wet in orange or dry in hot pink. Frankly, I don't think there's much difference in how bad I look in these outfits, but I'm not dressing to impress." I scanned the supplies on the coffee table. "Do you need me to get you anything else before I go?"

Luc inclined his head. "We're fine. Just be careful out there, okay? Promise me you'll take it slow. If you're in any doubt, take off the skis and walk."

I saluted him. "Yes, sir."

Sidney collapsed back onto his cushions. "In the

theater world, breaking a leg is wishing someone good luck. In your case...no. Try to stay upright."

"I'll do my best." The more I thought about it, the less inclined I was to believe that Luc was involved in whatever was happening at the chalet. All the same, I didn't feel entirely easy about leaving Sidney alone with him, pistol or no pistol.

I strapped on my backpack and carried my skis down the steps. Several of the steps that had been exposed when we'd arrived yesterday were now buried under snow. The air was crisp and cold. The brisk wind was a harsh reminder that this was the lull between storms. I had to make tracks fast to beat the next deluge of snow.

I tramped down to the chalet gates and walked down the snow-clogged road for ten minutes until I found a stretch with a satisfying slope and no apparent obstacles. As the snow was so high, scaling the fence that divided the road from the fields was a matter of stepping over it.

Before strapping on my skis, I checked my phone for a signal. Still nothing. I hadn't expected there to be one, but it was worth trying. I ran over my long-ago ski instructor's advice, filled my lungs with icy air, and pushed off.

The going was easy—deceptively so. Keeping to a sedate pace, I weaved a path down the mountain, past countless snow-heavy trees, partially exposed bushes, and half-buried fences. The Alps loomed around me, imposing and majestic with their dramatically pointed peaks that stretched far into the clouds.

The ease with which I traversed the first leg of my journey boosted my confidence. Maybe I'd underestimated my abilities. After all, that collision on the bunny slopes had occurred over ten years ago.

Buoyed with newfound self-assurance, I increased my speed to a small degree. When that proved unproblematic, I upped the pace another notch. Soon, I whizzed down the slope, relishing in the sensation of the wind whipping my hair. Objects flashed by in a blur. At this rate, I'd reach the village in no time.

You know that saying, "Pride comes before a fall?" Yeah...

The red object appeared out of nowhere. One moment, the slope was pure white. The next, a fire-engine red blob zoomed into view. The closer I got, the more human it appeared. A person was lying in the snow.

And I was speeding right for them.

I tried to brake, but my effort somehow loosened my right ski. Feeling like a spectator in someone else's drama, I could only look on with horror as it slid off my foot, leaving me juddering down the mountain on one ski. The inevitable happened, as I'd known it would from the instant I spotted that blasted red blob. I stumbled, tumbled, and face-planted into an unintentional snow angel.

The impact sent spikes of pain into my sore nose

and bruised ribs. I lay there for a few moments, too stunned to move. Then I pushed myself onto my knees and raised my head.

And stared into a familiar, frozen face.

My manager, Maurice, lay half-buried in the snow, bringing our corpse collection up to number five.

23

I collapsed back into the snow, too tired and too shocked to think straight. After discovering four corpses in the space of a few hours, I should've been used to the sight of death. I wasn't. This fifth dead body felt personal. I hadn't liked Maurice, nor had he liked me. Our relationship had been contentious from the moment my mother announced I was his new part-time employee. However strained our interaction, I'd never wished him dead.

What was Maurice doing in Switzerland? My mother had explicitly ordered him to stay in Nice. His job was to oversee the businesses that acted as camouflage for the Omega Group. Why had he defied her? And if he'd wanted to get involved in the Crofton-Lowe case, why on earth had he chosen to follow Sidney and me to the chalet? Apart from Luc, none of the Omega Group team knew we were snowed in with a killer.

I shivered despite my too-tight snowsuit and took another look at Maurice. Had I stumbled across our mystery murderer? Had he been involved in the plot to steal the Egyptian artifacts? Is that why he'd come to Höllenberg? If so, why was he dead on the mountain slope? Was he the killer, or the killer's fifth victim?

The first thing I needed to do was figure out how he'd died. Accident? Or foul play?

I pushed to my knees and gingerly checked myself for injuries. My already bruised face and chest were on fire. I wasn't in great shape, but at least I wouldn't have to add myself to the list of invalids at the chalet.

I turned my attention to Maurice. He lay on his back, half-submerged, his snowshoes poking through the snow. He looked like Hercule Poirot in a red snowsuit. A backpack lay beside him, the contents spilling out. I spied a black leather case and a gun. I pocketed the gun.

Scooping snow off Maurice's clothes, I checked for entry and exit wounds, starting at his head and working down. I'd reached his knees when his chest heaved with a crackling wheeze.

My heart high-jumped, and my gaze flew to his face.

Two blurry green eyes stared back at me, befuddled and mystified. "Angel?" His voice was a low croak, barely audible—barely human.

"You're alive." I sucked in air like oxygen was running out of stock and made my ribs vibrate with pain.

Violent coughing overcame Maurice. The only color in his gray cheeks was frostbite.

I helped him sit, opened my backpack, and wrapped him in the silver emergency blanket Luc had insisted I bring. Now he looked more like Poirot in Space than Poirot in the Alps. I found my water bottle and held it to his lips. I knew little about hypothermia, but I guessed he was experiencing the effects of some stage of exposure.

I let him drink half the bottle before forcing an energy bar on him. He ate it with slow, deliberate bites. I joined him in a morning snack, washing chocolate down with coffee. Then I checked my phone for a signal, but no luck. I slipped it back into my pocket and pulled my snowshoes out of my pack. "Can you walk?"

He looked at his legs as though he'd forgotten they existed. "I don't know. I can try."

"I'll strap on my snowshoes, and we'll get moving. We can't risk another snowstorm." I tugged on my snowshoes and then strapped my backpack onto my back and Maurice's onto my front. Dressed like this, I'd better not fall. If I did, I'd roll down the mountain like a human snowball.

I helped Maurice to his feet, no mean feat considering his snowshoes were the old-fashioned duck-feet kind. I winced when he gripped me around my sore ribs. "How long have you been lying here?"

"An hour? Two?" His frozen eyebrows formed an ice-tipped V. "I set out as soon as the storm eased. Snowshoes seemed the surest way to get to the chalet under these conditions."

"Dude, are you crazy? It's a long way up, especially at your age. No wonder you ran out of energy."

He looked up at the sky, now a brilliant gray-white. "Believe it or not, I used to be an intrepid snow trekker back in the day. Perhaps I am past my prime. When I realized I was exhausted, I lit my emergency flare and hoped someone would come. No one did—not until you."

Gone was the angry, arrogant ball of vitriol that I'd come to know and dislike. This was a subdued Maurice, too weak to care that the person helping him was me. "What are you doing on this mountain? Why aren't you at home in sunny Nice?"

"Pursuing a hunch." His smile was the first he'd ever directed at me. "After our meeting on Thursday, I did some digging, and I didn't like what I found. I was worried that you and Sidney might be in danger, so I followed you to Switzerland."

The idea that Maurice would give a hoot about my safety astounded me. Was this a lie to get me to trust him? I side-eyed the man leaning on me for support—one of the few men short enough for me to look straight in the eye. "That doesn't explain why you're on this slope this morning. What prompted you to brave the elements?"

"My original plan was to stakeout the chalet. Yesterday, when the storm got bad, I realized the road was impassable, so I took a room down in the village. By five a.m., I realized sleep would never happen. And then I checked your car tracker and panicked when I realized it had disappeared."

My eyes flew to his. "What tracking device? Why would the Peugeot have one?"

"It's standard procedure for all agents' cars when we're away on assignments."

The story sounded plausible, but why had no one bothered to inform Sidney and me we were driving a bugged vehicle?

"I used the tracker to follow you around Switzerland," Maurice continued. "You led me a merry dance, I must say. I wondered if the tracking device was faulty when you kept stopping at casinos. What was that all about?"

"A story for another time. I want to know more about the tracker."

"When I checked it this morning, I almost had heart failure when I checked it and realized it had stopped working hours earlier."

"A car bomb," I said, feigning nonchalance. "It happens."

He looked suitably stunned. "Good grief. You're serious."

"Deadly serious. You have no idea how much so."

"When I realized your tracker was dead, I tried calling you."

"And got voicemail. We suspect signal jammers are to blame."

"Then I called Desirée, but all she did was bawl me out for coming to Switzerland against her orders. I suspect the 5 a.m. wakeup call didn't help her mood. The storm had eased by then, so I decided to snowshoe up to the chalet."

Maurice succumbed to a bout of coughing. When he was done, he looked exhausted, totally spent. He didn't look like a person plotting an elaborate scheme to ambush me. Besides which, he'd had ample time to attack. I'd lain down in the snow for a good two minutes before I'd checked him out.

Some primal instinct told me to trust him—at least for the present. I looked down the slope, straining to see the rooftops of the village. But all I saw were trees and snow and more snow. I judged us to be maybe a quarter of the way down the mountain. Maurice wouldn't survive much longer in this giant refrigerator. "We're going to have to hike up to the chalet. Can you manage?"

Maurice nodded and pulled his space blanket close. A tremor ran through his body like an electric shock. Potential killer or not, I needed to get him moving before he turned into an ice sculpture.

Our progress was painful and painfully slow.

Paranoid about an attack, I remained hypervigilant. The physical and mental strain wiped all thoughts and questions from my mind. It was all I could do to put one big-ass snowshoe in front of the other and half-carry, half-drag Maurice.

His breathing rattled, and he had several coughing fits during our forced trudge up the mountain. When the chalet came into view, I almost cried. Not from joy or relief. It was a mixed bag of emotions, ranging from fear to frustration. I'd wanted to get help from the village, but all I'd done was add another patient to my nursing roster. At this rate, I should set up shop as a reluctant nurse.

The ultimate challenge was making it up the slippery steps to the front door. Whatever boost the water and energy bar had given Maurice, it had long since worn out. I had to turn around and pull him up each step, pausing to pant and moan through the pain of my poor battered ribs. I'm not sure how, but we made it.

When we stumbled into the entrance hall, the welcome warmth hit my frozen face. My legs turned to jelly, and I almost fell. This time, Maurice bore my weight. In a parody of the three-legged race, we staggered into the living room, clinging to one another for support.

Leg injuries notwithstanding, Luc and Sidney practically leaped off their respective sofas. They gawked at us—one dark, one fair, both slack-jawed.

Luc was the first to find his voice. "Is that Maurice? What's he doing here?"

"I don't know, but we've run out of sofas." I turned to Maurice. "Lean on the back of Luc's while I drag an armchair over to the fire. We need to get you warm."

"No." Luc's bark was worthy of a sergeant-major. "Leave the armchair where it is. If he's suffering from exposure, we can't warm him up too quickly. Help get his outer layers off and put the emergency blanket back on. Then make him a warm tea with a splash of schnapps."

"How do you know I'll find schnapps?"

"We're in Switzerland. Every household has schnapps."

I followed his directions to the letter. Once I'd settled Maurice in an armchair with his blanket and cushions, I made a pot of spiked fruit tea for us to share. While the kettle was boiling, I stripped off my snow gear, moved the gun to my jeans pocket, and ran upstairs to check on Charlotte. Because I had all the energy in the universe...

Her response to my knocking was a grumpy tirade. Hearing her rudeness was a relief. At least she was safe and warm in her room. "Are you certain you don't want to come down and have tea with us?"

"I told you. Leave. Me. Alone."

"Can I at least bring you up a cup? And maybe a biscuit?" I tried to copy Sidney's soothing signature tone—low, slow, and in control. But I sounded more like a stoned snowboarder.

A heavy object thudded against the door. My relief at knowing Charlotte was safe and sound waned. "Fine. Have it your way. You'll have to eat at some point. My plan to raise the alarm in the village got derailed. I don't know when I'll get down there now. Not for at least a couple of hours."

I couldn't imagine venturing into the snowpocalypse again today, but I knew I had to. Have I mentioned that I was the only able-bodied adult? Without me, they'd all petrify in place. Once I'd refilled my tank with warm tea and loads of chocolate, I'd make another attempt to fetch help.

Back in the living room, Sidney had hobbled around and unearthed a fruitcake and plates and was serving generous slices all around. He handed me a giant portion. "You deserve it after this morning's failed rescue mission."

I took the remaining armchair and poured myself a cup of tea. "I didn't get far enough for a phone signal. Whoever set up the signal jammers did a phenomenal job. Speaking of tech, did you know there was a tracking device on the Peugeot?"

"No way." Sidney appeared to be delighted by this revelation. "Who put it there? The thugs?"

Luc raised his hand. "I installed it when I changed the Peugeot's tires. When we go on assignments, all the agents' cars are tracked in case one of us gets into trouble and needs help. Didn't Desirée tell you that?"

"Desirée kept the facts to the bare minimum." Sidney's tone was dry. "We hadn't a clue we were driving a tracked vehicle."

"Never mind that for now," Luc fixed his powerful gaze on Maurice. "I want to know how you wound up on this mountain. Are you friend or foe?"

Maurice, who'd been drinking tea, spluttered. "Friend, of course. Why else would I risk my life getting here? And what are *you* doing at the chalet? Why aren't you running around with the others, chasing antique thieves?"

Luc's expression darkened. "I encountered Dario Giannelli. He was overly eager to put me out of the running to find the stolen cache. The only good news is that I broke his hand, so he's as much use to Rocco as I am to the Omega Group."

Maurice tut-tutted. Now that he was starting to thaw, he looked more like his old self. "I said pitting two rival P.I. agencies against each other was a bad idea. And that extravagant bonus? Pure madness." He shook his head, making the curled-up corners of his ridiculous mustache bounce. "That amount of money turns any group of otherwise reasonable people into cutthroat animals. Why should P.I.s be any different? We already knew that Rocco's crowd was corrupt."

"Sounds like an omnishambles." Sidney refilled his plate with a second slice of cake. "To be fair, though, it's not as if our first Omega Group assignment has gone to plan."

Maurice switched his attention from his teacup to Sidney's visibly swollen ankle. "What happened up here?" The question was razor-sharp and imbued with intensity. "I need to know exactly what's been going on."

Sidney looked at me and shrugged. "Angel should fill you in. It's a long story, and she knows how to be succinct."

I swallowed a mouthful of the seriously delicious fruitcake. "You want succinct? I can give you succinct. It all began with the dead dude in the tub."

In a few concise paragraphs, I described the series of catastrophes that had befallen us since our arrival at the chalet. As I recounted my tale, Maurice's jowls tightened to such an extent that I feared for his back teeth.

"And then I fell off my skis and face-planted beside you. Gotta say, for the first few minutes, I was sure you were Dead Body Number Five." I treated Maurice to my don't-screw-with-me super stare. "Now it's time for you to tell us your story. You mentioned wanting to warn Sidney and me we were in danger. As you've just heard, your fears were justified. How did you know we were in trouble?"

He broke eye contact and cradled his teacup between his pudgy hands. "Your mother's announcement at the meeting set off alarm bells. Her description of the Crofton-Lowe case sounded... wrong?" He put the cup on the table and massaged his purplish fingers. "Look, I haven't been an active agent for a couple of years. I know my career ended on a low. I'm excruciatingly aware of how Desirée rates my abilities. But the fact is, art and antiquities were my fields. I worked in that world for thirty years. I have knowledge and contacts way beyond Desirée's information-gathering clique. The moment she mentioned the exorbitant bonus, I smelled a rat."

That *Titanic*-hitting-the-iceberg sensation was back with a vengeance. "What are you trying to tell us? That my mother lied?"

Maurice met me stare for stare. "Either Desirée's in way over her head. Or she's part of the Crofton-Lowe plot."

24

Maurice's words created a booming echo in my mind. I wanted to shoot down his theory, deny that my mother was corrupt. But what did I truly know about Desirée Chablis? She'd flitted in and out of my life, staying long enough to build up my hopes before smashing them into smithereens.

My father was a small-time crook working for a medium-time gangster. Desirée was a soft porn star who'd married him and stuck around long enough to give birth to me. I'd spent my life assuming that while my mother associated with shady characters, she herself was not a criminal.

But then, I'd also assumed my flighty mother made her living from royalties from her film career and present-day strip gigs. The revelation that she helped run an international P.I. agency had flabbergasted me. I'd been equally astounded when I'd discovered she owned an impressive real estate portfolio. Clever Desirée.

What if she was using her connection with the Omega Group to feather her nest? After all, she'd been the one who'd pushed for a merger with Rocco Casetti's P.I. agency, an operation known for its unscrupulous dealings.

I sipped my tea and focused on Maurice. "Can you elaborate? Why do you suspect my mother of wrongdoings?"

Maurice spread his hands wide and looked at Luc, Sidney, and me. "I'm not saying Desirée *is* breaking the law. I'm hypothesizing she *might be*."

"Hypothesize away," I said. "I want to know why you suspect her."

"So do I." Sidney propped his leg on a cushion. "Desirée's always seemed legit to me, although coy about sharing information, as Angel and I have discovered. To our detriment."

The little man fixed me with an intense stare that I found unsettling. Not in a pervy way. I was confident I wasn't Maurice's type—assuming he had a type. I had him down as one of life's confirmed bachelors, more content to live with cats than people. This stare was the soul-scouring variety, like he was solving one of his beloved jigsaw puzzles, and he thought I'd stolen a few key pieces.

I met his intense stare with one of my own. "I know you don't trust me, Maurice. That's okay. I don't entirely trust you, either. But you can speak openly about Desirée in front of me. Anything you say stays on the mountain. I have no reason to go blabbing to her. I barely know the woman, and I guarantee she barely knows me."

He inclined his bald head. "All right then. I'll share my thoughts. Desirée is excellent in the field, but she's a lousy team manager. Jerry never should've allowed her to become his second-in-command."

Luc adjusted the bandage around his leg, his brow furrowed. "Doubting Desirée's abilities as a manager is one thing. Accusing her of corruption is in a whole other league."

The schnapps-laced tea had almost transformed Maurice back to his old bossy self. He rested his elbows on the armrests and steepled his fingers like a TV lawyer. "Best-case scenario, Desirée has bitten off more than she can chew with the Crofton-Lowe case. Even before Jerry was attacked, she pushed him to expand the agency. First, she wanted us to accept bigger, flashier cases. Next, she coaxed Jerry to consider a merger with Rocco's agency."

"The merger was a bad idea," Luc interjected, "but expanding the agency is the only way to keep us competitive in today's market."

"Yet you expressed your doubts at the meeting," I pointed out. "You wondered if the team could handle the job."

Luc's gaze snapped to mine. "Yes, I did. I was

referring to the scope of the job and the size of our team, especially when pitted against Rocco's crowd. I've never doubted Desirée's integrity."

"Is the team too small for the Crofton-Lowe case?" Sidney asked. "Is that why Desirée asked Angel and me to help with this assignment?"

"Yes, to the first question. Probably, to the second." Maurice tried to keep the smug I-knew-better attitude under wraps, but it seeped through. "Desirée wouldn't usually send two untrained P.I.s to do any job, no matter how low the risk. The Crofton-Lowe case is one example of her accepting cases that require more trained investigators than we currently employ. The Omega Group is a small team of highly trained professionals. Still, we can't compete on the level of Rocco's crowd. He has seventeen full-time active P.I.s, plus an office staff of five. Compare that to our six active P.I.s, one of whom is still recuperating from his injuries."

"Why would my mother take on cases the agency can't handle?" I asked, not quite willing to cast my mother in the role of the villainess, however strained our relationship. "Even if she's corrupt, she's shown every sign of wanting the agency to succeed. Pushing for the merger with Rocco, for example."

"Desirée overestimates her own abilities and the agency's." Maurice's frostbite glowed in the reflected firelight, lending him a demonic air. "Without Jerry around to keep her ambitions in check, she's out of control."

Luc held up his one hand. "Steady on, old friend. You're blowing the situation out of proportion. I agree that Jerry's a good foil for Desirée. He thinks small, she thinks big, and they compromise at the just-right spot. Recently, she's accepted cases that are a stretch for the agency, but none are impossible for a staff of our size. Including this one. The team Desirée dispatched on this case is the same size as Rocco sent."

"You didn't find her negotiations with Rocco fishy?" Maurice demanded. "We've never been able to prove Rocco works for a crime syndicate, but the clues are hidden in plain sight."

"According to you." Luc's chin had a stubborn tilt. "Desirée's ambitious streak borders on ruthless. Yet I've never had a reason to believe that she crossed a line, morally or legally. And the quarter-million bonus from the Crofton-Lowe case would give the agency an infusion of cash that we badly need."

This was news to me. It hadn't occurred to me that the Omega Group could be in financial trouble. "Is the agency having money problems?"

Maurice twisted his lips into a mockery of a smile. "Put it this way: the costumier, the yarn shop, and Luc's contribution from the café have kept us afloat. And we originally intended those businesses to deflect what the Omega Group truly was."

I pictured the dilapidated building that housed the

agency headquarters. The costumier and Jerry's office had a threadbare air, but Jerry's apartment on the top floor was nicely decorated. I'd assumed the shabby vibe was intentional, designed to put people off the scent of how Jerry Gallo earned his living. And even if the Omega Group was struggling financially, my mother didn't appear to have any cash flow problems.

"Are money issues why Desirée is dragging her heels about allowing Angel and me to train as P.I.s? Is it the cost factor that's holding her back?" Sidney, who'd remained atypically silent for most of the conversation, helped himself to a third slice of fruitcake. "Because if Desirée wants to expand the agency and take on more challenging cases, hiring new P.I.s is a must."

Maurice and Luc exchanged meaningful glances. Luc rose to the challenge. "Partly. Jerry sent all of us to an exclusive boot camp in the US. He paid the training upfront, and we reimbursed him for a portion of the cost once we started work for the agency." His eyes slid to me. "I believe Desirée's reluctance to commit to allowing you to join us is at least partially down to her wanting to keep you safe."

I erupted into peals of laughter. "If that's her goal, she did an excellent job this weekend. She sent us up here armed with a bag of makeup."

A look of pitying amusement crossed over Maurice's face. "Valentina likes to think she's wonderful at everything, but her German's only so-so.

Did she get a call from her Swiss contact or a text message?"

"A call." Luc grinned. "You're right about her German. Mine isn't perfect, but Valentina's German pronunciation has a fingernails-down-a-blackboard quality."

"The number Valentina's contact gave her was 636, not 663." Maurice was basking in this moment of glory, his complexion almost normal again. "Germans express thirty-six as six-and-thirty."

Sidney slapped his thigh. "Of course. That makes perfect sense. Why didn't that occur to us?"

"Because we were cold and tired and worried about our missing charge?" I turned to Maurice. "How do you know this? Did you speak to Valentina's contact?"

His smug smile settled into pure Cheshire Cat. "No need. I went to the train station, saw the mess you'd made of Locker 663 and the sabotaged security camera, and figured something had gone awry. Using logical deduction, I picked the lock of Locker 636 and found your bag." He pointed to his backpack. "Unzip it. The black leather case is yours."

I blinked at him, found the case, and flipped the catch. Two pepper sprays, two stun guns—just as Luc had described. "All right, clever clogs. You've told us how you followed us, but you haven't yet explained why you didn't just find us at one of the *many* places we stopped yesterday and tell us we were in danger.

Wouldn't that have been simpler than sneaking around?"

"When I called Desirée with the information I'd found, she dismissed my fears as sour grapes. I didn't want to risk her firing me before I had proof. I figured the best thing to do was go to Höllenberg and stake out the chalet. Then I'd be on hand if it transpired you and Sidney truly were in danger."

It all seemed a tad too convenient for my liking. Was Maurice in on the plot to steal the artifacts? Or did he hope to prove to my mother that he still had it in him to crack cases for the Omega Group?

Sidney's face split into a grin. "Hey, does the danger have anything to do with bears? A fortune-teller told Angel to watch out for bears this weekend."

I tossed a cushion, hitting him squarely in the face. "Traitor. I told you that story in confidence."

Maurice unhunched his drooping shoulders, his eyes alert. "What was that you said about bears?"

I cringed with embarrassment while Sidney repeated Ghiselle's psychic prediction.

Instead of dismissing the idea with a casual wrist-flick as I'd expected him to, Maurice chewed his lower lip, deep in thought. "Funny you should mention bears and danger in the same sentence."

"What connection can there be?" I demanded. "Canton Bern has a bear on its flag, but we're in Canton Valais."

Maurice released a labored sigh. "Didn't any of you learn Latin at school?"

Luc and I shook our heads, but Sidney nodded. "Yeah, but only for a couple of years."

"A couple of years should've been plenty of time to learn the Latin word for bear. I'll give you a clue. It's very similar to the French."

Sidney's face underwent a metamorphosis. "*Urs. Urs* means bear."

"Urs?" I sounded squeaky, as if I needed a touch of oil. "As in Urs Hauri?"

"Urs is a common male name in Switzerland," Maurice told us, "and it originates from the Latin word for bear. If your psychic warned you about bears, I want her number. She was on to something."

Or was Ghiselle an accomplice? Had she approached Luc with her ridiculous request, knowing he'd fob her off onto Sidney and me? None of this made any sense.

"Wow." I was unable to muster anything resembling an intelligent response. "So you think Urs Hauri is behind what's happened at the chalet? That doesn't make sense. Why would he put his daughter in danger?"

The older man made a throaty noise that sounded suspiciously like a chuckle. "I don't have all the answers, Angel. Quit interrupting me, and I'll finish my story. Maybe then we'll figure out the answer to this puzzle."

I sat back in my chair and folded my arms. "Okay. We'll shut up, maestro. You have the floor."

"To start at the beginning, I smelled a rat when Desirée told us about the Crofton-Lowe robbery. My expertise was—is—art and antiquities. I've worked countless robberies, forgeries, and auction house shenanigans. I know that world and its players. Including Colin Jones." Maurice paused here to replenish his tea. "I'm sorry. I'm still parched after being outside for so long."

"That's fine," I said. "You need fluids."

He took a long drink and continued his story. "The idea that suave and collected Colin Jones would harbor a grudge against an auction house CEO for years just because he'd had him questioned by police didn't tally with my experience of the man. Jones is—or *was*, according to what you've just told me—a slippery customer. However, I've never known him to take a slight to something as minor as being questioned by the police."

The information he was sharing fascinated me, but how trustworthy was Maurice? What if his story was a bluff to disguise his true reason for coming to Höllenberg? I glanced at Sidney, trying to read his thoughts, but he was cheerfully tucking into his cake. Was he acting, or was I the only one who found Maurice's tale plausible—and plausibly far-fetched?

I turned back to Maurice. He met my stare with one of bland interest. "My only encounter with Jones was post-mortem," I said, "but that detail in my mother's story stood out. Especially if Jones was a frequent person of interest in criminal investigations."

Maurice gave me an approving nod. "Exactly. Jones could wriggle out of most scenarios. There must have been a more serious reason for him to bear a grudge against Urs Hauri. And even then, I couldn't imagine Jones threatening to harm Hauri's daughter. That was never his style."

"Dude, don't leave us hanging," I urged, stuffing my face with more cake. "Get to the point and tell us what you found out."

"After Desirée's meeting, I made a few calls, wrote a few emails. And waited. This morning, I received a message from an old informant." Maurice leaned forward, positively vibrating with glee. "Word among the black marketeers is that Urs Hauri used Colin Jones to source most of his medieval weapons."

"The CEO of an esteemed auction house purchased his private collection on the black market?" I made a throat-slitting gesture. "If that got out, it'd be career suicide."

Maurice's nod was vigorous. "Precisely. At some point, Jones accused Hauri of cheating him. Hauri retaliated by threatening to shop Jones to the police. Jones said that he had plenty of dirt on Hauri to share with the authorities."

"I'm moving into speculation here," Sidney said, "but I wonder if the house Hauri's ex and daughter lived in contained any items from that illicit collection. From your description of Jones, it would be more in character for him to want to show Hauri he could grab one of the items he'd stolen on his behalf whenever he wanted to, rather than for him to threaten Hauri's family."

"Perhaps. All I know is that Hauri used Jones to source medieval weapons on the black market. That arrangement ended when they fell out over money. Cue the end of a profitable, if an illicit, business relationship."

"Until this week," Luc said. "What's the story? Why would Hauri suddenly help Jones steal the Egyptian artifacts?"

Maurice shrugged. "It's conceivable that Hauri facilitated the robbery, either due to pressure from Jones or because he was complicit in the plot. Bernard Roulez's lawyers kept the details of the Roulez estate sale a tight-lipped secret. No one was supposed to know Crofton-Lowe was handling the auction. The bidders received exclusive invitations and weren't told the details."

Sidney perked up at this information. "Is that a common practice? Wouldn't people want to know in advance what was coming up for auction?"

"It's standard for auctions of this value. The secrecy reduces the danger of a robbery."

"It didn't work this time." Luc picked up one of the celebrity magazines he'd been perusing and tossed it to

Maurice. "Check out these photos taken at a society ball held last month in Cannes. Urs Hauri was photographed with Nancy Roulez, one of Bernard Roulez's daughters. And they look mighty friendly."

Maurice caught the magazine and spread it on his lap. I leaned over to take a peek. Urs Hauri was pictured with his arm around an elegant woman in her forties. Hauri's emotions were hard to read—a complacent smile for the camera, but otherwise inscrutable. Nancy Roulez was a different matter. She stared up at his blandly handsome face in blatant adoration.

I made a low whistle. "Well done, Luc. Do you think he helped Nancy enlarge her portion of the inheritance?"

"It's a possibility. This proves Hauri knows Nancy, and presumably the other members of the Roulez family who attended that party."

"Assuming you're correct, where would Colin Jones fit into this equation?" Sidney asked. "Maurice said Hauri and Jones hated each other."

"I said they'd had a known falling out a few years ago," Maurice corrected. "For all I know, they patched up their differences. Maybe Hauri offered Jones the chance to steal the Egyptian artifacts as a way to reimburse the money he'd failed to pay years ago."

Luc frowned into his teacup as though the beverage had offended him. "Assuming Urs Hauri helped Colin Jones to steal the artifacts before the auction, why would he send his daughter to the chalet for the weekend? And why would he ask for her to have extra protection?"

"Maybe he didn't know Jones planned to hide the loot here," I suggested. "Maybe Jones went rogue."

Maurice snapped to attention. "You think the Egyptian artifacts are here in the chalet?"

I slid him a look. I wasn't entirely sold on his Guardian Angel story, despite his confidences. How could we be sure that Maurice wasn't here to steal the loot? There was one way to find out.

I looked at each of the men in turn. "We have to find those artifacts. Luc and I made no headway with my map, and Sidney and I found nothing during our search. The only one among us who knows this house inside-out is barricaded upstairs in her bedroom. I'm going to persuade Charlotte to help us in the search."

"She was disinclined to cooperate with you before," Luc pointed out. "Why do you think she'll listen to you now?"

"I'll tell her the truth. I'll tell her everything about Jones and his alleged connection with her father and the stolen Egyptian artifacts. Who could resist a treasure hunt?"

I trudged up the stairs, my legs still aching after the trek up the slope with Maurice. Exhaustion washed over me in waves. I needed a shower and a ten-hour sleep. But until we got off this mountain, I'd get neither.

When I reached Charlotte's door, I knocked using our code. "Can you please let me in? I need to tell you why we think people are attacking the chalet."

No answer. Not even a thrown object. Dratted girl. I'd have to pick the lock. I examined the keyhole to ascertain the best method of cracking this particular lock. Then I went to my bedroom and rooted in my toiletry bag for my nail scissors.

The scissors worked a treat, and the handle turned. "I'm coming in. No missiles, please."

Charlotte made no response. My heart rate kicked up a notch. Had the killer found her? Had I endangered her by not insisting she come downstairs? I pulled Maurice's gun out of my pocket and kicked the door open. I stepped inside, gun held high, copying movements I'd only seen on TV.

The bedroom was empty, the balcony door wide open. Charlotte Hauri was gone, leaving behind a wig of brown dreadlocks and a note pinned to the wall with a medieval dagger.

I tore the note free.

Ticktock, Angel. Better run while you can.

I froze in place, my stomach in free fall. Charlotte had left a bomb in the building.

Charlotte's note had a galvanizing effect that overrode my exhaustion. Adrenaline spiked my veins, and I was on the move before my brain had processed what I'd just seen. I thundered down the stairs and erupted into the living room.

"Everybody out," I shouted between gasps. "There's a bomb in the house."

The three men stared at me as though I'd performed an impromptu strip show.

"I'm serious. Charlotte's in on the plot." I held up the scraggly note. "She's done a bunk and left a bomb in the chalet."

Luc, the most incapacitated of the three, was the first to react. He got to his feet with surprising alacrity, given his one-armed, one-legged state. "Come on," he said to the other two. "We have to get out of here."

Sidney opened and shut his mouth, reminding me of my father's pet carp. Still clutching the magazine, Maurice hauled himself to standing and pulled Sidney off the sofa. With the aid of his spear crutch, Sidney limped to the door and had the presence of mind to grab several coats from the coat rack on his way out. We might get blown to smithereens but wouldn't freeze to death.

Maurice and I supported Luc, a situation that would've been hilarious had we not been in a life-or-death scenario. We were so much shorter than him that poor Luc had to stoop to lean on us.

Somehow, we all made it down the slippery steps without falling. When we reached the slope, we weren't so lucky. Sidney's spear stuck in the snow, jerking him off balance. He tumbled and rolled for several meters, finally coming to rest just shy of a tree stump.

"Not a bad plan," Luc remarked. "It'd get us down the slope faster."

"It'd also get us covered in snow," Maurice said reprovingly, "something I've had enough of for one day."

In the end, gravity assisted our progress. The three of us stumbled down the slope after Sidney, grabbing fallen coats when we passed them and eventually collapsing in a group heap.

It took a moment to sort out our tangled limbs and scramble into coats. None of us wore snow pants, but our top halves were protected from the elements, and we wouldn't freeze.

Luc shielded his eyes from the winter sun and scanned the terrain. "Okay, guys. We're far enough down from the house that we should be protected from falling debris in the event of an explosion. We can't rule out a potential avalanche, but there's nothing we can do to circumnavigate that danger. I suggest we keep moving down the mountain. And while we walk, Angel can tell us what the heck is going on."

We stagger-stumbled down the incline, Sidney leaning on me, Luc squashing Maurice. We followed the tracks Maurice and I had made earlier, making our progress faster.

"When I went into Charlotte's room," I began after we'd put another few meters between us and the chalet, "she was gone, leaving her dreadlocks and this note pinned to the wall with a dagger."

"Leaving her dreadlocks?" This information excited Sidney into a trot, and we almost fell. After a brief stagger, we righted ourselves. "Do you mean to say she was wearing a wig?"

"Precisely. No wonder the dreadlocks had a bedraggled appearance. She'd probably pinched them from Herr Hauri's carnival costume collection."

"That would explain the ransacked wardrobe. She must have grabbed them in a hurry. But why?"

"She was slow opening the door when we arrived

yesterday evening," I reminded him. "Perhaps she used the time to throw on a disguise."

We took a few uneven steps, got stuck in a particularly deep patch, and continued down the slope.

"May I see the note?" Luc took it from me and frowned at the scrawled words. "She addressed this to you, Angel. How did she know you'd be the one to find it?"

In my panic, this aspect hadn't occurred to me. "I don't know. Maybe she felt a connection with me because I was the only other woman in the house."

"Or she overheard us talking and knew you were on your way upstairs," Sidney suggested. "It's a short note—quick to scribble. Then all she needed to do was whip off the wig and pin both in place with the dagger, adding yet another dramatic flourish to her performance. It all ties in with accessorizing Colin Jones."

"Even so, she'd have had to act fast. I was slower than usual getting up the stairs, but not that slow. On the other hand..." I pictured the scene in my mind, focusing on the room and ignoring my reaction to the note. "The balcony door was open, and I didn't check her bathroom. I saw the wig, read the note, and panicked."

"The wig intrigues me," Luc mused. "Why would she bother to wear one?"

"The obvious reason. To hide her hair." I glanced at Maurice, who still clutched the ridiculous celebrity magazine in one frozen hand. I doubted he realized he still had it. "What if the girl we've been calling Charlotte *isn't* Charlotte Hauri? During yesterday's craziness, Sidney and I wondered if she was a fake. We triple-checked the photo my mother sent us and compared it to the other photos in the chalet. When she looked enough like the girl in the pictures, we struck her off our suspect list."

"Not just because of her looks," Sidney added. "We figured out the timing and decided Charlotte, or whoever she is, couldn't have killed the security guards. She was with one of us the whole time between the second explosion and Angel and me finding them dead."

It was Maurice's turn to trip. Luc almost lost his balance, forcing him to put weight on his bad leg. He gave a white-faced, tight-lipped groan.

"Sorry." Maurice wheezed from the effort of the downhill trek while supporting a man so much larger than he was.

"No worries, man. It's all good." A muscle in Luc's jaw flexed. "So we can conclude that Charlotte, or Fake Charlotte, has an accomplice. We've suspected an outside force all along."

"Didn't you rule out the possibility of a secret hiding place in the house?" Maurice asked, his brow puckering.

"We did," I said. "I drew a detailed map, and Luc and I couldn't spot any potential hidey-holes. But what we weren't able to do was search outside. For all we know, there's a shed somewhere on the property, perhaps camouflaged by the trees above the chalet."

Maurice looked back at the house. "I should've asked to check that map. Maybe another set of eyes would've spotted something you two missed."

"I doubt it. I stared at that darn map until I knew it by heart. But by all means, have a gander." Luc shoved his one good hand into his pocket and drew out the now-crumpled map. "Here you go."

"You brought the map with you?" Sidney peered over Maurice's shoulder.

"Not intentionally." Luc's smile held a hint of irony. "I kept staring at it all night. I guess I must've kept it on me."

Maurice scrutinized the map and then shook his head. "You're right. This is no help." He folded it and made to hand it back to Luc.

"No, wait a sec," Sidney said, a note of excitement in his voice. "Can I take another peek at the basement?"

We all stared at him. Maurice shrugged. "Why not?"

Sidney took the map. As he examined it, twin lines rippled across his forehead. "This can't be right. Where's the bunker?"

"Bunker?" I stared at him blankly. "Why would the Hauris have a bunker?"

His frown lines deepened. "Because we're in

Switzerland. I don't recall the precise rules, but all Swiss households are required to have their own nuclear bunker or a place in a community shelter. It's a leftover of Cold War policy."

Luc's intake of breath was audible. "Are you certain?"

"Absolutely. I attended a Swiss school for a year. A highlight was exploring the school's bunker." Sidney pointed back at the chalet. "We're out in the middle of nowhere. I'd bet my grandfather's watch that house has its own bunker."

I followed the direction of his gaze. "Aren't bunkers supposed to be underground, though? The chalet has an exposed basement, and I didn't see any sign of a trapdoor."

"Take another look at the chalet, Angel." Luc pointed up the slope. "The front of the basement is exposed, but see the side of the house? No sign of the basement. The rest of that floor is built into the mountain."

I released a slow breath. "I need to see the map again."

Sidney handed it to me, and I looked at my amateur sketch. I closed my eyes and recalled the basement, taking an imaginary walk through each section. Before I'd created the mess of broken weapons, the basement had been the tidiest I'd ever seen. Except for one area.

My eyes flew open, and the pulse in my neck

fluttered. "I know where the bunker is. In the room with the deep freeze, there's a stack of shelves shoved against the back wall. It's a mess of random items. It stood out because the rest of the place is obsessively neat."

"So there's a bunker in the house. What's the significance?" Maurice peered back up the incline. "What difference does it make to our situation?"

"The bunker is required to be easily accessible," Sidney said. "My only foray into the basement was my tumble down the stairs, so I didn't notice much. But if the place is as tidy as Angel says, the Hauri household isn't likely to break bunker regulations. That door should never be blocked."

"And if they blocked it in a hurry, it'd explain the untidy shelves," I added. "Whoever did that wanted to hide the entrance."

"The Egyptian artifacts." Luc breathed deeply and stopped in his tracks, straining to see the house against the low sun. "That's where they hid the cache."

"Most probably, but there's another possibility." My breath stuck at throat level. "The real Charlotte Hauri could be in that bunker."

26

I stumbled to a halt and stared at the chalet. My fear morphed into terror. When we'd been fleeing from a potential explosion, the house had seemed way too close for comfort. Now that we were faced with the prospect of rescuing a trapped teenager from a literal ticking bomb, the distance seemed infinite.

Luc broke the silence that had descended since my pronouncement. "You don't know that Charlotte is in the chalet. You don't even know that the girl we met *isn't* Charlotte Hauri."

"It's a reasonable assumption. Why else would she wear a wig?"

"We can't tear back to a building with a bomb in it on a hunch, Angel. This isn't a fictional thriller. In real life, there are rarely last-second reprieves. If we go back into that house, we'll die."

I jutted my jaw in a bellicose fashion. "I'm telling you, Charlotte's in that bunker. I can feel it with every fiber of my body."

Luc's eyebrow formed a sardonic arch. "Have Ghiselle's psychic abilities rubbed off on you?"

I glared up at him, regretting the difference in our heights that always put me at a disadvantage. "I've never claimed to have a sixth sense, yet my gut seldom lets me down. I'm convinced the real Charlotte is in the chalet. I always thought the girl we met struck an odd note. Her clothes and hair were full-on eco-warrior, yet the look clashed with her ultra-fashionable eyebrows. I don't know who that person is, but she clearly cashed in on her resemblance to Charlotte."

Sidney groaned. "We were so naïve. We should've pursued that hunch and pushed harder, asked more questions."

"I'm kicking myself too," I said, "but Luc didn't smell a rat, and he's a pro investigator."

"A pro with a bullet wound, courtesy of you." His words were hard, but his eyes glinted with amusement. "I haven't been operating at full capacity."

Maurice looked at the magazine as though he'd just noticed it clutched in his fist. "I believe Angel's right. That premonition you mentioned had something to do with a bear, right?"

I nodded. "Right. And you helped us identify Urs Hauri as a possible suspect. Not that I believe what Ghiselle says, of course." I delivered this last sentence with a dismissive note that fooled no one. Either Ghiselle truly possessed psychic powers, or she was somehow involved in the plot.

"Perhaps she's more right than we both realized." Maurice shook open the magazine, returning to the two-page spread of the red-carpet event in Cannes. "I remember now what I wanted to say before you ran downstairs with the bomb threat. That party where Urs Hauri was photographed beside Nancy Roulez? Nancy wasn't the only Roulez family member in attendance. Her sister Beatrice was there, as were their nieces." He tapped the very captions I'd been too lazy to read when Luc and I had laughed over identikit self-tans and eyebrows. "See here? Bernard's granddaughters were also at the party, modeling in the charity fashion show. Marianne and Jeanne-Ursine Monet-Roulez."

"Ursine? Like a female version of Urs?" I snatched the magazine out of his pudgy paws and stared down at a familiar pair of eyebrows. I swore in several languages. "Jeanne-Ursine pretended to be Charlotte. They're very alike, apart from the hair color. Jeanne-Ursine used that ridiculous wig to conceal her blond hair."

"It must've been a last-minute costume choice," Sidney said. "The whole outfit was an over-the-top version of what an eco-conscious teen might wear."

"The magazine describes Jeanne-Ursine as a medical student. That accounts for her knowledge of livor mortis when we examined Colin Jones's body. A much more likely explanation than a sixteen-year-old true crime fan knowing forensic details. And look at the description of her sister, Marianne." I handed Sidney the magazine and pointed to the caption. "Marianne is studying for her master's degree in chemistry. A chemist would know how to make a bomb. I bet she's the unknown factor, the one helping her sister from outside the house. We have to go back to the chalet and look for Charlotte."

Luc held up a hand. "Absolutely not. All of this is guesswork. And even if you're right, a nuclear bunker is probably the safest place for Charlotte to be if that bomb goes off."

I opened my mouth to argue, but the roar of engines drew my attention down the slope. Two red snowmobiles powered up the incline at an impressive speed. Friend, or foe? My heart banged against my ribs, and I closed my hand around the pistol.

My panic lasted all of a few seconds. The snowmobiles drew level with us, and I recognized my mother and Valentina on one and Armin and Urs Hauri on the other. I'd only seen photographs of the guys, but they were easy to recognize, even in their snow gear.

When Armin stopped their snowmobile, Urs Hauri leaped off, breathing hard, searching our faces for one he didn't see. "Where's my daughter?" he demanded. "Where's Charlotte?"

This didn't look like a man who'd just masterminded a theft. This was a frightened father, terrified for his daughter's safety.

"We suspect she's trapped in the nuclear bunker," Sidney said. "How likely is the bunker to withstand an explosion?"

"What?" Hauri's haggard expression stiffened into a rictus of horror. "Do you think the chalet will blow up?"

I handed him the note left behind by Jeanne-Ursine. "We believe there's a bomb in the building. How secure is your bunker?"

Hauri crumpled the note, and his wide-eyed gaze fixed on the chalet. "The door failed its last inspection."

"And you didn't fix it?" Luc sounded justifiably outraged.

"I don't know." Hauri's focus was solely on the chalet, his mind on his daughter. "I left all arrangements to my housekeeper, Frau Lenz. I assume she got it fixed, but I can't be certain." He tore his gaze away from the house. "If there's a chance my daughter is still in there, I'm going to rescue her."

Without waiting for us to respond, he pushed Armin into the snow, leaped onto the snowmobile, and shot up the hill.

I didn't wait for anyone to react. I grabbed my mother's arm and hauled her off her snowmobile, then took her place behind Valentina. I took immense satisfaction in pressing Maurice's gun into Valentina's back. "I don't know how to drive one of these things, so you're gonna do it for me. Unless you want to test my shooting skills, I suggest you follow Hauri. And if you don't believe I'd shoot you, take a look at Luc's leg."

Valentina's eyes moved to Luc. He shrugged. "It's true. Angel's a mean shot."

Wordlessly, Valentina started the engine.

We zoomed up the slope after Urs Hauri, reaching the chalet seconds after he leaped off his snowmobile and unlocked the garage door. Valentina swerved into a downward parking position. "Pro tip—always park with a getaway in mind."

"Duly noted." I got off the snowmobile and raced after Hauri.

My guess as to the bunker's whereabouts was spot-on. By the time Valentina and I caught up with him, Urs Hauri was tearing down the shelves near the deep freeze. We helped him shove the shelves out of the way and soon exposed the bunker's solid white door. A metal chain was looped around the door handle and secured with a large padlock.

Hauri's voice broke on a sob. "They've chained it shut."

"Bolt cutters," I said, summing up the situation in an instant. "I saw some next door."

I legged it to the neighboring room and located the bolt cutters from the shelves of DIY tools that I'd noticed during my tour of the basement. When I returned, Valentina helped me get them around the chains. It only took a few seconds to cut through the metal, but those seconds felt unending. When the chain finally gave, Valentina unlooped it from the handle, and I yanked open the door.

Inside the small room, a brown-haired girl was gagged and bound to a chair. She stared at us through frightened hazel eyes. I whipped out a medieval dagger from my pocket and cut her free.

Her father eased the duct tape from her mouth and enveloped her in a bear hug. "Sweetheart, are you okay?"

"I thought you'd never come, Papa." She choked on her tears. "They killed Frau Lenz. I thought they were going to kill me."

"Come on," Valentina urged. "The reunion can keep until you're out of here."

Keeping his arm around his daughter, Urs Hauri retraced his steps through the garage. Valentina and I hurried after them.

Outside the chalet, Hauri helped Charlotte onto their snowmobile.

"Get back down to the others," Valentina ordered. "We'll be along in a moment."

"Wait a sec," I called. "Is there another building somewhere on your property? Maybe a shed?"

Hauri pointed at the crescent of trees above the chalet. "There's a shed up there. Our gardener uses it in summer."

"I bet that was where the sisters kept the artifacts," I murmured to Valentina.

Urs Hauri started the snowmobile, and he and Charlotte shot down the slope, blowing snow in our faces.

I turned to Valentina. "What now?"

Her lips set in a grim line. "Now you get on our snowmobile and follow them. Meanwhile, I'll look for the bomb."

"No way." I crossed my arms over my chest. "I'm not leaving you to search on your own."

She cocked an eyebrow. "Do you have any experience defusing bombs?"

"No, but I've spent almost twenty-four hours in this house. I can help you search for it."

She shrugged. "Suit yourself. If that bomb detonates, we're dead either way. If the house explosion doesn't kill us, the resulting avalanche will."

I whipped around and peered down the slope to where Sidney and the others waited. My heart froze in my chest. I couldn't let any harm come to my friends. "Then I have nothing to lose by helping you look. We should start in the basement and work our way up."

To my surprise, Valentina didn't contradict my suggestion. We worked our way around the basement as quickly as possible, checking every nook and cranny. While we searched, I filled her in on our adventures to date.

"Sounds like a plot that got way out of hand,"

Valentina remarked when I'd finished. "We passed two women in a Range Rover on our way up the slope. I bet that was them."

"And I bet they had the artifacts with them," I said grimly. "They must've hidden them in the shed."

"Very likely." Valentina looked around the basement and shook her head. "There's nothing here. Did the fake Charlotte spend an inordinate amount of time in any one area of the house?"

"Charlotte's bedroom. And she spent the night in the living room with us."

Valentina nodded. "Okay. We'll split up and check those two rooms next. If her bomb threat isn't a hoax, we don't know when she set it to go off."

I led her up the stairs to the entrance floor. "I'll take the bedroom, seeing as I know where it is. You can check the living room."

"Good grief. That's an impressive pile of anime plush," Valentina called from the living room.

The mention of the plush brought me up short. I paused at the foot of the stairs, my mind a whirl. Charlotte—or Jeanne-Ursine—insisted on bringing down her stuffed toys. Understandable if she'd been the real Charlotte Hauri and had wanted the comfort of the familiar. Seeing as that wasn't the case, why had she been so adamant that they join us overnight? And why had she freaked out when I'd picked up the pig-girl?

An icy sensation spread across my shoulders. "Valentina, I think I know where she hid the bomb."

I raced back into the living room and rooted through the pile of toys. The pig-girl sat buried at the bottom. A coincidence? I didn't think so. Without pausing to consider my actions, I picked up the toy. "This is the one."

Valentina didn't question me. She whipped out a penknife and carefully cut up the toy's back seam. When she exposed the ticking timer, I almost dropped the toy. As if anticipating my reaction, Valentina put her hands around mine. "Easy there. You're doing great. Put it down gently on that armchair and let me do the rest."

My hands shook beneath Valentina's, but I did as I was told. Maybe I'd never like the woman, but in this life-or-death situation, she was the professional, and I was the amateur. I knew which one of us I trusted to deactivate that bomb, and it wasn't me.

"You need to leave, Angel," she said, not taking her eyes off the bomb. "Take the snowmobile and join the others. Get as far away on a direct path down from the chalet as you can. I'll join you when I'm done."

Or not at all if you fail. I swallowed hard and tasted bile. "I'm staying with you. It's the least I can do after forcing you up the slope at gunpoint."

For the first time since we'd met, Valentina's low, sultry laugh didn't grate on my nerves. "For what it's worth, I'd have done the same. You followed your gut, and your gut was right."

The next couple of minutes were agonizing. Valentina pulled wires out of the pig-girl and examined each with minute precision. When she finally produced scissors and cut a wire, it took me a full minute to register that the danger was over.

I sank to the ground, struggling to breathe. "Is it out?"

"Not out, defused." She held up the pig-girl with an air of triumph. "We could play football with this, and we'd be just fine."

I shuddered. "All I want to do is get away from it."

Valentina grinned and tossed the toy onto the table. "Come on then, partner. Let's make tracks. You did good for your first assignment."

27

Outside the chalet, the snow had begun to fall in dense clumps. The frigid Alpine wind whipped my exposed face and jean-clad legs, making me regret not wearing snow pants. Valentina swung herself onto the snowmobile, and I slid behind her onto the passenger seat. She started the vehicle, and we zoomed down the slope and away from the house of horrors.

"Where to now?" she yelled over the engine's roar. "Wanna see if we can catch the deadly sisters?"

"Heck, yeah. I want the satisfaction of seeing them brought to justice."

Whatever one thought about Colin Jones and the security guards, Frau Lenz hadn't deserved to wind up dead in a deep freeze. And what the sisters had done to Charlotte? Unpardonable. They'd held a sixteen-year-old girl hostage in her own home and left her to die.

As well as wanting Monet-Roulez siblings to get their comeuppance, I had a selfish reason to catch the crooks. If they had the stolen artifacts in their possession, the Omega Group would get the quarter-million bonus. After what Sidney and I had been through in the last twenty-four hours, I intended to make sure part of that money paid for our P.I. training. Thanks to underestimating the threat against Charlotte and taking a slapdash approach to organizing our bag drop-off, my mother had put us in danger. She owed us big time.

At the speed Valentina was driving, we reached the others in record time. Luc and Sidney sat on a snowbank, eating energy bars. Urs Hauri had climbed off his snowmobile and was hugging his daughter while my mother and Maurice talked to him. From their respective expressions, I could tell my mother was in full damage control mode. She'd messed up, but she'd doubtless pretend everything we'd achieved was thanks to her superior investigative skills.

Valentina drew up beside the group but didn't kill the engine. "We're going after the artifacts. Angel thinks she knows where they are."

My mother's face was a mask of controlled emotion. "The Range Rover we passed on the way up? Armin hiked down far enough to get a phone signal. The police are on their way."

"What are you doing here, Desirée?" The question

had occurred to me several times during all the commotion, but we'd had more pressing priorities. "How did you know we were in trouble?"

Still, my mother's expression stayed blankly neutral. "Maurice's phone call bothered me."

"Wrecked your beauty sleep?" I didn't hide my scorn.

A flicker of an emotion I couldn't pinpoint flashed in her eyes, but it was gone in a millisecond. "When Maurice told me he was worried about you all, I got concerned. I'd dismissed the lack of phone contact as a casualty of the storm. Still, when your car tracker and Luc's disappeared from the radar, we decided to abandon the search for the artifacts and headed to Höllenberg."

I nodded at my manager. "Thanks, boss. I appreciate you looking out for Sidney and me."

A half-smile broke through his severe countenance. "Happy to help. We won't turn you into a stellar yarn seller, but we might make a private investigator out of you."

"After you risked your life to get to us, I'd say we'll make one out of you again too." I stared pointedly at my mother. "Right, Desirée?"

She didn't say anything, but my words had caused an angry flush.

Valentina revved the snowmobile. "Time to make tracks. Hold on tight, Angel. This'll be a bumpy ride."

She wasn't joking. We sped down the slope, edging closer to the road. The lower we got, the easier it was to see where the fields ended, and the road began. The heavy snow had bent some trees to an alarming degree, and several branches were strewn in our path. Valentina neatly zigzagged to avoid them, giving me whiplash in the process.

We'd driven for a quarter of an hour when I spotted the olive green Range Rover. I couldn't resist a triumphant fist bump. A snow-laden tree lay across the road, blocking the Range Rover's path. A falling branch had damaged the front of the vehicle. With a line of trees on one side of the road and a wall of snow on the other, the sisters were unable to turn their car.

When Valentina drew up beside the fence, the person I'd known as Charlotte Hauri was screaming at a second blond woman in a mixture of French and German. We didn't need to conduct a search of the Range Rover to discover if they had the artifacts. The car was stuffed with objects of solid gold, some spilling out onto the road.

In wordless agreement, Valentina and I pulled our guns on them.

"Hands on your heads, faces on the ground," Valentina ordered. She tossed me a pair of cuffs. "You cuff the fake Charlotte. You have a history with her."

I didn't need to be told twice. The fake Charlotte looked older than sixteen without the dreadlocks and dressed in a fashionable cashmere coat. Still, she couldn't have been more than in her early twenties. The heavy eye makeup and baggy clothes were effective ways to shave five years off her age.

I grabbed her wrists and twisted them hard, snapping the cuffs in place. "Jeanne-Ursine, I presume?"

Her answer was a snarl. "Why didn't you leave? How many hints did we need to give you?"

"You—or should I say, your sister—blew up our cars. How were we supposed to leave in the middle of a blizzard?"

"If it hadn't been for the storm, we'd have been halfway to Paris by now." Her words were a petulant whine. "It was the perfect plan. No one was supposed to get hurt."

I snorted. "Please. You left Charlotte Hauri to die. If we hadn't rescued her, she'd probably be dead, bunker or no bunker."

"I knew you'd find her, eventually." She was pleading now, trying to win my sympathy. "Why do you think I left you the note? You were so clever at working everything out. You even suspected me. I saw it in your eyes last night."

She was utterly shameless. This woman had left a child to die and had murdered or helped to murder four people. I shivered and huddled into my orange jacket. "I should've picked up on the exaggerated way you played the bratty rich kid. You butchered the bread last night. Way over-the-top. I'm sure the real Charlotte knows how to make a sandwich."

Jeanne-Ursine's laugh made my blood curdle. "Don't bet on it. She's grown up with every luxury. Did you see all the gadgets in her room? And that's just *one* house. And all the nauseatingly posed holiday snaps? I doubt that kid's ever wanted for anything."

"Whereas you, Jeanne-*Ursine*, were ignored and unacknowledged by your biological father and your mother's family. This was your opportunity to claim your stake in the Roulez fortune and get revenge on Urs Hauri for abandoning you. Am I correct in assuming he's your father?"

Her cold eyes narrowed to serpentine slits. "He's the sperm donor, yes. He dumped my mother as soon as he found out she was pregnant and has denied paternity ever since."

I looked at the woman Valentina had wrestled into handcuffs. Marianne Monet-Roulez had her sister's fair hair, but her heart-shaped face and baby-blue eyes could never pass for Charlotte Hauri. Marianne caught me examining her and smirked. "Different father, similar story. Our mother had horrible taste in men."

"Am I supposed to hear violins in the background?" I turned to her sister. "What about that cashmere coat? I bet that didn't come cheap."

Jeanne-Ursine smirked. "I can't afford a coat like this. I liberated it from one of the wardrobes in the chalet."

As someone with a long history of liberating items that didn't belong to me, I wasn't in a position to judge. The dead bodies and the kidnapped kid were a whole other story. I tightened her cuffs and hauled her to her feet. "I hope you enjoyed your luxurious stay at the chalet. I have the feeling your next accommodations won't be as fancy."

Sure enough, sirens echoed through the valley, and flashing lights soon came into view. Marianne attempted to break free from Valentina's grasp, but the Spaniard was having none of it. "Oh, no, you don't. I'll shoot you if you move so much as a muscle."

A red snowmobile zoomed down the slope, Sidney at the controls, Luc as co-pilot. When they halted a couple of meters away from us, I cocked an eyebrow. "I didn't know you could drive a snowmobile."

Sidney's wide, open grin had a mischievous air. "You never asked. It's not a comfortable way to travel with a sprained ankle and a busted leg, but I figured Luc and I deserved to be here when our crooks got hauled away by the boys in blue."

The police vehicles stopped in front of the fallen tree, and several armed police officers leaped out. While they read the wicked sisters their rights, Luc handed Valentina and me bars of Swiss chocolate. "Courtesy of Urs Hauri. Apparently, he goes nowhere without a supply of chocolate."

I bit into mine and moaned appreciatively. "I approve."

"So," Luc dropped his voice and spoke directly into my ear. "What was that you were saying about not being a team player? Seems to me you managed just fine. You even cooperated with Maurice and Valentina, and I know you're not their greatest fan."

I swallowed the chocolate and tried not to think about how close his lips were to my earlobe. "I can work with others if they let me do what I do best, and they get on with their jobs."

His low laugh sent a shiver down my spine that had nothing to do with the cold. "Would it interest you to know that Maurice sang your praises to Desirée? So much so that she's placing a call to the school in Florida where the rest of us trained to see if she can score you and Sidney places on the next boot camp."

A ripple of excitement set off a chorus of butterflies in my stomach. Were Sidney and I finally getting to train as P.I.s? And all because of Maurice? This time yesterday, the idea of my manager sticking up for me would've shocked me. Today, after all we'd been through, I sent a silent thanks up the slope to the little man. Maybe we'd never be friends, but I appreciated what he'd done for me. "Seriously?"

"Seriously." Luc touched my arm. "You guys did good. I'm sorry for what I said about July. You two handled yourselves like pros, then and now. I'm proud to call you my teammates."

I looked into his electric blue eyes, and a smile

spread across my face. "Housemates, teammates. You'll never be rid of me."

Luc stared down at me with a hot intensity that liquified any reserves I might've had about sitting this close to the man. "You know what? Having you around all the time doesn't sound so bad."

28

*I*f Sidney bounced any higher in his seat, he'd eject through the sunroof. "I keep pinching myself to be sure it's real. This is actually happening. After all the waiting, you and I are starting our P.I. training."

It was the day after the action at the chalet. Sidney and I sat in our rental car—final destination, Zürich Airport. So much had happened since we'd gotten off Hell Mountain that my mind hadn't processed it all. We'd spent the night at a hotel near Höllenberg, answering police questions and pumping my mother for information on the case. This morning, we were in a car, speeding toward a new career.

I swigged coffee and swiped my phone screen, opening the saved birthday message to my brother. My thumb hovered over the send button. "Yeah, it's happening. Desirée sent me our plane tickets and the course registration details. In five hours, we'll be in the skies."

I was thrilled my mother had booked Sidney and me places on the next P.I. boot camp, but I hadn't expected it to kick off on Monday. Not least because of that conversation with Luc. I didn't know what was happening between us. Maybe something, maybe nothing. All I knew was I didn't want to be away from him for six whole months.

Unfortunately, the Florida boot camp only ran twice a year. Sidney and I were faced with scrambling to get on the next flight to Florida, or with waiting until May for the next course to begin. Deciding we could live without our stuff in Nice, we opted to get on the next available flight. Once we got to America, we'd hit the shops and buy whatever we needed.

"Just think, Angel. In six months, we'll be fully qualified members of the Omega Group." Sidney beamed at me from behind the wheel of our snow-worthy SUV. "This is a dream come true. Totally worth battling crazed killers in a snowpocalypse."

"Hmm..." I re-read the belated birthday text I'd written to my brother Del. Took a deep breath, and hit send. I lowered the phone. "Not sure I'd like to repeat the near-death experience part. The Monet-Roulez sisters are a piece of work. What do you think will happen to them? Will the judge buy their 'poor victims' story?"

"They're young, beautiful, and first-time

offenders," Sidney said dryly. "And they're insisting they didn't murder anyone, nor intend to kill Charlotte. In the case of the housekeeper and Colin Jones, they might be telling the truth."

"That story about the housekeeper resisting their plan to lock her and Charlotte in the bunker? And then stabbing Jones with a spear?" I shook my head. "That tale stinks. Even if the housekeeper killed Jones, it's mighty convenient that a crossbow just happened to go off in close proximity to her chest right after."

"Marianne admits she dressed up Colin Jones's dead body as a way to scare you and me away from the chalet, but she denies any involvement in the murders. I mean, someone stabbed Guido and Luigi, and we're pretty sure it couldn't have been Jeanne-Ursine. The guards didn't kill themselves. My money is on Marianne."

"And the sisters blame Jones and the security guards for the theft, claiming Jones duped them into helping." I breathed out a sigh. "Money brings out the worst in people. They could've waited to see how their court case went rather than stealing from the Roulez estate."

Snow began to fall, and Sidney switched on the wipers. "Luc says they were unlikely to win, though, and litigation is expensive. His grandfather is familiar with the case. He thinks Bernard Roulez's will is rock solid."

"I'm not condoning their actions," I said, "but it's

rough that they got nothing. You'd think the old man would at least acknowledge his only granddaughters."

"According to your mother, he threw his daughter out when she got pregnant with Jeanne-Ursine and ignored all attempts at reconciliation, even when she was dying. He sounds like a piece of work, but he was entitled to distribute his wealth as he wished."

"It sounds like the whole family is twisted," I mused. "Speaking of family, did you believe Urs Hauri's denials about Jeanne-Ursine being his daughter? Her resemblance to Charlotte is remarkable."

Sidney snorted. "Nah. He only said that because Charlotte was present. Jeanne-Ursine is his daughter, acknowledged or not."

I nodded. "I'm inclined to agree. The name is a clue, as is the sisters' decision to hide the stolen goods at Urs Hauri's chalet. What better way to get revenge on the man than implicating him in the crime? That aspect would've also appealed to Colin Jones. Leaving an artifact or two on the premises for the police would've guaranteed a bumpy ride for Hauri."

"Right. The Crofton-Lowe theft covered a lot of bases. The sisters wanted revenge on their mother's family for stripping them of what they believed to be their rightful inheritance. And Jeanne-Ursine wanted to destroy the father who'd ignored her all her life. What better way to get retribution than to destroy his career and kill the daughter he'd chosen over her?"

I pulled my orange jacket tight around my chest. At least this was one item of clothing I'd be able to ditch before we reached sunny Florida. "Did you notice that Jeanne-Ursine was scathing about her father whenever he came up in conversation? That contrasted with the information in her file. Charlotte was described as a true daddy's girl. I should've picked up on that."

"Hey, don't beat yourself up. We got there eventually. We saved the day—with a little help—and we recovered the stolen artifacts. Not bad for our first Omega Group assignment."

The robotic voice of the satnav told Sidney to take the next exit. As we pulled off the motorway and headed toward the village of Simplon, I checked the list we'd compiled last night. The René Bateau who lived in Simplon was the last possible candidate to be the Undead Pierre Dubois.

I glanced at my watch. "We can't hang around for too long or we'll be late getting to the airport. If the guy's not home, we'll get back in the car and forget about this case. We can tell Ghiselle we did our best, and the case is a lost cause."

"I have a good feeling about René Bateau of Simplon." Sidney drummed a tune on the steering wheel. "Maybe yesterday's crime-solving magic will last into today."

A few minutes later, we drew up in front of an attractive detached house on a small plot of land and climbed out of the car. A man was outside the house, building a snowman with a toddler. My pulse quickened when he turned around. Fair hair and a matching mustache, just as the receptionist at Crans-Montana had described. Other than that, this man was Pierre Dubois' doppelgänger.

He watched us approach with wary eyes, shooting a glance at the toddler, and then to the curtained kitchen window where a woman stood, washing dishes.

"Pierre Dubois?" I asked the question firmly in a low voice.

The man stiffened, and his Adam's apple bobbed. He looked at the toddler. "Go inside for your snack. I'll follow in a moment."

The toddler seemed unsure, watching us with unabashed curiosity. Then the lure of the promised snack won, and he turned and ran to the house, all loose limbs and full-body energy.

His father fixed his gaze on us. "Did Ghiselle send you?"

"Yeah," Sidney said. "She's convinced you're alive."

His laugh was laced with bitterness. "Of course she is. She helped me die."

Sidney and I exchanged a loaded look. "Ghiselle helped you to fake your death? But why?"

"The insurance money. My grandfather took out a generous policy when we got married. I was worth more dead than alive." He scratched the back of his neck, looking tired and ten years older than he had when we'd gotten out of the car. "We were going to start a new life in the Caribbean. I'd lie low for a few months, let the insurance money clear, then she'd join me."

"What went wrong?" I asked. "And why are you telling us all this? I thought you'd deny everything."

Pierre's gaze went back to the window. The woman was no longer visible, presumably dealing with the toddler's snack. "I deny nothing. Those few months on my own were a wake-up call. I was forty-seven years old, and I'd never made a decision for myself in my entire life. I realized how miserable I'd been married to Ghiselle. We were all wrong for each other. So when the money showed up in our new bank account, I transferred it to one I'd set up using a different fake name and moved to Switzerland."

"Where you met your current partner and started a family," I finished for him. "Does she know?"

"About Ghiselle?" He looked up in surprise. "Oh, yes. We have no secrets. I told her everything when we started to get serious. She had a right to know."

We all stood there in awkward silence, none of us knowing what to say next.

In the end, Pierre was the one who spoke. His voice was gruff and rough with emotion. "Will you tell Ghiselle?"

Sidney glanced at me, reading my expression.

"No," he said. "We won't tell her where you are or your new name."

"On one condition," I added, surprised at such a sentiment coming from me, Angel Doyle, semi-reformed thief. "You defrauded the insurance company. You need to pay them back."

I expected him to demur, but instead, he nodded. "I've been meaning to get in touch with my grandfather. We were never close, but I'd like him to meet my son while there's still time. He's always been big on respectability and keeping the family name out of the press." A sly smile curved the ends of his mustache. "I have a feeling I can persuade him to help me out of this situation."

Sidney produced one of our ridiculous, glittery business cards and handed it to Pierre. "See that you keep your word. We'll be in touch."

The man watched us get into our car and drive away from the home and life he'd created, far from his controlling family and overbearing wife.

"Do you think he'll follow through?" I asked when Pierre had disappeared from the rearview mirror.

"Probably." Sidney slid me a slow-burn smile. "I'm not sure I care."

"What do we tell Ghiselle? If Pierre makes a clean breast of things to the cops, she'll know he's alive."

"We tell her we looked and we didn't find Pierre Dubois. Simple as that. Whatever happens after isn't our problem." He slid a sly look. "I must say, her psychic powers mustn't be all bunkum. She was right about the bear."

But was she right about my feelings for Luc? Maybe I'd know once the next six months were over. I leaned back in my seat and stretched my neck from side to side. "So, partner, two cases nailed in two days. Not bad for Sparkle and Shine's first investigations."

He laughed. "Are you warming to the name? I knew the glitter cards would wear you down in the end."

"Steady there, tiger. All I'm saying is we did well."

"We have to admit we had help from the Omega Team. We couldn't have put all the clues together on our own."

"Yeah, you're right." I wrinkled my nose. "I hate to say it, but maybe teamwork isn't all that bad. Even when it includes Maurice and Valentina."

"See? We'll fit right in at the Omega Group. And once we're qualified, we'll get all the cool gadgets and cases, just like the others." Sidney happy-sighed. "From here on in, life is going to be awesome."

In my pocket, my phone pinged with an incoming message. Probably my mother with a last-minute instruction. I slid it out of my pocket and glanced at the screen.

My eyes skimmed my brother's words, and my mouth went bone dry.

> *Is what Dad says true? Are you some kind of P.I.? 'Cause I need your help. Monterosso al Mare, Italy. Life or death. Please come, Sis. You're the only one I can trust.*
>
> *Del xx*

~

Thanks so much for reading ***Ambushed in the Alps***. I hope you enjoyed Angel and Sidney's second international adventure!

They're back in ***Murdered in Monterosso***. Can Angel make it to Italy, save her brother, and get back in time for the first day of her course? Or will murderous hijinks (and Sidney's love of gelato) slow them down?

Join my VIP mailing list to get notified when the next book launches (and I'll send you a **FREE** story). **Sign up at zarakeane.com/travelpinewsletter**

Happy Reading!

Zara x

Join my mailing list and get news, giveaways, and free stories!

Sign up on
zarakeane.com/travelpinewsletter

Angel Doyle, semi-reformed thief and accidental P.I., is back for a third electrifying adventure in *Murdered in Monterosso*, out now.

Angel and her friend and sidekick, Sidney, are ecstatic to fly to Florida for a six-month P.I. boot camp. They'll finally become licensed team members of the Omega Group, the super-secret international P.I. agency co-run by Angel's mother, former adult movie actress Desirée Chablis.

On the way to the airport, Angel receives a message from her estranged brother. He's in mortal danger, and she's the only person who can save him. Apart from the name of an Italian town, Angel has no idea where to find him, or what mess he's landed himself in this time. She's forced to decide between fulfilling her dream and saving her brother.

Can Angel make it to Italy and back in time for the first day of her course? Or will murderous hijinks (and Sidney's love of gelato) slow them down?

***Murdered in Monterosso* is available at all major book stores.**

EXCERPT FROM *MURDERED IN MONTEROSSO*

My estranged brother's text message was about as welcome as an outbreak of crotch crabs. Actually, with the benefit of hindsight, I'd have preferred pubic lice. I didn't like surprises. I especially didn't like surprises involving my crazy family derailing my career plans.

Before my phone heralded impending doom, I was in a buoyant mood. After months of hope and hard work, I, Angel Doyle, semi-reformed thief and accidental P.I., was about to realize my dream. I was in a rental car with my friend Sidney, speeding toward Zürich Airport. We were on our way to Florida and an all-expenses-paid P.I. training camp. In six months, Sidney and I would be fully qualified private investigators and full-time employees of the Omega Group, the supersecret international P.I. agency based in Nice, France, that my mother co-ran with her ex-husband.

Scoring a job with the Omega Group was my dream come true—Sidney's, too. And it was right within our grasp. Or it had been, until thirty seconds ago, when my phone had pinged with news of my brother Del's latest imbroglio.

"Hey, earth to Angel." Sidney took one hand off the steering wheel and waved it in front of my face. "You feeling okay? Was the weapons-grade espresso I bought you too strong, even by your stomach-stripping standards?"

I put my phone facedown on my lap and forced a smile. "The coffee's fine. I'm just tired."

Sidney's expression radiated skepticism. I didn't blame him. Lacking his years at drama school, I sounded as believable as a politician denying a sex scandal. The sick sensation in my stomach turned into a cramp. I couldn't drag Sidney into this mess. He'd be devastated if I told him I was considering skipping our flight. And if I told him why, he'd insist on accompanying me to Italy.

His gaze lingered on me for an uncomfortable moment before he returned his attention to the snow-dusted motorway. "I get it. We've had an insane weekend."

This was the understatement of the millennium. Over the last couple of days, Sidney and I had battled a blizzard, vanquished violent criminals, and rescued a teenager from a literal ticking bomb. Our success in cracking our case had finally convinced my mother we'd make excellent additions to her team. She'd pulled strings to secure two last-minute places in a six-month P.I. boot camp.

A boot camp that I might have to bail on.

My fingers tensed around my phone, but I didn't pick it up. I didn't need to reread Del's message. When his text had arrived, I'd stared at the screen so hard the words had seared into my brain with laser-like precision.

Is what Dad says true? Are you some kind of P.I.? 'Cause I need your help. Monterosso al Mare, Italy. Life or death. Please come, sis. You're the only one I can trust.
Del xx

Eight months of no contact, and now this mad missive? What on earth had my brother gotten himself into this time? And how did our father know about my P.I. experience? I hadn't spoken to Dad in almost two years.

Del and I were half-siblings and shared the dubious honor of a career criminal father. Dad was a low-level crook working for a mid-tier London gangster. Two years ago, I'd given evidence against my abusive ex-boyfriend—Dad's boss's son.

Instead of supporting me, my paternal family had branded me a traitor.

Following the fallout, Del had been the only one to keep in touch. I didn't kid myself that he'd chosen my side. More likely, he'd simply forgotten that I was persona non grata. That would be typical of Del. He'd always been slow on the uptake. For months, he'd continued to include me in silly forwards and generic "Yo, whazzup?"-style messages. Nothing personal. Nothing that showed he cared.

Earlier this year, he'd gone radio silent. I was hurt, but not surprised. I assumed he'd finally gotten the memo. Eight months had passed, and my brother hadn't responded to my attempts to get in touch.

Until today.

What's that trite saying? Be careful what you wish for? Yeah. Totally that.

Sidney flipped the indicator and filtered into the lane for the Zürich Airport exit. "We'll have enough time to grab breakfast before our flight. Seeing as we checked in online and just have carry-on baggage, all we need to do is drop off the rental car and get through security."

Our lack of baggage wasn't planned. The Swiss assignment had wrapped up yesterday, leaving us no time to get back to our house in France to pack our stuff. We'd buy clothes once we reached the US. Until then, we each had a small backpack with essentials. The idea of an imminent shopping trip thrilled the fashion-conscious Sidney. All I cared about was weather-appropriate clothing, regardless of my location.

I closed my eyes and tried to rally my racing thoughts. There were several explanations for Del's message. Few reflected well on my brother. None boded well for me.

The most likely scenario was that Del had fallen afoul of a London gang and fled to Italy to hide out. Depending on what sort of scam he'd pulled, it might be the life-or-death situation he described. Or he might simply be on a drug-fueled high.

Memories of past Del disasters flashed before me like a Worst-Of clip collection. The dude was a bona fide mayhem magnet. Take the time he'd forgotten a sports bag full of cash on the London Underground, necessitating a trip to Morocco to outrun his gangster boss. Or the art gallery heist when he'd mistaken an unmarked police vehicle for his getaway car. Del's life was a litany of calamities worthy of an Oscar-winning slapstick comedy. The best part? He had a tendency to drag others into his disaster du jour. Today, it was apparently my turn.

Sidney took the exit, and the airport buildings loomed into view—gray and snow-dipped against the pale blue sky. I had to decide what to do, but my heart beat so fast I could barely breathe, let alone think. I prided myself on my ability to keep my head, but my nerves were shot after yesterday. In the space of twenty-four hours, I'd survived an ambush, two explosions, and a shoot-out. No wonder my fight-or-flight mode was permanently on.

I inhaled slowly and held my breath, allowing my stomach to expand. All I'd wanted was to wish my brother a happy birthday. I'd assumed he'd ignore my text, just as he'd ignored all the others I'd sent him over the last eight months. I hadn't expected my message to generate such a response.

With a controlled exhale, I picked up my phone and began to type. Then I stopped, my thumb hovering over the delete button. Knowing Del, it'd require several incoherent replies for me to decipher the mess he'd landed himself in on this occasion. Calling was the smarter move.

The connection went straight to voicemail. Frustrated, I made a couple more attempts. When I received voicemail for the third time, I released a silent sigh. I loathed leaving voice messages, but it seemed I had no choice. I kept it terse and to the point. "Hey, I got your text. Call me back ASAP."

Aware of Sidney sitting beside me, I tried to keep my voice neutral. I needn't have bothered. My friend had an unerring ability to pick up on other people's emotions, and he was particularly good at reading mine.

He glanced my way, a crease marring his otherwise smooth forehead. "What's wrong?"

"Nothing." Catching his pointedly raised eyebrow, I amended my statement. "Nothing I can't handle."

The crease in his forehead deepened. "That sounds ominous. Who are you trying to call? Your mother? Is there a problem with the boot camp?"

"There's no problem with the course." Or there wouldn't be, if I got on that plane.

I massaged my temples and ran through my options. Could I drive to Italy, find Del, and then fly to Florida before class started? Unlikely. However, I could book a flight from an Italian airport and fly out tomorrow. I'd be a day late, but I'd plead a family emergency. Depending on whatever Del was embroiled in, it wouldn't be a lie.

When Sidney pulled into a space in the rental car company's parking lot, I still hadn't heard from my brother. The concern that had gnawed at me since I'd first read his message had morphed into a full-blown, bile-inducing panic. An icy trickle of sweat slithered down my spine. What should I do? Drop everything and run to Del's rescue? For all I knew, he'd been out of it when he'd composed that text. It had the hallmarks of a bad trip. But what if he was in genuine danger?

Sidney unbuckled his seat belt. "We'd better get moving. A shuttle bus to the terminal leaves in five minutes."

Fear had switched on my stomach's high-speed spin cycle. I reached into the space under the dashboard computer and groped for the key fob. My fingers closed around it with white-knuckled strength, mainly to stop them from shaking. Drug-fueled hoax or not, my brother's message had pushed me close to a panic attack. Why was my reaction this intense? Del and I had been close as kids, but we'd drifted apart by our late teens, long before he'd gone no-contact eight months ago. Old times' sake? A stronger sibling bond than I'd assumed we shared? A premonition of danger?

Still clutching the key, I climbed out of the car.

Sidney leaned into the boot and took out our backpacks, unfurling to his full height. He was so much taller than me—not that beating my five feet two was difficult. His skinny frame made him appear even taller than his six feet two. He had an angular face with enormous blue eyes, a straight nose, and cheekbones sharp enough to cut granite. His were the sort of uniquely striking looks that'd fit right in on a Paris runway.

He shrugged his backpack over his shoulders and handed me mine, examining one of my loose curls. "I know you're not convinced, but I love your natural shade."

"Don't you mean my *unnatural* natural shade?" I quipped. "Dying my hair back to strawberry blond hardly embraces Mother Nature."

In a fit of drunken celebration before we left for Florida, I'd allowed Sidney to dye my hair, changing my curls back to something resembling my natural color for the first time in a decade. His handiwork thrilled him. I felt uncomfortably *seen*. Until I'd woken up this morning and seen my reflection through sober eyes, I hadn't realized how much my dyed hair was part of my self-defense strategy. A reaction I'd ponder later, when I had time to navel-gaze.

He nudged me with my backpack, bringing me back to the here and now. "Why don't you check the car for anything we forgot? I'll drop off the key."

I took my backpack from Sidney's outstretched hand, but I didn't release my grip on the key. For all Del's faults, I couldn't abandon him. Even if it meant temporarily abandoning my course.

"I'm sorry, mate," I blurted. "Something's come up. I'll catch a later flight and join you tomorrow."

This time, both of Sidney's blond eyebrows arched into his shock of fair hair. "Are you serious? What's so important that you need to ditch the flight at the last second?"

I swallowed past a painful lump in my throat. "I'll tell you once I've dealt with it. Promise."

"Not good enough, Angel. You've been angling for this opportunity ever since we moved to Nice. Why would you bail on the chance to train to be a private investigator?" Concern tinged his tone, but his stare was so intense it felt like a mind probe.

I shifted my weight from one leg to the other, dropping my gaze from Sidney's confused face to my scuffed boots. "I'm sorry," I repeated. "I'm bailing on this flight, not on the course. I'll catch a later flight."

"Does your sudden change of mind have anything to do with that text message you got in the car? Who were you trying to call?"

I moved to the driver's side of the rental car without meeting his eye. "I'll tell you all about it when I get to Florida. The cocktails are on me."

"You can't just leave with no explanation, Angel. And what about the rental contract? The car's due back now."

"I'll call them later. Don't worry. I'll cover the extra cost."

His sigh expressed exasperation. "The cost isn't my concern. You're stressed, and I want to know why. No way you'd willingly turn your back on the opportunity to take this P.I. boot camp."

"I'm not quitting the course. I'm just not catching this flight." If I looked at him, I'd burst into tears.

I'd only known Sidney since July, but the situations we'd been through since our first encounter had made us close. Well, as close as I allowed myself to get to anyone. Regardless, he was a friend. A good friend. Probably the best friend I'd ever had.

Which was why I couldn't tell him the truth. Sidney would never let me go to Italy on my own. He'd insist on tagging along to help, even though he wanted to be a professional P.I. just as badly as I did. My showing up a day late for our boot camp was a major no-no. For all I knew, I'd get the proverbial middle finger and find myself on the next flight back to France. I couldn't let Sidney share that risk.

On impulse, I closed the space between us and hugged him tight. He smelled of shampoo, posh scent, and dependability. My tight shoulders relaxed, and a comforting warmth replaced the icy tension.

And then the text message flashed through my mind in glowing neon letters—a garish reminder of what I had to do.

I broke the embrace and stepped back, my cheeks growing warm. I didn't do physical affection. My sudden desire to hug Sidney had to be caused by stress.

Sidney stared down at me, agog and slightly pink. He affected a laugh. "Angel Doyle engaging in a PDA? The Apocalypse must be nigh."

"Not quite." I shifted my weight from one leg to the other. "I'll call you when you land in Florida and let you know when I'll arrive. It'll be tomorrow at the latest."

Without waiting for a response, I leaped into the car and started the engine, neatly reversing out of our space and speeding toward the exit. In the rearview mirror, Sidney watched me go for a second, hands in his hair, mouth open. Then his lips formed words I couldn't hear. He ran after the car, waving for me to stop.

Doubt crept over me. Did I want to face the Del situation on my own? No. How likely were Sidney and I to miss the start of our course if I booked us seats on a flight out of Italy this evening? Depending on the connections, we could still make it.

I switched my foot to the brake, about to press down on the pedal when my phone pinged with an incoming text. My innards lurched, and my clammy palms grew clammier. Ignoring road safety regulations, I pulled my phone out of my pocket and scanned the screen.

Can't talk right now. Not alone. Can't give deets. I think my phone's hacked. Remember our hideout when we were kids? Meet me at the place that looks like it. Four p.m., Italian time. Come alone. No cops.

Our hideout? But that was in London. What place in Monterosso, a town I'd never been to, resembled the abandoned shed we'd transformed into our childhood fort? A shaft of unease pierced the dented armor of my self-control. The first message might have resulted from a bad trip, but the second? No. Del was in trouble.

I tossed the phone onto the passenger seat and took a last look in the rearview mirror. Sidney was still running after me, a lanky blond blob growing smaller by the second. If Del was in genuine danger, no way was I involving my friend. Blinking back tears, I hit the gas.

Murdered in Monterosso is available at all major book stores.

ABOUT THE AUTHOR

USA Today bestselling author Zara Keane grew up in Dublin, Ireland, but spent her summers in a small town very similar to the fictitious Whisper Island and Ballybeg.

She currently lives in Switzerland with her family. When she's not writing, Zara loves knitting, running, unplugged gaming, and adding to her insanely large lipstick collection.

Zara has an active Facebook reader group, **Zara Keane's Mystery Mavens**, where she chats, shares snippets of upcoming stories, and hosts members-only giveaways. She hopes to join you for a virtual pint very soon!

zarakeane.com